CAMERON BATTLE AND THE ESCAPE TRIALS

Also by Jamar J. Perry

Cameron Battle and the Hidden Kingdoms

CAMERON BATTLE AND THE ESCAPE TRIALS

JAMAR J. PERRY

BLOOMSBURY
CHILDREN'S BOOKS
NEW YORK   LONDON   OXFORD   NEW DELHI   SYDNEY

BLOOMSBURY CHILDREN'S BOOKS
Bloomsbury Publishing Inc., part of Bloomsbury Publishing Plc
1385 Broadway, New York, NY 10018

BLOOMSBURY, BLOOMSBURY CHILDREN'S BOOKS,
and the Diana logo are trademarks of Bloomsbury Publishing Plc

First published in the United States of America in February 2023
by Bloomsbury Children's Books
www.bloomsbury.com

Bloomsbury books may be purchased for business or promotional use.
For information on bulk purchases please contact Macmillan Corporate and
Premium Sales Department at specialmarkets@macmillan.com

Library of Congress Cataloging-in-Publication Data
Names: Perry, Jamar J., author.
Title: Cameron Battle and the escape trials / by Jamar J. Perry.
Description: New York: Bloomsbury Children's Books, 2023.
Series: Cameron Battle; book 2
Summary: With his mother trapped and his father still missing,
Cameron is desperate to return to Chidani, but when a nasty bully
in his new school is possessed by a mmo, Cameron and his trusty friends
Zion and Aliyah are transported to Chidani sooner than anticipated.
Identifiers: LCCN 2022037870 (print) | LCCN 2022037871 (e-book)
ISBN 978-1-5476-0725-9 (hardcover) • ISBN 978-1-5476-0869-0 (e-book)
Subjects: CYAC: Magic—Fiction. | Mythology, Igbo—Fiction. |
Friendship—Fiction. | Books—Fiction. | African Americans—Fiction. |
Fantasy. | LCGFT: Fantasy fiction. | Novels.
Classification: LCC PZ7.1.P44773 Cak 2022 (print) |
LCC PZ7.1.P44773 (e-book) | DDC [Fic]—dc23
LC record available at https://lccn.loc.gov/2022037870
LC e-book record available at https://lccn.loc.gov/2022037871

Book design by Jeanette Levy
Typeset by Westchester Publishing Services
Printed and bound in the U.S.A.
2 4 6 8 10 9 7 5 3 1

To find out more about our authors and books visit
www.bloomsbury.com and sign up for our newsletters.

To me—for making it through

The Three Gifts

Igbo Mountains

Asaba

Palacia

The Noble Road

Sanaga Forest

Supernatural Forest

Onitsha

Okeniyi

Temple to
Idemmili

ATLANTIC OCEAN

Atlanta

Georgia, U.S.

CAMERON BATTLE AND THE ESCAPE TRIALS

CHAPTER ONE

"Watch out!" I said, reaching out and grabbing Zion's backpack straps as he tumbled off the bus steps.

"Whoa," he said as I pulled him back. "That was close."

I pointed at the book in his hand. "Reading again instead of watching where you're going?"

He smirked at me, curls bouncing over his eyes, as he jumped down onto the concrete and started to walk to the bright yellow entrance of Sutton Middle School, our new school now that we had finished elementary. "Aww, so you care about me?"

"Not really," I said, running to keep in step with him as we went through the entrance. I snatched the book from him—the second in the Percy Jackson series—and stuffed it in my backpack. "I care more about *my* books, you know, the ones you keep stealing from me."

A crowd converged inside the large school building, which

was built with a mixture of red-and-gray brick on one side, with its center carved out of glass. Zion dug in his pocket, ignoring my accusation.

"You've had it all summer," I said, whispering this time. "You know . . . ever since . . ."

"Ahh," Zion said, fishing out a slip of paper. "There it is! My locker number and combination." He grabbed my hand and pushed through the crowd of scared-looking new middle schoolers, pulling me to the second-floor stairs as a large man stepped in the hallway and yelled, "Seventh graders! Let's get moving. First period starts soon!"

Zion had been waiting for middle school ever since we had come back from Chidani, talking about it nonstop. I hadn't particularly cared, though, because my mind was on saving my mama and figuring out what happened to Daddy.

I let Zion pull me upstairs, across the stainless marble, our new sneakers squeaking over the floor. I fished my slip from my pocket—"Don't forget this, Cam," Grandma had said on the way out of the house this morning—while Zion mumbled his locker number and combination to himself, stepping up to number 207. I folded my arms, leaning against mine, number 209, right next to his.

"We need to talk about it, Zion," I whispered again. "There's so much that happened—"

Zion sighed, opened his locker, and stuffed his things in, cutting me off. "Cam, can I just have one regular day?" he asked, taking out another sheet, his class schedule. He grabbed his leg, squeezing it as he gazed at the paper. "Can I just get one day where I get to be a kid? It's the first day of school, and you're acting like the world is going to end."

"But it *will* end if Amina gets what she wants," I hissed.

A quick look of concern appeared on Zion's face before it disappeared. "Listen, we have English with Ms. Maton first period. We should get there." He patted my shoulder. "If you want to talk about it, we can. But can it wait until after school?"

I sighed again, pulling the straps of my backpack tighter around my shoulders. "I guess so."

He tossed me one last glance before making his way through the crowds of bewildered-looking students to class. I stood there for a while, deep in thought. I guess I understood a bit; we had been through death and back in a matter of months, and Zion wanted to forget about it for a while. But, for me, I just didn't see a point. Nothing made sense any longer, including school.

There was a mixture of excitement and nervousness in the air as my elementary class experienced middle school for the first time. But I couldn't feel anything, except for an itch to return to Chidani to finish what we had started.

Before long, the hall had cleared and I was left with a few stragglers as the late bell rung. The large man from earlier stepped forward, a crease burrowing itself into his forehead, his lips pursed.

"Really?" he said, shaking his bald head, taking off a sheet of paper from his clipboard and beginning to write with a black pen. "Late on the first day of school? Let's get to class, son." He handed me the paper, a write-up. I scoffed as I opened my locker and stuffed my backpack inside after I removed my class notebooks and pens.

Written in red letters on the paper were the words Late to Class. Detention on Friday, 3:30 p.m.

"Already?" I said, snapping the locker shut with more vigor than I meant. By the time I got to Ms. Maton's class, every student was seated. Zion sat in the front, as we always did, but the seat next to him was occupied. He gestured with his hands as if to say, "I tried, bro."

"Mr. Battle, I presume," Ms. Maton said from the board, her eyes kind as she regarded me. "You're the only one who hasn't shown up yet."

"Yes, ma'am," I said, gripping my notebooks hard against my chest. Every eye in the class was on me.

She pointed to a seat in the back. "There's only one open seat left." She handed me a worksheet, then gestured to a cart of literature textbooks by the door. "Go ahead and take one, write your name on the first page, and then turn to page thirty, and we can get started. I'll record your textbook number later."

I did as I was told, and walked past Zion, grumbling "traitor" under my breath so that only he could hear it. He giggled behind his hands as I sat down.

I barely paid attention as Ms. Maton passed out the syllabus, going over the rules of her classroom. But I did turn to page thirty in the textbook like she asked, and read along with the class as we went through an excerpt from *Their Eyes Were Watching God* and filled out the worksheet on theme.

"Hey, you?" someone whispered to my right. I scrunched my forehead, turning my head as the class continued to read aloud.

"*You?*" I mouthed. "I do have a name," I whispered back.

The boy who said it chuckled a bit. He tapped his worksheet with his index finger, where "Vince" was scrawled at the top. "What's your name?"

I pursed my lips, my attention returning to my worksheet as Ms. Maton strolled past our desks and went back to the front of the class, holding her teacher's textbook. I heard a *tsk* coming from Vince's mouth, but I didn't turn to him again. Just then, a sharp pain ratcheted across my chest, and I struggled to keep the groan in. The pain vanished, though, in another second.

"Hey, yo, I need your help," Vince whispered again. This time, I looked at him from the corner of my eyes. He was a Black boy, just a little bit taller than me. He wore all-red Nike Foamposites, his dark jeans barely reaching the top of his shoes. An emblem of a basketball and the school sigil of an eagle was stitched into his black shirt, marking him as a basketball player.

"Hey, yo," he said once more.

"What?" I said, annoyed at this point.

"Do you have another pencil?"

I pointed at his worksheet. "How did you write your name?"

He held up a pencil with a broken tip. "The one I was using obviously stopped working."

I gestured at the entire classroom. "It's literally the first day of school, bro. How you forget to bring extras to class?"

"And how you forget to get to class on time?" he grumbled.

"Cameron, Vince, is there a problem back there?" Ms. Maton said from the board, annoyance flitting over her face, too. "We should be reading and filling out the worksheet."

"No, ma'am," Vince said, a smile brightening his face, his teeth the color of pearls. "Sorry about that. Won't happen again."

Her face softened at his response while I pursed my lips even harder.

"Brownnoser," I mouthed.

Zion shifted his head to me, but then he turned back around while I went back to reading.

"Yo, I said I need a pencil," Vince whispered. "I know you got one, nerd."

I slammed my pen down on my desk, looking at Vince once again. Red appeared in his eyes, but when I blinked, it had disappeared. I noticed how the hair on top of his head stood tall, while the back of his head was shaved bald. Designs were drawn into its sides. I shuffled through my pockets and handed him a pen. "Here."

"Thanks," he said, writing once, then putting it in his ear, and leaning back in his seat so far that the top rail of it was poised against the wall.

Really? You're gonna terrorize me about something to write with and then hardly even use it? Ms. Maton's eyes searched the back of the classroom where she saw Vince obviously not paying attention, with his seat leaning against the wall, and said nothing. I seethed, but kept my focus on the work at hand; it wasn't that I was angry at Vince. He was a basketball player, and he could probably get away with anything he wanted. I was annoyed that instead of figuring out a plan for Chidani, I was stuck dealing with pests like the one sitting right next to me.

As soon as the bell rung, I passed my work down the aisle and was the first to stand up, but not before a foot stuck out and crashed into my leg. I flipped over and hit the floor, my cheek banging against the linoleum.

"Ugh," I groaned as all the kids around me laughed.

"Cameron, are you okay?" Ms. Maton said.

Something clattered against the floor next to my mouth. My pen. I grabbed it and stood, sending dark glares Vince's way. He only smiled innocently and whispered quietly, only loud enough for me to hear.

"Next time, when I ask for something to write with, give

it to me." His eyes turned to my feet. "And what's up with the Converses? Nerd 2.0."

I pushed past the group of students crowding around me, my face hot, and went out of the classroom, Zion following close behind.

CHAPTER TWO

"Well, no one said bullies are the smartest people in the world," Aliyah said after Zion and I arrived for lunch and told her about our morning.

We stood in the lunch line, grabbing plates of slop—at least that was what it looked like. Administrators and teachers strolled the outskirts of the cafeteria, which were made up of long tables that set adjacent to each other in rows. It was seventh-grade lunch, and every last one of us was here— including that idiot Vince, who was sitting near the cafeteria doors with his friends, most of them wearing the same Eagle basketball shirts. Of course, he was leaning back in his seat like earlier, like the moron he was. I mentally hoped he would crash into the floor.

Zion pointed at another door that led to an outside area, where a sign was posted that read, *Entrance to Outside Lunch*

Area. "Maybe we should take this convo outside?" He sent a nervous glance Vince's way, who was staring straight at us.

"Sounds good to me," I said, following the small stream of students heading that way. Aliyah, her box braids bouncing over her shoulders, led us to a row of picnic seats, surrounded by greenery. It obscured our view a bit from the cafeteria doors.

"What is this?" she groaned, sticking her plastic fork into the slop and watching it plop back down to her plate. I wrinkled my nose when I caught a glimpse of a black bean in the grayness.

"I don't know," Zion said, his mouth already full. "But it's good to me."

I ignored them both, pushing my plate away. "Listen, it's time to plan."

Aliyah sighed. "Here we go again."

"We *have* to get back to Chidani," I said, touching the familiar place in my chest. "I have to save Mama. You *both* convinced me that we needed to fight, for both worlds."

"Yeah we did. But not without a plan," Zion said, gulping. "And your grandma told us not to talk about it until she had a chance to think it through."

"Well, she's taking too long," I argued. "It's been two months, and she hasn't mentioned it once." A deep place tugged in my heart at the memory of Mama as a mmo, Amina controlling her. "While we're sitting here dealing with trolls like Vince, Mama is in Chidani, suffering, and who knows what happened to Daddy? And out of respect for Grandma, I haven't pulled out *The Book of Chidani* not one time since we got back. Something's gotta give."

"Cameron . . . ," Aliyah said.

"I'm just trying to figure out a plan to get back to Chidani."

Zion picked up a dinner roll and swirled it around the slop, taking a huge bite. "You're not going to leave us alone about this, are you?"

"Nope," I said, smiling at him.

"Meaning, your grandma's suggestion to wait means nothing to you?"

"It did two months ago," I responded. "But I'm tired of waiting on her now, just as I was tired of her keeping the *Book* away from me when my parents disappeared."

"Hold on," Aliyah said, standing up. "Before we continue this conversation, we need to make sure that we're truly alone." She walked in the direction of the cafeteria, pulling back the foliage and stepping through to the other side. When she returned after a few minutes, dry leaves peppered her hair.

"We're pretty far from the cafeteria," she said, plucking off and throwing the leaves to the ground. "No one should be able to hear or find us as we talk."

Aliyah let out a heavy sigh as she sat, her eyes darting to

Zion before speaking again. "Okay, Cam. Let's discuss." She tapped my chest. "If you need to read the *Book*, do it."

"I thought you'd never ask," I said, concentrating hard, closing my eyes. A lump appeared in my throat as it started to water, and the feeling made me nauseous. A deep intentional feeling settled upon my shoulders and then into my chest as I willed the *Book* forward, from its hidden place in my soul. An image of Agbala, the goddess of healing and justice, emerged in my mind as I pushed even deeper. Sweat beaded against my forehead with the effort.

"Whoa," I said as I mentally *pushed* one last time, my eyes flying open. Shining in light the color of rubies was the *Book* in all its splendor, translucent, hovering over us and turning in a circle.

"Ahh!" Zion screamed, grabbing it immediately and slamming it against the picnic table. When he did, the light disappeared and the *Book* became solid. He shifted his eyes from left to right, checking out for any onlookers. "Whew, that was close."

Zion handed it over to me, and I caressed it lovingly, memories of our last trip to Chidani surfacing in my mind's eye. It had been two months since I had seen it last, two months since it had given me magic, making me one of the most powerful people in the world.

With trembling hands, I opened the *Book*, riffling through its pages.

"What are we looking for, exactly?" Aliyah said.

"Dunno," I said. "Something that will help us when we get back to Chidani, most likely."

"We can't just go back to the Palacia?" Zion asked.

"We can," I said, continuing to shuffle through the pages. "And probably should. But Makai and the others won't let us go off alone. And I *need* my mama." A warm presence settled on my hand. Aliyah. Her eyes bored into mine when I looked up.

"Here, let me try," Aliyah said. "I can see if I can find something."

"Good, 'cause I'm too hyped up right now," I said, handing it to her.

As Aliyah flipped, Zion leaned over to read with her, his lips silently moving.

"Wait!" Zion said after a while, turning to a page that Aliyah just passed. "I don't remember seeing this last time, or when Cam's mom and dad read to us."

"Let me see," I said, my forehead scrunched.

"It's about Descendants," Zion said, handing it back over to me.

When I touched it, I gasped as golden light seemed to spread from my fingers, filtering down to the *Book*'s pages, adding more words to the selection Zion had found:

Agbala created the Descendants when she gave the *Book* to the enslaved Igbos as they were forcefully taken to the Americas. The *Book* followed them across the ocean, and Nneka was the first one who touched it, becoming the first Descendant, tasked with power and knowledge, to keep Igbo history alive.

"Well, we knew that part," I said.
"Just keep reading," Aliyah suggested.

The *Book* was thrown overboard when it was found; however, it made its way back to Nneka. When she touched it again, she not only was able to read Igbo history and learn about Chidani and share it with others, magic also filled her entire body, giving her the unique abilities of Sight and Summoning. These allowed her to return to her homeland of Chidani. On her deathbed, after attempting a powerful spell, she prophesized that the enslaved would one day be free. When the *Book* passed to the next person in her family, they too gained a unique ability.

The passage ended there, along with a moving image of a woman standing in a field, magic swirling around her like wind.

"I wonder if this is the passage we were supposed to see," I whispered.

"It's gotta be," Aliyah said, flipping page after page. The rest were all blank.

"There was also gold coming out of your hands," Zion said. "Sounds like the right one to me."

"But what does it all mean?" I asked. "Why would the *Book* show us this? How does it help us with any type of plan?"

They both grew quiet, allowing me to think hard. Agbala had never told me about this part of the story; I knew that she gave the Igbo people the *Book*, and that she had been punished for interfering with human affairs. But she had never told me that each Descendant held a special power.

"Agbala never told me that I had some special skill, outside of the powers I already have as the Descendant to open barriers."

Zion stuck his plastic fork out at me. "Literal *gold* just came out your fingertips. Maybe that's it? Gold dust fingers?" He waggled his fingers.

Aliyah scoffed. "Really, Zion?"

He shrugged. "I'm just sayin'."

I shook my head. "No, that can't be it. The *Book* has always been able to show us pictures and words when I commanded it to. There's something else. Something else we haven't considered."

We sat in silence for a while, Zion eating while Aliyah stared off in the distance. When I spotted a trash can, I went over to dump my food, thinking as I did. *What if I don't have a special power? What was Mama's?* I couldn't shake the fact that after all the progress I had made, I was still inferior, still not reaching the pinnacle of my magic, of my true power. I had felt powerful enough in Chidani, but was there something else I was missing? Something else that Mama had that I needed to inherit from her somehow?

When I returned, Aliyah and Zion were whispering among themselves.

"Why would the *Book* show us that, though?" Zion was saying. "That's not really a plan."

"Well, it's never been wrong," Aliyah said, touching the page. "Just . . ."

"Just testy," Zion finished for her.

"I meant not all the way forthcoming," Aliyah said.

"I agree with you both," I said, sitting down again. "The *Book* has never steered us wrong, but it never tells us the outright answer."

"Which is?" Zion said.

I pored over the words inside once again, trying to find something beyond the fact that I felt inadequate.

"Okay, well, what about the ring? We still haven't found that one, the last gift," I said.

"Well, turn to the page where we found the story of Anyanwu and Ramala," Aliyah suggested. "Maybe we missed something."

"We already did that, but here goes," I said, turning the pages. They all were blank; it wasn't until I turned another page toward the back that it stopped midpage, like a barrier was making it stuck in place. "I think we're here." When I forced the page down, the scene appeared once again, a picture of the sun god Anyanwu at Ramala's coronation, shrouded in flames, words writing themselves across the page.

"It's different!" Zion gasped, pointing. There was an imprint of a throne this time, etched into the sky. A ring hovered above it, revolving over and over again.

"It is," I said. "But I wonder what it means?"

"It can't be Ramala's throne," Aliyah said. "We know what that one looks like."

"Whose throne is it?" Zion asked. "Maybe Ekwensu's? Cam, you said you went to Shukti."

"No, it's not his," I said, shaking my head, shuddering a bit. "His was made of bone."

"Then it has to be Anyanwu's," Zion said, a determined look in his eyes. "I know it is. The ring belongs to him, right? It would make sense Amina might keep it there, in his kingdom."

"That makes no sense, though," I said, rubbing my eyes. "Why would she keep it there? We can't get to the Sun Kingdom. And didn't we discuss this a few months ago in Chidani?"

"*We* can't," Aliyah said, pointing toward herself and Zion. "But you probably can."

"Yep," Zion said. "You have the powers of gods, Cam. If anyone can do it, it's you."

I laughed a bit. "So we find Anyanwu? The god that Ramala doesn't even like to talk about? Sounds like a death wish to me." When I groaned, Aliyah reached over and grasped my hand, squeezing hard.

"Cam, we will figure this out."

"It's not that easy, Aliyah," I said, tears smarting in my eyes. It was like being in the fighting arena once again, watching them succeed before me. "I need my mama. You don't understand."

Zion reached out and grabbed my other hand. "I was there, Cam. I know—"

"No, you don't," I said, with more anger than I really meant. I sighed. "I'm sorry, I—I didn't mean—"

"Well, what's going on here?" a familiar voice sounded through the bushes near the cafeteria doors. It was Vince, stepping past the foliage, two of his friends following along with him like he was their king. Which he probably was.

Aliyah snatched the *Book* from the table, putting it behind her back. "None of your business." She glared. "Step off."

"Aliyah!" Zion said, his eyes growing wide.

"I was just asking a question," Vince sneered, staring at me. There it was again, that red glint in his eyes. As soon as he blinked, it was gone, returning them to their full whiteness. "Ain't your name Dameron, or something like that? Or is it really Nerd 2.0?"

His friends behind him thought that was the funniest

thing ever, laughing their heads off. I wanted to knock them off their shoulders. I balled my fists.

"Cameron," I said through clenched teeth. Fear trickled through me, betraying my tough exterior. "My name is Cameron."

He pointed to Zion. "And is this your little friend? The one who sits in the front of the classroom?"

His friends snickered as I stood, Aliyah standing with me. Zion followed, too, but he was trembling like a leaf.

"Yes, my best friend," I said. "And what of it?"

"Are y'all always so . . . ?" Vince trailed off, a faraway look appearing in his eyes.

"You mean, *bookish*? *Studious*? *Intelligent*?" Aliyah said, taking a step forward. "Can't find the right word?"

"Aliyah!" Zion said again, screaming this time, grabbing her arm.

"Come on," Vince said, rolling his eyes, gesturing to his friends. "Let's get out of here, away from these weirdos."

"Yeah, you better run!" I said, not feeling as confident as I wanted to.

They laughed as they walked away. "What kinda voice is that?" Vince said as he disappeared behind the trees. "*Yeah, you better run*," he said, mocking me.

I balled my fists even tighter. "Who does he think he is? He already tripped me in first period, now he's finding me just to pick on me and Zion?"

"You gotta stand up for yourself," Aliyah said, closing the *Book* and handing it back to us. "That's the only way they learn."

Zion checked his watch, his hands trembling. "It's almost time for our next class." He took out his crumpled schedule. "It says we have science next."

They picked up their trays, and started to walk back.

"Wait," I said, opening the *Book* once again. They crowded around me as we went back to the same passage. "What about Chidani? We need to decide now."

"Not until your grandma gives us permission," Zion said.

"We can't wait for her anymore," I said, staring intently at them both. "We have two pieces of the puzzle. There's a special power that all Descendants have. And they are all different. I need to find mine. And we need to find Anyanwu. The *Book* is showing this to me for a reason; if I find my power and the ring, I can defeat Amina for good and get Mama back."

"And possibly your dad," Aliyah said, finally coming around to my thinking.

"Exactly," I responded.

"I vote we go back," Aliyah said.

I turned to Zion. "What about you? You in or you out?"

"I'm in," Zion sighed. "It's the only way we'll really know for sure. Your power is there, most likely. And so is the ring."

I held out my hand to both of them, which they grasped.

"Then we go back. I've always had the ability to send us back. If Grandma doesn't give us permission by this weekend . . ."

"We go back," Zion finished for me.

"And we figure it out along the way," Aliyah said.

"Welcome to middle school," Zion groaned as we walked inside together.

CHAPTER THREE

The sun filtered through the blinds in the living room as I prepared for school the next day. I sat between Grandma's legs, rolling my eyes as she slathered my hair and face with Vaseline. Zion was at the kitchen table—he had spent the night—eating breakfast, already dressed and ready.

"Grandma, we need to talk about Chidani," I said as she took a rattail comb and ran it through my naps. "Ow! I'm tender-headed, remember?"

She handed me the comb, distracted for a bit. "Here, just do it yourself."

I did as she said, gingerly combing upward through my curls so that they stood like soldiers, high to the sky. "We need to talk," I repeated. "We have to get back to Chidani."

"I need to find Mama," I said as I stood and grabbed my backpack from the kitchen table. "And I need to figure out what happened to Daddy."

Grandma snapped her fingers. "Don't forget to tuck in your shirt."

I rolled my eyes again, but did as she said. "Come on, Zion. She's not listening."

He gestured at his half-eaten plate of eggs and toast, his curls bouncing over his eyes. "Don't you see I'm tryin' to eat here?"

"We're gonna be late for the bus," I said.

"I am listening, and I just don't know, Cameron," Grandma said, swiping Zion's plate from the table and placing it in the sink along with the rest of the dishes.

"Hey!" he said.

The woman Grandma had been a few months ago was no more; she moved with extra vigor now, her eyes were clear, and her voice was commanding. Every night since we had come back, she had been sleeping in the attic, watching out to see if any mmo would return to attack us. None did, so she had assumed that everything was *relatively* good in Chidani. She would never admit it, but I think she was happy that Mama was alive . . . well, *almost* alive. She'd spent the last two years not knowing where her daughter was, but now that I had returned safe, she carried herself with strength. She also assumed that the portal opened in the attic; if she slept there, she could keep us from going back until she gave us express permission.

I turned to her, incredulous. "What do you mean you 'don't know'?" I said. "I need to go back to Chidani and save

Mama. Just because the barrier has not been overrun with mmo since we returned, does not mean that we are safe." I felt like stamping my feet, but that definitely wouldn't make Grandma soften to any of my plans. A sliver of pain shot through my chest, and I grasped it, a reminder that I still had something to do, still had a mission to complete. "I can go back if I want to," I whispered. "I have that power. You can't keep me away forever."

Grandma saw the movement, and her eyes welled with tears. She kneeled in front of me, clutching my hands. "I'm just trying to protect you, Cam. You have to believe me. Yes, you have the power to go back, but . . . I can't allow you to just go back there when I don't know if you'll be safe. Plus, I can't lose you like I lost your mama and daddy."

"But Mama isn't dead," I pleaded. "I saw her."

She wiped the sweat from my forehead. "I know you saw her, baby. And I don't want you to see her like that again. We have to save her and we will. We just need more time."

I removed my hand from hers and narrowed my eyes, speaking softly. "I'm going back."

Sighing, she stood up straight, shaking her head. "Just like your mother, always headstrong. Brave. Confident to a fault. Just like me, too. At least you get it honest. But you forget, Cam. I was the Descendant before you and your mama." She raised an eyebrow. "So if you think you can get past me, think again."

"Come on, Zion," I said, smacking his hand that was

reaching for a blueberry muffin in the fridge. I wrapped my hand around his, feeling how warm it was. "We have to get to the bus."

"'Bye, Grandma Battle!" Zion yelled as I pulled him out the door.

We walked to the bus stop in Grandma's neighborhood. Unlike two months ago, the sun was a constant in our lives, shining down relentlessly. It was early in the morning, but it had already begun to peek outside of the clouds. I kept my fingers laced with his.

"I mean . . . ," Zion began to say as we passed the trickling pond in the woods and got to the one-lane road that led to the bus stop.

"You're not changing your mind about going back this weekend, are you?" I said.

"No," Zion said, his eyes beginning to sparkle in the sunlight. "That doesn't mean I'm not scared, though." He shivered a bit. "I was seriously hurt last time. I wouldn't wish that pain on anyone." He stared down at his right leg and grasped it as a faraway expression appeared in his eyes. "I still feel it every now and then."

I stopped in my tracks, concern for him flowing through me. I felt foolish as I remembered seeing him grab his leg yesterday at school; I had been so focused on me that I hadn't thought of the mark Chidani had left on him. I stared into his eyes. "I . . . I didn't know. But Agbala healed you, right? And you never told me this."

"Yeah," he said, sadness permeating his tone. "I feel it sometimes, like a phantom. It's completely healed, but it's a reminder that what we went through was . . . *real*. A reminder that we have to go back at some point. Sometimes, I think about what it would mean if we *didn't* have to go back. And the nightmares . . ."

"You've had nightmares?"

He nodded. "All the time. Why do you think I've been spending even more time with you this summer? Spending more nights at your house? I'm scared to be alone, but, at least, when I'm with you, I'm not as afraid."

We continued to walk in silence, our fingers intertwined. I was lost in thought about Zion, about his nightmares, about the pain he was feeling. I couldn't help but blame myself, even though I knew I had nothing to do with Princess Amina trying to take over Chidani and our world. There was a deeper side of me, though, that knew that I had no choice but to save everyone.

The *Book* in my chest wouldn't allow me to think otherwise.

When we reached the bus stop, Zion untangled his hands from mine and we got on the bus, heading to school.

CHAPTER FOUR

Snap!

"Ow!" I said, stepping back as Zion giggled behind the shirt he had just whipped at me. We were in the boys' locker room for PE, another class we shared with Aliyah. I was already nervous about changing in front of people, but, of course, Zion just had to make it even more awkward. I cut my eyes at him, dodged the next shirt attack, and went inside one of the bathroom stalls to change, far away from the lockers. I could hear the soft pattering of his shoes as he followed. "Zion, just give me a second. Go ahead; I'll be there in a minute."

"But Coach said we only had five minutes—"

"Just do it, Zion."

I was *not* about to change in full sight of a group of rowdy boys.

When I came out of the stall with my PE shorts and white

T-shirt on, I forced my school clothes into my gym bag. A shadow passed across my vision.

"Hey, Nerd 2.0, too scared to change in front of the boys?" I zipped my bag and looked up to see Vince, leaning against the row of sinks. His arms were crossed over his chest, and even though he was twelve years of age, they were already corded with muscles. A smirk wrapped around his face as his eyes narrowed like snake slits.

"Again?" I groaned, straightening my shirt as I went to the wide mirror opposite the sinks. Fear gripped me as I side-stepped him. He really was a big dude.

A sharp, twitchy pain suddenly appeared in my chest; I moaned and hunched over a bit. There was the *Book* again.

"Something wrong, Dameron?" Vince said, continuing to smirk.

I finished straightening the collar on my shirt, gathering my courage, and started to push past him. "Move, Vince. Or I'll make you move. I don't have time for this. I'm gonna be late to gym."

His hand came down on my shoulder and tightened, stopping me in my tracks. I stared upward into his eyes. I could've sworn they flashed red again, but they turned back white as soon as I blinked.

"Did I tell you that you could leave?" he asked, his voice turning dark.

"Yo, what's your problem?" I said, pulling at his hand. But it only tightened more. "You gotta stand up for yourself," Aliyah had said. I pushed against his hand, and when it moved slightly, I maneuvered around him.

Something pushed me, hard, from behind, and I fell to the floor, dropping my gym bag in the process. I turned around and there was Vince, standing over me, that same smirk on his face. I thought I saw a red tinge of light surround his body, flickering in and out in the space.

"Wimp," he said.

Dambe, the fighting style we had learned in Chidani, caught me so quickly that it made me breathless, making the hairs stand up on my arm. In one second, I lay on the floor, and in the next, I was standing, watching as Vince's smirk turned to a frown in slow motion. My hands involuntarily pushed out and slammed into his chest, causing him to fly across the room. When he screamed, an unnatural wind kicked up in the space, ruffling my clothes. With a grunt, Vince crashed into the locker near the bathroom, leaving a huge dent in it, and crumpled on the floor.

What in the . . . ? I looked down at my chest to see a blue light shining there, the same light that had opened the portal to Chidani a couple of months ago. My hands shook from the force of my push as time settled back into place.

My breath returned to me as I ran over to Vince, barely believing what had just happened. "Vince? Vince? Please wake up," I said, bending over him and rubbing his face, pushing on his shoulders. He groaned as I touched him, his eyes flickering open.

"What happened?" he moaned.

"Um . . . ," I said, not knowing what to say. I hadn't known that I could use Dambe in my world. I hadn't felt it in months. Also, why didn't Vince remember what he had done?

The coach's whistle brought me out of my reverie. "Um . . . you fell," I said, helping him to his feet. "I'll see you outside." I grabbed my bag and then went to my gym locker and stuffed it inside. Once that was done, I hurried out of the room and onto the basketball court. I chanced one glance behind me to see Vince rubbing the back of his head, his eyes following mine.

"You did *what*?" Aliyah screamed at me. Her braids were tied in a tight bun at the top of her head, and her dark skin gleamed in the sunlight. After Coach had explained to us what the expectations were for gym—mostly to do a lot of exercise that I had no intention of doing—he had blown his whistle again and escorted us outside to the track where he told us the first assignment due in a few weeks was to run a mile, full-out, without stopping.

Before then, it was just practice.

Zion, Aliyah, and I spent this time talking instead of running.

"Shh," I said, walking in the middle of them, talking fast. "You're too loud. We can't risk anyone hearing about this. Plus, you were the one who told me to stand up for myself."

"Yeah, but not like that!" Aliyah cried.

I shook my head. "The *Book* caused me pain when I sat next to Vince yesterday. But in the locker room, the pain was twenty times that. It's been trying to tell me something is off."

"You need to speak slower," Zion said, wiping his brow as we passed under the cover of a group of cedar trees.

"Okay," I said, taking a breath to clear my mind. "I was in the locker room, and I guess Vince stayed behind to talk to me. Well, 'talk' isn't the right word. He was just . . . acting weird. I don't know . . . y'all, he seemed different. Evil, actually. When he pushed me, I used Dambe to fight him off me. Yesterday, I saw red flash through his eyes. And today, it happened again! I wasn't sure if I was just seeing things, but now I'm sure something is wrong."

"Wait," Aliyah said, stopping in her tracks. "Dambe? Are you sure about this, Cam? We haven't been able to use that since we came back from Chidani."

"Correction," Zion said, stopping with her. "We haven't *tried* to use it since coming back. Maybe we can here."

Coach Marcus ran past us in his green track suit, giving us disapproving looks. "I'm seeing a lot of walking and talking! Get to steppin'!" he barked. We sped up, pretending to run, but then fell back into a brisk walk as he rounded the corner. We stayed close to the trees, so as not to be seen easily.

"But that doesn't make sense," I whispered. "Makai told me that nature hums at a different frequency in Chidani than it does here, which is why we could use Dambe there. That means that . . ."

Aliyah gasped. "I'm starting to remember how it was before. Remember how much it rained before the portal opened the first time? It was unnatural."

"A clear sign that the barrier was breaking down," I responded. "When things change . . ."

"Don't say it," Zion said, shivering. "Don't say it."

"If we can do Dambe here, then that means that something has happened in Chidani. Or . . . the barrier has continued to deteriorate."

We quieted as more of our classmates passed us, including Vince. He looked over, gave us a head nod, and kept it moving.

"He doesn't seem too different to me," Zion said. "If anything, he's doing what he usually does, which is being a jerk."

"I'm serious," I responded. "It was like a haze came over him or something in the locker room, like something had taken over his body. He seemed like a different person."

"Maybe you were just seeing things?" Aliyah suggested.

"Yeah, maybe," I said, but I was still unsure about the situation. I was *sure* Vince had changed right in front of me. Almost like . . . I shook my head to clear it. I refused to believe that could happen. "Let's go inside the woods," I whispered, pointing past the trees. "We need some privacy."

We went inside, walked a few paces, and then came to a

bench, situated behind a large tree. I steered them to it, where we sat down. "Listen, there's no coincidences."

Aliyah stared at me with concern. "Right. Experience tells me that something else is going on."

I nodded. "We need to figure out what's going on, and why Vince changed right in front of my eyes."

"Okay, bring out the *Book* again," Aliyah said. "Maybe it has something to say."

The *Book* swirled in me as I commanded it upward, until a peaceful sensation settled upon my shoulders.

"Let's do this," I muttered.

CHAPTER FIVE

The *Book* solidified and dropped on the bench, flipping to a page. We all peered at it, hoping that we would see something different.

"It's the same thing we read before," Aliyah said, then read aloud:

> "The ring of immortality was created by Chukwu, the creator of all things. He gave his favorite son, Anyanwu, dominion over the sun and gave him the Sun Kingdom to rule. For millennia, Anyanwu rose in the sky and settled into darkness at night. For his faithfulness, Chukwu decided to give it to Anyanwu.
>
> "Anyanwu appeared at night with the other two gods when Ramala prayed to them for help. After she struck

the bargain with them, Anyanwu gave her the last gift, his ring."

"Look," I said, pointing as a drawing etched itself on the paper, right below the words. When I touched it, fire bloomed across the drawing. We gasped and jumped back. "There's something happening in Chidani. Or, something happened while we've been gone."

Deep lines appeared next, as if someone or something was using charcoal to draw. A tall man appeared, drowning in fire. It was Anyanwu, sitting on a gigantic throne watching an opening in the sky, his purple agbada falling to the floor, covering his feet. The moon emerged from the sky, a familiar woman resting there before descending into the temple, a staff held tightly in her hand.

A dark shadowy figure appeared behind the throne, its face obscured by black smoke.

"Ala," Zion whispered, pointing to the woman. "The mother goddess."

"Why would she be visiting Anyanwu?" Aliyah asked.

"I mean . . . he *is* her son," I pointed out.

"Yeah, but why show us this scene?" Aliyah asked. "What does this have to do with Dambe, and Vince? There must be some connection."

"The *Book* hasn't been wrong yet," Zion said, turning to me. "Cam? Any thoughts?"

"It must be something important that has to deal with the ring," I said. "Look, the drawing is still moving!"

Ala glided across the page, from the temple's door to her son, who still rested upon his throne as if he were asleep. She touched his face, caressing it, as if she were waking him up from a long slumber. Something detached from the back of Anyanwu's throne, hovering in the sky, light from the opening in the ceiling glinting against it. It was a simple thing, a silver circle with an etching on its interior. The dark figure disappeared.

"The ring!" I said, pointing.

"Cam . . . you actin' like we can't see that," Zion said, hiding a laugh behind his hand.

"But we've been searching for it," I said, excitement blooming in my chest. "It's the second time we've seen it near his throne. We know where it is now."

"So this entire time Anyanwu had it?" Aliyah said, rolling her eyes. "I thought he gave it to Ramala and that's why she has eternal life? And that dark figure that just disappeared? Why does it look familiar?"

I snapped my fingers. "Think about it. Amina left the crown . . ."

"In the ocean surrounded by dark magic because she knew that Ramala wouldn't look there as it was Idemmili's domain," Zion finished for me.

"And she hid the scepter . . ."

"On Okeniyi!" Aliyah shouted. She quieted down when

Zion and I sent annoyed expressions her way. "On the island where Agwu lives; she knew Ramala wouldn't think to check there considering that she barred the trickster god from ever leaving."

"So that would mean that Anyanwu probably doesn't know that he has the ring," I continued, gesturing at the drawing. "If you look here, it seems that Ala wakes her son from his sleep. I guess life as the literal sun is the same over and over again. He probably hasn't moved in centuries."

"And with Ekwensu's power, Amina left it in his palace for safekeeping, knowing that Ramala wouldn't think to look there considering . . . how she denied Anyanwu's proposal," Aliyah said.

"You know what this means, right?" I said.

"What?" they both asked at the same time.

"It means that the ring, just like the other two gifts, has evil surrounding it." I clenched my fists. "Probably mmo controlled by Amina. And that dark figure didn't just appear in this picture for no reason; I bet it's a mmo." I stared at them, looking each in the eye, as a determination I never knew gripped me. "This isn't a coincidence. There's no way the *Book* would show us this—right after I used Dambe—if it's not telling us why Vince seems different."

"Well, well, well, sneaking off again?" a voice said before I could tell them what I knew for sure about Vince.

We all turned to see him strolling through the woods, leaves clinging to his gym clothes, a curious expression brightening his eyes. "It doesn't look like you should be out here."

I grabbed the *Book*, slamming it shut as my heart beat so loudly in my chest that I was sure Vince must have been able to hear it. "What do you want, Vince?" I said, narrowing my eyes.

"Coach just told everyone to dress in," he said, gazing at the *Book*, which was emitting a soft light now that I had closed it. "So, what's that?" He took a step forward.

Zion stood and stepped in front of me and Aliyah. "None of your business."

When Vince laughed, that same red glint appeared across his eyes again. "It *is* my business, though." He took another step forward.

"If Coach said that it was time to go back to the locker rooms, why aren't you there?" Zion asked.

"Because I was following you guys the entire time. Duh," Vince said.

"Just leave us alone, Vince," I said. "We have better things to do than to talk to you."

"Yeah . . . what he said," Zion responded.

Vince's lips curled upward into a snarl. He took another step and glared at Zion. "What is this? Is Cameron like your boyfriend or something? Get out of the way."

"Cam, something's wrong," Aliyah whispered in my ear, pointing to Vince. His appearance had started to change, to morph into something else. In one second, a dark smoke emerged from his body and a ruby illumination covered him. In another, it disappeared, and Vince became normal again. I knew what this was, but I was too scared to say it aloud, because if I did, then that meant it would be true.

Zion's face turned a deep shade of red before he yelled at Vince. "He's *not* my boyfriend. Go away!"

Vince moved so fast that he became a blur in the wind. He pushed Zion to the side with one strong swipe of his hand, sending him careening toward a nearby tree where he crashed into it and fell to the ground. Aliyah and I stood as Vince pushed the bench so hard that it shattered against the dirt. He grabbed the *Book* from me with such vigor that I was knocked back.

"Mmo!" I screamed. Vince's expression changed to one of pure torture, and a gray, pallid color spread over his face as his mouth opened in a wordless scream. He cradled the *Book* like a child would, as dry, gray patches formed along his mouth, his chin, and his cheeks. His eyes glowed scarlet as he barked at us. *"Book! Book! Book!"*

When he said those words, the sky opened and lightning struck the ground right behind Vince, forcing me to close my eyes. A ferocious wind picked up in the clearing as rain showered down, forming a deluge. A rip appeared in the sky, a dark vortex of wind emanating from it and dropping to the ground in the shape of a tornado. Zion stood and ran to Vince, trying to get ahold of the *Book*. Vince smiled, showing broken and rotten teeth, his mouth a cavern of blackness. He stepped backward into the vortex, and it lifted him upward. "Finally. Amina will be pleased," he said as he rose.

"Noooo!" Zion screamed, jumping into the vortex as Aliyah and I leaped into action. Zion grabbed Vince by the legs and pulled him back to the ground with all his strength. Vince maneuvered out of Zion's hands and kicked him in the stomach, sending him flying through the air. Dambe seized me as I moved, the music of the air a deep, haunting sound that reminded me of when we found Ramala's crown. I caught Zion right before he fell; he clutched at his midsection, yelping in pain. Vince snarled once and made to jump backward into the vortex again, but Aliyah appeared behind Vince, grabbing him around the waist, holding him so hard that he couldn't escape.

When he screamed, an unearthly growl released from his mouth, sending shivers up my spine. "He's a mmo," I said to Zion as I helped him to his feet. "He's here for the *Book*."

"How did he become a mmo?" Zion screamed in the ferocious wind.

I thought of the mmo we had seen in Grandma's house, the one she had killed in the attic. If one had escaped in our attic, that meant that more might be in our world, waiting to find me. I didn't have a choice now; I *had* to go back to Chidani and find that ring.

"Guys!" Aliyah called from where she was holding Vince. Her legs lifted in the air as Vince stepped forward, his shoes digging in the dirt. "Some help here?"

"Let's go!" I said to Zion. We both disappeared, going into Dambe. I closed and opened my eyes, directing myself toward Vince. Aliyah let him go as I smashed into him and a sickening *crunch* sounded as if a rib snapped in his chest. The *Book* fell from his hands, and Vince stumbled to the dirt, falling toward a cedar tree. Zion appeared in the air and dropped down, and he and Aliyah grabbed on to Vince now. I took a few steps back, then ran, planning to join them in trying to release the mmo's hold.

Vince narrowed his eyes and disappeared as soon as I got close to him. I crashed into Aliyah and Zion, falling to the ground. We all peered around the clearing, our clothes now soaking wet. Zion pointed to the cedar tree. "Cameron, get the *Book*!"

I scrambled to my feet and ran toward it, but I was too late. Vince appeared again, his entire visage almost changed to mmo now. Black blood spilled from his mouth, his hands turned gray and long, his nails brittle and yellow, as he pushed me in the chest. I flew back, but not before seeing him pick up the *Book*. "No! Give it back!" I screamed.

Aliyah, Zion, and I attempted to block him, but Vince barreled through us into the vortex. White light surrounded him, and his hair stood up on end, its tips soaring through the air. I stepped forward as Vince began to rise again to the rip in the sky.

"Cameron, no!" Zion said, grabbing my arm. I shrugged him off and ran, jumping into the air. I slammed into Vince's feet and climbed up his chest to wrench the *Book* from his hands.

"Cameron!" I heard Aliyah scream, as Vince and I struggled together.

I just managed to see Aliyah and Zion jumping into the vortex as Vince and I were sucked into the rip.

I'm going back to Chidani, plan or no plan.

CHAPTER SIX

Vince and I continued to struggle as we spiraled through lightning, darkness, and rain. The rip opened into a void; it was full of shadows, swirling around and around, the wind threatening to pull us apart. The tornado we flew in kept us afloat, but I had a horrible suspicion that if we stepped out of its confines, we'd fall into the spinning darkness.

Vince's eyes turned scarlet as he growled at me, trying to push me off.

"Give it back!" I screamed at him as he punched me in the eye. I felt it swell, but I held on to him so I wouldn't fall out of the vortex. "It's mine!"

"It's Amina's!" he growled, his face turning an even deeper shade of gray.

"Cameron!" I heard Aliyah and Zion say as they tumbled closer to me. I sent a hard kick to Vince's chest, and the *Book* dropped from his hands. I reached out to grab it, but it slipped out of my grasp. I let go of Vince and twirled away when he tried to strike at me again.

"Don't step out of the vortex!" I yelled to Aliyah and Zion.

"I caught the *Book*!" Zion called.

Before I could respond, bright cobalt lights blinded me. I scrambled in the air, unable to see until Aliyah and Zion grabbed my arms as the wind continued to whip around me.

"Where are we?" Zion screamed, handing the *Book* to me.

I couldn't form words. I thought we were going back to Chidani, but what I saw was a cacophony of things that didn't make sense. There was Vince, still struggling in the air, but . . . struggling with himself? A bright smattering of stars encircled us and so did lightning, striking every which way as we floated. Then, there was a sea of blue all around us. But when I looked closer, it really wasn't a sea. They were circles of blue, each one shining, each opening with ferocious roars. Below us was another circle, and if I narrowed my eyes, unlike the other fissures, I could just make out the broken bench, the cedar trees, the school track in the distance. A sudden realization dawned upon me.

"Cam, where are we?" Zion whimpered, clinging on to me.

"These are portals," I said. I stared at the *Book* in disbelief. "Either this did it or Vince opened them."

"I . . . I don't think that's Vince," Aliyah said.

When I turned to Vince, he was still struggling with himself as the mmo inside him tried to wrench free. In one moment, he was gray and decaying, and in the next, the boy I knew would return, his eyes pleading. "Please, help me," he begged. As soon as he said those words, his expression darkened again, his clothes ripped, and he roared in unmistakable agony. He moved toward us, his body angling too close to the edge of the swirling wind.

"Don't step out; you're going to fall!" I screamed to him.

He reached out to me, but slipped as he marched out of the vortex. He yelled as he fell into the spinning darkness.

"Cameron!" Vince howled. But there was nothing I could do to save him now. As quickly as he had screamed, he disappeared into one of the blue portals.

"What just happened? What just happened?" Zion yelled.

My heart beat so fast that it was hard for me to concentrate, to figure out what to do next.

"We have to save him!" Aliyah said through the roar of wind.

"He's a mmo!" Zion responded.

"But he's still Vince," I said, completely confused and disoriented. I snapped out of my reverie as a plan began to form in my mind. "Okay," I said, looking down to the portal we had just come through. "We can't go back down there, not back to our world. We have to find Vince. That creature has a hold on him because of Amina; it's not his fault."

Aliyah gestured to all the portals around and below us. "But which one leads to Chidani?"

"We go follow Vince," I said, unsure. "The *Book* should

45

be able to help us if we need it." I didn't know if that was true, but it was the only explanation I could come up with. One thing was clear, though: we could *not* go back to our world now that Vince was gone and taken over by a mmo, by Amina. It was my job as the Descendant to keep the barrier intact— and that meant finding Vince. Plus, it was my chance to get my mother back from Amina.

I looked at them both, evaluating the fear on Zion's face, his hazel eyes shining with tears, the fear that made Aliyah shake. I held out my free hand for them to grab.

"We only do this if you want to. If not, we go back home right now."

Aliyah raked her braids behind her back. "I'm with you."

Zion wiped the tears from his face. "We were gonna have to go back anyway. Let's do this."

I closed my eyes, taking a deep breath. When I opened them, I angled myself near the portal Vince had fallen into, bringing Aliyah and Zion with me.

We stepped out of the vortex, and fell immediately. I did my best to keep the scream in, but it released into the void as we went faster and faster. Blue light expanded and exploded through me as we drew closer to the portal. It enveloped us, and I prayed, with all my heart, that we would find safety on the other side.

CHAPTER SEVEN

My body rested upon a hard surface, soft whisperings reaching my ear. I couldn't decipher the words, couldn't bring vision back. I struggled, but found that I had no limbs, could feel nothing.

"Open your eyes, Descendant," a deep, feminine voice said. I complied, groaning as I did. My gaze alighted on a strong bare foot first, until the voice drove me to stare at its owner.

"Welcome back."

I groaned again, feeling a sharp pain from behind my head.

"You are fine," the woman said, staring down and reaching out to me. "Let me help you sit up." I grabbed her arm, feeling nothing but pure power surge through me as I regained my composure and control over my body.

The woman was undeniably beautiful, and immediately

recognizable. A crown crested her head, covering it from side to side, silver spikes striking the air around her. A star sat on top of the middle spike, its light almost blinding me. What looked like seashells were fastened to her chest and upper arms, multicolored and heavy. Her midriff was almost bare, with a tattoo in the form of a sun emblazoned around her naval. Her iro was cerulean, a skirt that flowed along the wooden floor I was lying on. I gasped when she stepped forward, as one of her legs was in the shape of a mermaid's tail.

"Mmiri?" I said, stunned at her appearance. And a bit fearful.

She nodded before gesturing around her with her staff. "Welcome to my domain."

I stood, marveling at the open space encircling me, an expansive void, stars and galaxies whirling around, dust particles emitting light. We moved through this domain on a boat, as if we were floating through water. Blue portals spread all around us.

"My *domains*," she corrected herself. "For I am the protector and the goddess of the cosmos, of the dimensions."

"Where . . . where are my friends?" I managed to say. Every time I met a new god or goddess, it was an experience that I couldn't quite put into words.

"Behind you."

I went to them as they lay on the boat's floor, shaking them awake. I explained the situation, and we all went to the side of the boat, marveling as we spanned through open space.

"Descendant," Mmiri said to me. We turned to her as she handed the *Book* over to me. "I think you need to keep this with you. You almost lost it on your fall here, but I caught it for you." She leaned her head to the side, her eyes changing colors as she did. "I can distinctly hear my sister Agbala telling you to keep it close to your heart. Maybe you should listen to her."

I nodded, doing as I was told, commanding the *Book* back into my chest.

Zion wiped the sleep out of his eyes. "This is a strange place."

"It's nowhere. And everywhere," Mmiri said. "The place in between everything."

"No more riddles, please," Aliyah groaned.

Mmiri laughed a hearty laugh, so loud that the boat rocked from side to side. She was as tall as a building, her crown striking passing stars. When she laughed, it was like a mountain were moving.

"Whoa! I get seasick easily!" Zion yelled, holding on to me.

I scrunched my forehead. "I thought I was the portal, the place in between both worlds."

The goddess sighed and approached me, touching my chest. As she did, golden light spread from her touch to all around my shoulders and back. "You're but one of them, my dear. Agbala, Agbala, Agbala. I'm afraid she has become one with the humans in such a way that she forgets that she is a goddess."

"She gave some of her powers to me," I said. "In the *Book*."

Her eyes found mine, dipped in the color of honey now. "That she did. It's the reason why you are able to enter here, to see me. You're the first humans to ever accomplish that." It reminded me of what Agwu had said, how Ramala had been granted the powers of a god and how she didn't deserve it.

I felt myself getting defensive. "If it weren't for me, Amina would have taken over everything. Agbala made a plan because she knew evil was coming."

Mmiri nodded. "She did. And I thank her for that every single day. However, she lost herself in the process . . ." Agbala said she had sacrificed to make the *Book*, but she hadn't gone into detail. And I had a feeling Mmiri wouldn't tell me what she meant by it, either. She became quiet now, as we spun through the galaxies, stars, and multiple voids.

I shivered as we traveled. "We need to find Vince."

"You are right about that," Mmiri said, thrusting her staff into the dust surrounding us to pull the boat forward, making us go even faster.

"He fell into the same portal we did," Aliyah said.

"Shouldn't he be here with us?" Zion asked.

Mmiri's face turned sad, her changing mood causing the boat to rock even more. She waved her hand, and seats appeared underneath our feet, making us sit down as we traveled. "I wanted to catch him, but it was either him or you." Her eyes found ours again. "I chose to save the Descendant.

"As Agbala has undoubtedly told you, gods cannot directly intervene in human affairs. Only indirectly. Because . . . Vince is his name?" We nodded. "Because Amina's machinations caused Vince's affliction, only she or you can help him. So that means you'll have to find him. When you opened the portal moons ago, a few mmo escaped. One possessed your friend, using Amina's magic to anchor itself to him. That mmo was tasked to find you. And it did."

"How do you know all of that?" I asked.

"My dear, I am the goddess of the cosmos. I see and hear everything, even the past. Time and space mean nothing here."

"Amina was captured in the last battle," I said. "That means she can't control the mmo anymore, right?"

"She still has a connection to them," Mmiri said, shaking her head. "Which means she still has a connection to Ekwensu. But, no. She can feel them, but she can't direct them to attack any longer."

"Then it's my fault that Vince was attacked, because I opened the portal months ago? I didn't mean to."

She shook her head. "No, it's not your fault. Amina did this; you didn't. However, it has happened now, and that problem lies on your shoulders to fix. Unfortunately, that's how life seems to work, at least for humans."

I wanted my mama. I wanted my daddy. And I wanted to protect my friends and family. Vince was neither.

"It's not fair."

"One cannot escape their destiny," Mmiri said, plunging her staff into the dust again and pulling us forward.

I groaned. "You sound just like Agbala."

She laughed a bit. "Yes, that is Agbala."

"Is Vince dead? Is he a mmo?" I shivered at the thought. Although he was no friend, I still didn't want anyone to die.

The goddess closed her eyes, as if she were mentally searching for him. "No, no, he is not. He is struggling, though, somewhere in between human and mmo. He waits for you in Chidani. I cannot tell you more than that, for that would be . . ."

"Interfering in human affairs," we all said at the same time.

"But I can tell you this," she said, her eyes opening, her expression turning dark. "Something that you must know. A mmo has possessed this person you call Vince. That is the first step in his soul being irreparably damaged." She turned her diamond eyes my way. "Which means that you don't have long before Vince dies and becomes a mmo permanently. Before he becomes Amina's servant."

I gulped. "How long do we have to save him?"

She closed her eyes again, and I imagined her consciousness expanding, seeing all the routes we could take. "Two moons. The rest you will have to figure out for yourself." When she opened her eyes, she stared at me so intensely that I knew that she wanted to tell me something, something else that I hadn't considered yet, but she couldn't. "Your magic is powerful, Descendant. Even if you haven't tapped into its full might yet. Save the boy. Believe me. Save him and everything else will fall into place."

"What do you mean?" I whispered.

She shook her head. "I cannot tell you more than that."

Save him and everything else will fall into place. What did she mean by that?

She strolled away from us and sat on the bow of the skiff, her foot and tail dangling in the stars and dust as we traveled through the cosmos. Leaving us to speak alone with one another.

"So, we know Vince isn't dead," I whispered to Zion and Aliyah.

"And we know where the ring is," Aliyah whispered back.

"At least, we *think* we do," Zion said.

"So, what do we do first?" I asked. "We either try to save him, find the ring, or save my parents." I put both hands over my eyes, rubbing them vigorously. "There's just so much we have to do. But from what Mmiri just told me, I almost feel like we have to get Vince before we do anything else; I think it connects to everything. Save him, save the world."

"But we're still in gym clothes!" Zion said. "There's no

way we can try to go anywhere to find *anything* dressed like this."

Aliyah sent us both a small smile. "Only one thing we can do: we go back to the Palacia, where it's safest. We should be able to find armor, protection, and possibly answers to all of our questions. I don't suggest we do this alone."

"Some help the gods and Ramala were last time," Zion muttered darkly.

"Aliyah has a point," I said. "It's the one place where we were safe last time . . . I mean, safe until the mmo attacked the castle. However, Princess Amina is captured, and we can find out answers from her, maybe, on how to get the ring." I clenched my fists as my voice shook. "She also has my mama. I need my mama back."

"We're going back to the Palacia, then," Zion said.

I called to Mmiri, who inclined her spiked crown to us. "We've decided that we are going back to Queen Ramala."

"Good answer," she said, standing. "Now, hold on to your seats. We have traveled far into the cosmos. It will be a bumpy ride."

When she thrust her staff into the stardust this time, the boat shook so violently that we almost toppled over. The goddess pushed and pulled with thunderous force. My heart thumped through my chest as a blue light bloomed below us, indicating another portal opening.

"Wait, you're not gonna—" Zion said.

"Yes," the goddess responded serenely, cutting him off.

She pushed the staff into the dust again, this time looping it under the boat. "I said, hold tight." With a pull, we flipped upside down and the boat fell so fast that I could barely catch my breath. My ears filled with Zion's and Aliyah's screams as we careened through the stars toward the blue.

"I wish you luck, little ones," Mmiri sighed.

My fingers began to slip from the stern seats. "No, no, no!" I yelled, but to no avail. There was a pressure on them, giving me no control over my grip. With a *creak*, our fingers released from the boat and we were free-falling toward the open portal. The *Book* pulsed against my chest, more painful than I could ever imagine. But the pain was a release, was a reminder that I was still alive, that the portal would bring me back to the place where Mama and Daddy had disappeared.

I grabbed Aliyah's and Zion's hands, closing my eyes and accepting my new mission.

We bounced on grass and dirt in a clearing, and the pain of the *Book* subsided.

Zion groaned and stood, holding his stomach.

"Zion?" I called, but he shook his head. He stumbled behind a tree, and we could hear him vomiting.

Aliyah looked queasy as well. "I'm beginning to *hate* the gods."

I laughed. "They can be cagey."

"No, I don't mind the caginess," she said. "I do mind their methods of travel, though."

Zion came back into the clearing, his light brown face still a shade of green. "Can we at least travel by . . . something normal for once? You know, like a car? Or a bus? Heck, I'll even accept a *train* at this point."

I stumbled to my feet, looking around in apprehension. "This is the Supernatural Forest. We should probably—" As soon as the thought came to me, the wind shifted, strong gusts flowing into the clearing. A smile came to my face as I thought of the gryphons. They swooped into the woods from above, their enormous wingspans cracking the tree branches under their weight.

I pushed Zion and Aliyah behind me, stepping back farther and farther. "We might want to get out of their way."

The gryphons crashed into the dirt, sending up a cyclone of dust. Their lion legs were like boulders, every step making a slight depression in the dirt and crushing the leaves. Their eagle faces were large and striking, their beaks long and sharp enough to impale us if we got too close or were struck by them. When they shook, some of their feathers fell to the ground and sent up another flurry of dust into the air.

I stepped forward to Ugo, my snow-white gryphon, awe drowning out any fear I felt at being away from him for so long that he wouldn't recognize me. As soon as I touched him, I gasped at the familiar sensation of connecting with him. Tears filled my eyes, and in a second, Ugo placed me back in

his world, the vision shining with bright light, my feet stepping into damp sand on an island in the middle of a blue
sea. Our mental connection grew stronger as my hands found
his head, winding through his ivory feathers that felt like gos-
samer strings. He chirped in pleasure underneath the soft
pressure.

"I've missed you," I said. His familiar scent of sandalwood
and oranges reminded me of Mama. I realized that it was
Ugo's way of connecting me with her memory, making me
feel her because he had once belonged to her, too. Missing
Ugo was the same as missing her; her presence was always
going to be with me through him.

"Thank you for giving me this." His scent evoked visions
of Mama in the mornings, jumping out of the shower and
coming into the room to wake me up, her body still warm as
she hugged and tickled me awake. It smelled of the loving
embraces she and Daddy would give me when they prepared
me for school, brushing my hair with rough strokes, sliding
hair grease through it, massaging my scalp with their fingers.
And of the Sunday morning peppermints she would pass out
on the way to church.

As the gratefulness flowed through me, I awakened back
in the clearing with Aliyah and Zion. Aliyah was already sitting on top of Odum, her dark skin striking against its auburn
coloring. With a grunt, Zion was using the foot straps to get
on top of Ike, his gryphon the color of deep, warm sand. Ugo
inclined his head toward me, his large wings wrapping around

me, sending ivory feathers flying all over. He clucked at me with a large tongue.

"Okay, okay, okay," I said, laughing and jumping on top of him.

"To the Palacia!" Aliyah said. With a strong gust of wind, all three of us were lifted off into the air. My stomach tumbled over and over until I settled on Ugo's back, my hands grabbing the reins. I stifled a scream as he soared over the Supernatural Forest and straight up. We were so high that my ears clogged with the pressure. When we broke through the clouds, rain soaked me to the bone. I shivered on top of Ugo, remembering that we were still in our gym clothes.

We flew so fast that I could barely see our surroundings, although at this point it was only just clouds. As quickly as we had started flying, it was over. Without warning, Ugo dipped quickly into the clouds once again, this time shifting directions, leading us over the Atlantic Ocean. The sight was as I remembered; the sun had given way to the moon, but it was cut in half, one side of it bright with light and the other side dark. The same could be said for the water; in some parts, it flowed with reckless abandon, crashing against the rocks on the shore, while the other was shrouded in darkness, unmoving, stagnant like wastewater. I remembered the last time we had touched the barrier that separated our world from Chidani and how painful it was, like my body was on fire.

The gryphons switched directions again, leading us to our desired destination.

We're coming up on the Palacia! Zion telepathically screamed from his perch, pointing forward. The castle spread between two peaks of the Igbo mountain range, having been built right into the rock face. When it was filled with people, pullies connected to the base of the mountain ferried them from the ground to different sections of the palace, all the way up to its spacious courtyard lined with stone. Well, it *used* to be.

Aliyah flew closer to me, leaning over. *Looks like we haven't been gone that long. They haven't even fixed the damage.* Right where pieces of the stone wall should have been was the large hole blasted into it, and at the top of the Palacia was our chambers, its towers the largest in the entire structure, a large depression bored into the ceiling. Looking at the ruined palace, the place that had provided us refuge for so many months, sent rage through me like hot flame.

The *Book* conjured memories of our time there, calming my anger. Images flooded back to me: the grueling training, eating too much food, deepening my friendships. Finding out Bakari was my ancestor, an adult I could rely on. It was so good to be back in a land that, for so long, I had only dreamed of. It reminded me that anything and everything was possible. Including saving my parents.

We landed inside the courtyard with a hard *thump* and

jumped down immediately. The place looked deserted; the once luscious green grass was sparse in areas, and cool air rippled dust throughout the space.

"Looks like nobody has cleaned up since we left," Zion said.

"We never know how time affects this place," I said.

"I guess we're about to find out," Aliyah said.

CHAPTER EIGHT

As soon as we strolled forward, the golden Palacia doors opened and Makai stepped outside, peering into the night, his hand holding on to his sword.

"Makai!" I yelled as we ran to him. "We're back!" A look of glee and satisfaction spread over his face as he pulled us to him in a huge bear hug. I distinctly remembered being mad at him before we left the first time, but that seemed so far away now. There were so many shifting priorities now; my old behavior made no sense to me in the face of what I had to do. Saving Vince, finding the ring, and saving my parents were all that mattered. It was time to forget the petty arguments of the past.

Makai's embrace was warm and inviting and tight, unlike his presence in my life before.

"I knew you would be back," he said. "Agbala said you would."

"What's going on?" Zion asked, struggling out of Makai's hug. "How long have we been gone? For us it was about two months."

"You were gone for just a few days," Makai said, his eyes gazing over the destroyed courtyard. "As you can see, not much has changed here. We thank the gods, though, for Queen Ramala's continued health. Thanks to you, her condition is stable, although she is still in danger of dying if the third gift is not found."

He stared at me with such intensity that I had to look away. "Come inside." We followed him through the doors into the great hall. Workers walked through it, using tools to repair the hole the mmo had caused when they blasted through the marble floors. At least progress was being made. Even some of the broken statues and paintings had been repaired. Makai led us through the great hall and straight into the doors that opened into the Throne Room.

It was much like I had remembered it, its location untouched by mmo violence. The room was crowded with nobles, talking among themselves so loudly that no one noticed us coming in, not like last time. Ivory towers rose from the floor like sentries, their surfaces embossed in gold leaf. The deep ebony marble floor had swirls etched into it in intricate patterns. Paintings hung on the walls, many of them depicting the queen and her sister. Gone, though, were the aziza flitting through the air, showering healing magic on the citizens.

The throne rose from the floor like a giant, its head almost touching the ceiling. Like always, the queen sat in it, tall and sure, her hair gray, Amadioha's scepter of thunder and lightning positioned in her left hand as she gazed at the onlookers. On top of her head was Ala's crown of wisdom and knowledge. It seemed that she had gotten stronger with every moment that passed.

"Looks like she's still doing well," Aliyah whispered to me. A sense of pride surged through me as I thought about how we had risked our lives for the world, how we had helped her and her country in their time of need. Now, though, it was *her* time to help me.

"Cam, look, Agbala is here, too," Zion said. Like always, the goddess of justice and healing stood right next to Ramala, standing at her side, her crown stretching to the ceiling, a snowy light engulfing her entire body. Her silver kaftan seemed to float in the breeze, and when I looked closer, she *was* floating, her feet barely touching the floor. The warmth emanating from her filled the room, wrapping around me like a hug. Previously, I would have leaned away from that feeling because it felt too close to Mama, but now, it was something that I coveted. And probably another reason why I wanted to come back to Chidani.

As Makai led us forward, the crowd parted, gasping as they did. Different variations of "the heroes are back" could be heard as we walked. Agbala turned her head our way as the crowd grew silent and then whispered into the queen's ear, who leaned forward in anticipation.

"Queen Ramala, they have returned as Agbala said they would," Makai said, bowing deeply to her.

Ramala gestured, beckoning us forward. We walked up the large steps, Zion tripping along the way. I grabbed him under the shoulders, and we continued.

"What . . . what are you wearing?" Ramala asked, a slight smile lifting the left side of her mouth.

"Gym clothes," Aliyah said, laughing. "We actually hadn't planned to come back so early."

Agbala turned a gaze to me, which made me a bit uncomfortable. "We've been watching you since you've returned home," she began. "Ramala and I. Witnessing your eagerness to return and your willingness to make plans. I was concerned when you first left, but you are steadfast with helping to save us, just like your parents were. I thank you for that. Our connection through the *Book* remains strong." Her expression turned confused now. "I admit, though, that I didn't see you come through the portal."

"We came back to help save my parents," I whispered. "That means we have to find that ring."

Agbala's eyes turned stormy as she regarded us, going from dark brown to a gray that sent a chill down my spine. "Something's wrong," she said as they returned to normal. "I knew I felt a disturbance not too long ago."

Zion raised his hand. "Um . . . that probably would've been us going through the portal."

Agbala shook her head. "No, not you. I would have sensed if Cameron had opened a portal with his magic. And would have sent the gryphons to you almost immediately. But this was different. This *felt* different. It was the *Book* . . . but, not. I'm not used to my vision being clouded."

"What happened?" Ramala said, growing serious, sitting straight in her seat. "Tell us everything."

I looked at Aliyah and Zion, who had both grown silent. I guessed it was up to me to tell them. "Well, some kid we know—I mean, he goes to school with us . . . and . . ." What I was saying sounded too fantastical to be true. It was hard to put words to it, but Chidani had taught me over the last long months that anything and everything was real, or at least had some truth to it.

Aliyah took up the tale, saving me. "It was a boy named Vince. He took the *Book* from Cameron, opening a portal to Chidani. Multiple portals, actually."

"We tried to fight him," Zion continued rapidly. "But we were pulled into the portals with him."

"We got the *Book* back, but something happened to him," I said, shivering a bit at the thought. "He turned into a mmo and then morphed back, over and over again. At certain points he was trying to get us to help him, but in other moments, he was back into mmo form. It was scary. He fell into one of the portals. And then Mmiri picked us up, bringing us here."

"The goddess of the cosmos," Agbala sighed. "My sister. I haven't seen her in centuries."

"We need to find Vince and help him," I said. "He doesn't deserve what happened to him. Mmiri says we have two moons before his soul is lost. We also need to get the ring, to close the barrier for good. It's . . . the only way to get my mom back." I looked down at my hands as I spoke. "When I opened the barrier the first time, mmo escaped into our world. Mmiri watches the universe. She told us that she saw the mmo attach itself to Vince, trying to find us. Trying to find me. And bring the *Book* back to Amina."

I declined to tell them that we knew where the ring was; *that* would have to be a conversation after we figured out a plan to save Vince. Zion and Aliyah must've had caught on to my omission; they both sent me side-eyes of confusion. I would tell them why later, but I knew from experience that Ramala and Agbala would want us to focus on the ring first for the queen's health, and leave Vince for later. I wasn't going to allow that to happen, not after Mmiri had told us that finding Vince would put everything into place.

Ramala scrunched her eyebrows together, and when she spoke, anger coated her voice. "Amina. Always one step ahead."

"We must consult her," Agbala whispered to Ramala.

Ramala's eyes turned steely. "No, we will not. We can't risk her escaping once again. If she does, all might be lost."

I cleared my throat. "Look, she knows things we don't know. We don't have a choice but to talk to her." We knew where the ring was, but Amina might have answers about Vince, too, that we could use to save him.

"He's right, Ramala," Agbala said.

"Can you ensure that she will not escape?" Ramala asked.

Agbala nodded. "I ensure it."

"Then I insist that I be there with you," Ramala said, gripping her scepter tightly, so tightly that I thought it would break. "It's time to speak to my sister once again."

———

The dungeons were dark and dank, empty except for a small stream that coursed through the large palace. We followed Agbala and Ramala into its depths, Makai guarding the entrance.

I saw the light before I saw Amina. It was a blazing thing, swirling in reds, blues, and oranges, like the sun had wrapped itself into the dungeons. Then, I saw the cage Agbala stopped us in front of. The light was inside it; something struggled within its depths. I could just make out Amina, almost seeming as if she were sleeping. The sun encircled

JAMAR J. PERRY

her like chains, binding her into one place as she floated above the ground.

"This is her prison," Agbala said. "We've kept her here ever since you left."

"Serves her right," Zion said, darkly, gripping the leg that had been broken.

Ramala took a deep breath and held her scepter high. Lightning crackled through it as she swung it forward, clanking against the cell door. Amina awakened with a start, staring at me. She struggled, but the sun only tightened itself around her with its impenetrable bonds.

"The *Book*!" she said, her mouth hanging open greedily.

"Never," I said, taking a step forward. Aliyah pulled me back, shaking her head.

"What did you do, Amina?" Ramala said, scorn drowning her voice.

Amina took on a tone of mocking as she spoke. "Besides taking your gifts for myself?"

We said nothing.

She laughed as she floated in the air, her eyes narrowing. "Well, you've already taken the crown and scepter back from me, and you know I'll *never* tell you where the ring is. This could only mean one thing." A wave of nausea washed over me as she turned her gaze to me again. "Mmo have escaped into your world, haven't they? I can feel it even now, see it all in my mind's eye. Two, by my count. You killed one, but one is still alive. They will always stay loyal to me, no matter how

68

long you keep me bound here, no matter how long I don't have direct power over them. They are trying to finish the mission I gave them moons ago."

Her words gave me horrible pause. Whatever happened to Mama would happen to Vince if I didn't save him in time. No one deserved that pain. No one.

"Vince," I said, the words barely able to leave my mouth. "It took Vince."

"All in service to me, of course," Amina said, an impassive look crossing her expression.

"Amina," Ramala said, raising her scepter. "Tell us what we need to know."

"It took Vince and almost stole the *Book* from me," I said. "It didn't succeed."

"But it did succeed in taking Vince," Amina said dispassionately.

I groaned, closing my eyes and squeezing my fingers together in the middle of my forehead. "He is still alive." "Two moons," Mmiri had said.

"He is. Not for long, though."

I opened my eyes. "Where is he?"

Amina smiled. "Now why would I tell you that? There's nothing in it for me." Her grin grew wider as she continued speaking.

Anger was like flame, licking through my body and incinerating me from the inside out. I thrust my right hand down as magic coursed in my chest. Shadow and gold shrouded my fingers as a sword appeared there, the same one the *Book* had given me months ago. I pulled it up, ready to lunge at Amina.

A hand lightly touched my shoulder, a calmness reverberating through me. "Wait. Did you just try to heal my anger—"

"Cameron, no," Agbala said. "Now is not the time to kill. It is the time for answers."

I shrugged off Agbala's hand. "Leave me alone," I said, storming away into the darkness. Zion tried to follow me, but the look I gave stopped him. "Just let me go."

As soon as I rounded the corner, I could hear Amina speaking in a mocking tone. "Agbala, the goddess of healing and justice, always using her magic to calm people. I remember you did the same to me, trying to make me forgive Ramala for what she did to our people. For taking their ability to age from them, all so you could erect a barrier between us and our enslaved descendants." Her voice broke. "For not saving them. I wonder when Cameron will realize that you do nothing but *use* people, that you only care about yourself."

I remembered that understanding, how I thought Agbala was using me, and how I had refused to find the rest of the gifts for her. Zion and Aliyah had taught me that I was being selfish, that they and their families were in danger, too. I stumbled into the darkness, found a space near a wall, and just sat there, letting my thoughts take over. In the corner of my eye, the sun prison's light appeared, but I did my best to ignore it, to ignore the constant drone of Ramala and Agbala pleading with the princess. I knew that it would do nothing to try to negotiate with Amina, someone whose entire soul was corrupted. I shivered, recalling the vision I had of Ekwensu using his blade to take a piece of Amina, turning her into his acolyte. This would be Vince's fate, too, if we didn't save him.

The *Book* pounded in my chest, so hard and painful that I had to close my eyes. In these moments, though it was unbearable, I knew it was trying to tell me something, trying to help me get through an impossible situation. I thought hard, mentally riffling through its pages. I found the words, but not the solution. Reading the *Book* was like looking at a movie, the pictures moving and the words writing across pages like a fantasy to me, tinged with gold.

When I opened my eyes, Zion and Aliyah were standing in front of me. And I had an idea.

"Are you okay?" Aliyah said, reaching out to me.

"Amina didn't have any answers, did she?" I asked.

Zion shook his head. "She only spoke in riddles."

I twirled my sword in the air. "She told more than she thought possible."

Hearing Agbala and Ramala still speaking with Amina made me lower my voice. "Think on what she said. She said two escaped into our world, right? One that we killed, and one that is alive, connected to Vince. That means that Mmiri was right; she still has a connection to the mmo even though she can't control them."

"Meaning?" Aliyah said.

"Meaning that our world is safe. For now. Grandma killed the first one. We still have to find the one that took Vince," I said. "She is clever, but she slipped up when she mentioned that."

Aliyah and Zion breathed a sigh of relief, and I felt it too. At least Grandma would be safe while we were in Chidani.

"Why didn't you tell them we know where the ring might be?" Zion asked.

The *Book* thumped in my chest once again, and I cried out. "They would just focus all of their attention on it instead of Vince. You know how they are; they care for us, but they want Ramala healed more. If we save him on our own, we might save my mom." I cried out again as my chest thumped. "The *Book* is trying to tell me something, trying to show me something. I think I might know how to find Vince."

Aliyah gasped. "Mmiri did say that saving him would solve everything. What could she have meant?"

Something was needling my brain, but I couldn't put it into words just yet. I needed to get them alone so that we could discuss it. "I don't know, but I'm willing to find out. *Without* Agbala and Ramala's help. What's the point of telling them everything when they will just try to keep us here, protected from my destiny? Why tell them when Ramala might not even let me *try* to get Amina to give me back my mama?"

Agbala and Ramala returned to the dark hallway, saying nothing about Amina's reluctance to help us.

"Go to your chambers," Ramala said, strolling past us. "We need to prepare you for the work that needs to be done."

"See?" I said, whispering to Aliyah and Zion as we walked. "We need privacy for this. Let's go to the library. We've got two moons to get Vince back. And Mama. Let's make the most of it."

CHAPTER NINE

By the time Makai led us to our chambers, I had already commanded the *Book* out of me so that we could read together. Although I was exhausted, I knew that time was of the essence if we wanted to find Vince before going to the Sun Kingdom to find Anyanwu's ring.

We tiptoed out of our chambers after Makai left, heading to the library Ramala had shown me. We marched through the gardens past the Throne Room, but I couldn't help but appreciate the peace and calm of the fountains shooting water, the fish jumping from glittering ponds, and the trees of jackalberry, granadilla, pineapple, mango, and plantains. When we got to the familiar tall building, I stopped, chewing my lips. I jiggled the door handle, but of course, it was locked.

Zion gasped. "We've never been here before."

"Ramala brought me here to discuss finding the gifts," I said, placing my palm on the door. "She showed me how to operate one of the Maps. We need it so that we can plan." I concentrated hard, closing my eyes, and commanding the doors to open. When I opened my eyes, my hands were showered in gold, and the doors unlocked.

"Good," I said, leading the way in. We marched up the stairs and into the great room. It was empty inside, but the books in the library soared from one place to another, placing themselves in the right positions, glowing with an emerald light. The shelves rose from the marble floor, the ground the color of rich browns and deep burgundy.

"Whoa," Aliyah said. "I can't believe we haven't seen this."

"This is so cool," Zion whispered.

"It is pretty cool," I agreed, leading them to the room with the Map. The door opened without a problem.

I gently pushed the Map aside and placed the *Book* down on the large, iroko wood table, furiously flipping through the pages. Zion took one of the pillows off the large chair near the table, placing it in his lap as he sat.

"When Mmiri said she couldn't intervene in human affairs, it reminded me of when Zion shattered his leg and we couldn't heal him with azizan magic."

Zion groaned. "We had to get Agbala to do it for us because a god, Agwu, hurt me. Although, I was in too much pain to remember any of that."

"But that doesn't help us," Aliyah said. "Vince wasn't harmed by a god, so Agbala wouldn't be able to heal him."

"Exactly," I said, winking. "It would mean the opposite."

"Wait," Zion said, standing up as my hand settled on a page. "If Agbala was able to heal me, but the azizan light couldn't—"

"Then that means azizan light would probably cure Vince," I said.

"But Vince isn't injured, right?" Aliyah said, her left eyebrow arching. "He's possessed. Why would azizan magic cure him?"

"It's the only play we have," I insisted. "From what we know, only two things can heal quickly in this world: the gods and azizan magic. We know Agbala can't do it because a god didn't hurt Vince."

Aliyah nodded. "So that leaves the azizan magic."

"So . . . we still got nothing," Zion said, staring at me. "Mmiri let him fall in the portal. We don't know where he would be."

"I do and you do, too," I said, staring down at the words as they formed on the page. "You just don't remember this part in the *Book*. Even I forgot, until it nudged me to the right answer."

Zion peered over the *Book* and read aloud as a picture of a female aziza drew itself on the page, with see-through golden wings, a choker wrapped around her neck, a silver iro dripping down to the ground, and an arrow brimming with light in her hand:

"Centuries ago, the Supreme Mother, Ala, helped dying humans, liberating them, assisting their souls into the

afterlife. However, she began to create anew, birthing the aziza, giving them a sliver of her healing power so that they could help the humans when she could not. The aziza nestled their kingdom in the trees of the Igbo people, hiding in secret, but honoring their duty to the humans by healing them when needed. People believed in them, but none had ever seen them, for they had retreated once it was known that colonizers had breached Nigeria's waters.

"Once Ramala prayed for the barrier, sensing that the danger of enslavement was over, they came out of hiding, spreading their healing again to the world. Known for their magnificent feats, they built the Crystal City in the desert so that all could witness their power. Over the centuries, they invited anyone and everyone into their domains, to take part in their benevolence. Some were known to enter human lands, saving those who needed saving, healing those who needed healing.

"However, humans are fickle beings. They betrayed the aziza many times, killing them for sport and overutilizing their magic. In response, the azizan queen, Ala, closed off their borders and punished the humans by making their city invisible to human eyes. Ala understood that, even though they had been mistreated by enslavers, humans were capable of forgetting who and what protected them when they needed it most. It is said only one with great power can access the Crystal City's hallowed halls once again."

The writing ended there. Zion frowned, staring at Aliyah and me.

"Hmm, do you think—"

"That Vince is with the aziza?" Aliyah finished.

I nodded. "I have a feeling that he will be in the Crystal City. You read it; the aziza are known to heal injured humans. My gut feelings have never been wrong up to this point."

"I mean, you're right," Zion said. "But did you understand what I read? The *Book* says that their city is hidden from human eyes."

I smiled. "Remember our gryphon training? I saw an 'empty city' in the desert."

"Wait," Aliyah said, snapping her fingers. "I saw it, too!"

Zion raised his hand. "So did I. You think what we saw was the Crystal City?"

"I'm sure of it," I said. "We didn't see anyone there, and it makes sense that we would be some of the only ones who could see it. The *Book* says only those of immense power could. And Ramala told me when she took me to the Map of Chidani that the azizan queen had called the aziza back to their city. That must be Ala. And Ramala is powerful and could open barriers at will." I smiled at them. "And so can I."

Zion rubbed his hands through his curls, which needed to be washed. "That's the plan? To go to the Crystal City? I don't know, Cam; I think I'm tired of tinkering around with gods and goddesses. And even if we are allowed there, we would come face-to-face with Ala of all people, Agbala's mother. Heck, she's *all* of their mothers! The mother of gods!"

I smirked. "You scared?"

"Always."

"Good," I responded. "You should be. That'll keep us all alert."

"Something else Agbala said is making me think that Vince could be there," Aliyah said, pacing the room, nervous excitement drifting from her in waves. "She can find *anyone*, especially when we call her. She couldn't find Vince; she only *sensed* a disturbance. Just as she sent the gryphons for us the first time we came here, she would've done the same for Vince if she had known exactly where he was."

"She . . ." I cleared my throat. "She also found the *Book*, too, before it returned to Grandma and me."

Zion grabbed my hand, looking deeply in my eyes to help me return to the present. I returned his gaze, feeling the shaky sensation drift away as soon as it came.

"It's settled," I said, closing the *Book* and returning it back to my soul. "We go to the Crystal City tomorrow. The faster we find Vince, the faster we get that ring."

"Makai and the others will want to go with us," Aliyah pointed out.

I smiled again. "When have we ever listened to rules?"

After servants brought us food when we returned to our chambers, we took a much-needed bath and settled into our respective rooms. Zion snuggled close to me, wrapping his arms around me like a baby. I fell asleep quickly, but a knock sounding on the door woke me up hours later.

I extricated myself from Zion's arms, and crawled out of the bed so as not to wake him up. "Who is it?"

A familiar voice spoke. "Bakari," the soldier said.

I opened the door quickly, closing it behind me silently. There he stood, towering over me, looking like a grown version of me. A sheepish look crossed his face as he gazed at me, one of his hands resting against the back of his head. He was already dressed in his soldier's uniform, heavy boots and armor. The scar on his cheek looked harsh in the dawn light.

"I . . . I heard you had come back, and I just wanted—"

I enfolded myself in his arms. He grunted in surprise, picked me up, and just held me for a long while, before letting me down. "I wasn't sure if you were coming back."

"Of course, I was," I laughed. "There's still work to be done here."

He led me to one of the couches, sitting down with me. "Amina doesn't seem to be forthcoming about anything."

"She doesn't have to be," I said. "I already know what I need to know."

"What about your mother?" Bakari gulped, a look of anger dashing across his face. "We all saw what she did to her. She's still alive . . . but as a mmo."

"She didn't give us any information about that." I tapped my chest. "But the *Book* hasn't failed me yet. I have a plan."

His eyes turned sharp. "Cameron, don't do anything without our support. We are here to help you." He reached out to grab my hand, sending warmth flowing straight through me. "I can't let what happened to your mother happen to you."

I squeezed his hand in return. "Do you think we can save her?" I said, my voice catching.

Without speaking, he looked away, effectively answering my question.

"Bakari?" I pleaded.

"No one has ever been known to come back from being a mmo," he said softly. "Death is the only thing that's permanent in our lives. We either go to paradise or we go to . . . Ekwensu, either in servitude for the wrongs we have done or when our deaths are so traumatic that we *can't* pass on." When he turned back to me, his eyes were sparkling with tears. "That's what happened to your mother. And possibly your father. I don't think you can save her."

I looked around me, at the artifacts and memories Mama had left behind. There were the Ikengas sitting in every corner of the room, signifying her courage and her relationships with the gods. Each pillow, cushion, and embroidered tapestry held her, too, showing how long she had lived in Chidani, how she had become a hero. How she had *earned* a place with the Igbo, how she lived in the tallest place in the kingdom. She and Daddy had been heroic, had fought for something greater than themselves.

"I refuse to believe they both are truly dead," I said, gesturing around me. "I will find them. And I will save them both."

Bakari decided to change the subject. "Agbala told me that you were a Summoner, able to pull things from the *Book* at will. We will have to train you in that, as one hasn't been seen since Nneka, the first Descendant."

"She told you *what*?"

"Didn't you pull your sword out of thin air earlier when you were speaking with Amina?"

"Oh, yeah . . . I did do that. I thought it was just an expression of my anger."

"No, Cameron," he said, looking deeply into my eyes. "It's something that hasn't been seen in centuries. It makes you powerful, almost on the level of a god. More powerful than your own mother."

"So I do have a special ability?" I said. "The *Book* told us that all the Descendants had one, but I was unsure if I did. Now, not only am I walking in Mama's legacy, but Nneka's as well."

I sighed, feeling the inadequacy, but also the purpose that

came with having so much power. "Another thing I have to train for."

Bakari grunted. "There's always a need to train. Makai wouldn't see it any other way."

I stood. "Of course, he would see it that way."

"I will see you later," Bakari said, standing up.

I gave him another hug. "Yes, later," I lied.

After Bakari closed our chamber doors behind him, Aliyah came out of her room, dressed in a bathrobe the color of snow. Her braids fell down her back as she rubbed at her eyes. "I couldn't help but hear the end of your conversation," she said, yawning. "You don't want to train? Why?"

"I . . ."

"You have this new power that we don't understand yet," Aliyah said, grabbing my hand. "Maybe we should wait before going to the Crystal City. I . . . I don't want you hurt if we make a rash decision without first making sure you know how to use your power to help us. Mmiri said we had two moons; we can spare two or three days here."

I shook my head, closing my eyes tight as tears formed in my eyes. "I can't keep waiting around when Mama's life is at stake. I keep thinking about it, Aliyah. The pain she must be in. How Amina tortured her soul by turning her into a mmo. About . . . what I saw in the Cave of Shadows. We have to move, and training only delays me. At the end of it all, Mama has to be saved, Daddy has to be found, and Amina has to die. For good."

Aliyah's soft voice made me open my eyes. "What about your power? What about finding what it is and how to use it? I can't lose you, Cam."

"The *Book* hasn't done me wrong yet, has it?" I asked. "Whatever I need, it has given to me. Trust me on this, Aliyah."

She was silent for a moment before nodding, squeezing my hand. "Okay, Cam. I trust you. I always have and always will."

CHAPTER TEN

Zion yawned loudly, wiping the sleep from his eyes.

"Shh!" I said as we took off our sleeping robes. "Do you want our personal servants, Dabir, Amir, and Moro, to hear us?"

"Whew, no," Zion whispered, throwing open the door to our dressing room and looking through our armoires. I shivered at the thought of the magical pool, and how thoughts became actions there. I didn't want to experience that again, at least not now.

A soft knock sounded on the door, and Aliyah came in. "Moro is going to be up soon," she whispered, closing the door behind her with her pack already slung over her shoulders. "I made sure to pack a tent if we need it. We should hurry up."

"We're almost done," I said, putting on my riding clothes and helping Zion into his; he was still delirious with sleep. I popped him in the back of the head. "Wake up. Now."

"Okay," he groaned, but he did look more alert. "Let's just go."

We grabbed our riding packs, went back inside our bedding chambers, and tiptoed over to the window. Wordlessly, we called for our gryphons. Their wingspans beat against the air, loud and all-encompassing. They were sure to wake the guards tasked to watch over us.

"Hurry up!" I urged, opening the window clasp and jumping onto the windowsill. There was just enough room for Aliyah and Zion to join me. We wiggled on the sill, as the gryphons screeched in the distance. *Come on, come on, come on*, I thought. The wind roared again as the gryphons approached, so loud and fast that we teetered.

"Cameron, I can't hold on!" Zion screamed.

"Zion!" I yelled, but it was much too late. He slipped and fell, a bloodcurdling scream ripping the early morning. I didn't wait for Aliyah; I felt Ugo's presence before I even saw him, a heavy, but peaceful feeling wrapping around me with a warm embrace, and I knew he was close enough to save me. I jumped after Zion without taking a breath.

I urged Ugo on as I fell, could feel him pushing to me, so fast that I could feel his consciousness brush against mine. The wind shifted again as I fell, my body unconsciously orienting into a safe position. With a *thump*, I collided onto Ugo's back, and I immediately grabbed the reins around his neck and sat up straight. With a jolt, Ugo flew down like lightning, flipped over once, and then used his talons to catch the screaming Zion. With a screech, Zion's gryphon, Ike, careened out of the swirling gray of dawn, and Ugo released Zion onto the other gryphon's back. I breathed a sigh of relief as Aliyah flew above me on Odum.

Close call, Zion said telepathically.

The mental connection was complete. We flew over the castle, so high into the sky that we burst through the clouds and the only thing I could see was our tower's turret stretching past them.

I leaned down and whispered to Ugo. "Okay, now take us to the Crystal City."

He went even faster through the clouds, Zion and Aliyah following close behind.

Can we never do that again? Aliyah said. *Zion almost died.*

He was never in any danger, I said, trying to make the best of the situation.

I beg to differ, Zion said. *What if Ugo hadn't caught me?*

Did you think he was gonna catch you?

Zion was quiet for a while. *To be honest, it's strange. I did know he would catch me. When I was falling, I was certain he would.*

Well, let's not try that out again, okay? Aliyah said.

Deal, I said. I grew quiet as we flew downward, breaking through the clouds and flying over the ocean. When I looked behind me, the Palacia was not too far behind, but with every passing second, it grew smaller and smaller.

The *Book* swelled in my chest and shocked me, like I had put my hand into an electric socket. "Ow!"

The sky darkened, and everything disappeared as if some-one had turned off a light switch. Aliyah and Zion disap-peared and so did Ugo. It still felt as if I were flying, but there was nothing but inky blackness all around me. I had the urge to panic, but the warm feeling of a hug that enveloped me told me everything I needed to know.

"Yes, Agbala?" I said, a little annoyed.

She appeared in front of me, surrounded by the golden river I had seen before. It was all-encompassing, bringing me into her domain. A stern look appeared on her face as she regarded me, her lips poking out in protest. The light that encircled her turned from white to gold to scarlet as her mood changed.

"You left the Palacia," she said, walking to me. "You forget that I have a connection with the *Book,* too, as I was the one who created it. It tells me everything about you, and every decision you make. Of course, I've tried to give you your space, to try not to look in on you. But the feeling it gave me was too powerful."

I said nothing, so she repeated her accusation. "You left the Palacia."

"I did," I responded.

"I would guess that you think you can solve everything on your own."

"I'm not alone," I said, defending myself. "I took Aliyah and Zion with me. You were the one who told me that I needed to rely on the help of my friends in order to defeat Amina for good."

"I also realized that you're a Summoner, that you need more training. Why leave now when you're so close to clenching victory?"

"Agbala, at some point, you have to actually *let* me be the Descendant," I said, a warm sensation sweeping through me. At first, I thought it was her magic, trying to heal me. But, no, it was something else. After feeling Bakari's love for me, I recognized that this was the first instance that I actually felt love . . . for *Agbala*. For the goddess who had sacrificed everything to save both worlds in a time when strife was way too high, even when it meant that she would face consequences. Consequences she hadn't yet shared with me.

Catching on to my feelings, Agbala's tone softened as she floated in front of me. "I realize that I can't keep you from your destiny. But you must allow me to help you. To be a Summoner is to wield great power. You must learn to use it wisely."

I took a beat to think, before telling Agbala what we had learned. There were so many pieces I was holding inside. I had been thrust a "destiny" that I hadn't understood when I first came to Chidani, I became frustrated with that destiny when I was in training and when Vince was taken, and now I wanted Agbala to just leave me alone. There was a realization, too, that was higher than them all, that made me know that I had to live my destiny. Mmiri had told me that if I saved Vince, all the dots would connect. And Mama overshadowed all the doubts I had, all the anger I had let build up, all the frustration of walking in a fate that hadn't belonged to me at first. My parents were what I wanted, and I was going to save them, no matter what I had to do.

"I know where Vince is," I said, clenching my teeth.

"Where?"

"In Ala's domain, the aziza's Crystal City. We're going there now."

"Ahh," she sighed. "No wonder I couldn't see Vince. I can't see into the gods' sacred places anymore now that I have intervened. If he's being protected by a god, that's beyond my vision. But why wouldn't you tell us this?"

"Because you would have stopped me from going. Listen, if we find Vince now, I can spend more time looking for the ring and then save my parents. I can't do that if I'm training and wasting time."

As she regarded me, that same warm sensation filtered through me, as if the sun were shining through me. "Come back to the Palacia." She thrust her arm toward me. "I can force you."

Another feeling replaced the warmth as I brought my arm up to grasp hers, like icy tentacles covering my skin in shadows. It was as if I were a different person, as if something had taken hold of me. I didn't understand this new magic I had, that the *Book* was giving me, but it felt *good*.

"No," I said as Agbala looked at my arm in alarm. "I'm going to the Crystal City. Now, leave." I wasn't really telling *her* to leave; I was telling the vision to leave so I could do what I was meant to do.

"Descendant, don't cloak me—"

At my command, the vision did leave, the darkness vanished, and I was back in the warm sunlight, traveling across the ocean with my friends. When she was gone, I felt different, disoriented, as if I were alone even though Aliyah and Zion were nearby. It was disconcerting, not having Agbala with me, watching for danger. But I knew what needed to be done. I knew that I had to do this on my own, that I couldn't have anyone treating me like a child any longer.

Vince's life depended on it.

My parents' lives depended on it as well.

———

I had just finished telling Zion and Aliyah about Agbala's vision when the Crystal City came into view. The sky darkened as we soared over the desert, and the temperature dropped. However, as soon as a structure rose in the distance, the night was replaced with the sun in an instant.

Okay, well that's not weird at all, Zion said.

Weird, but expected for Chidani, Aliyah responded.

As I chuckled, Ugo dipped down to the sand, Odum and Ike following not too far behind. Their lion feet stamped the ground so hard that they kicked up a sandstorm. We coughed and wrapped extra dashikis around our mouths to keep the sand out.

When it finally dissipated, we looked around us. Sand stretched for miles in every direction, and the sun shined brightly on us, so hot that sweat poured down our faces. In a few seconds, my clothes were completely soaked.

I massaged the side of Ugo's head, contemplating what we should do next. For a second, I thought about what the *Book* said about the city, that no one could enter if they weren't powerful enough. Uncertainty floated through me, similar to how I felt when first coming to Chidani.

"Look!" I said, as the city came into focus, the sand sweeping aside.

"Now *that's* beautiful," Aliyah said.

In front of us stood a towering metropolis, its magnificence augmented by a wall that seemed to be made of diamonds. The air turned cool, but not cold. The sand underneath our gryphons' feet washed away, replaced with ice, crystals reflecting in its depths. Ahead of us, a large brass gate tinged with blazing gems closed off the city. Turrets and parapets rose from each corner of the wall, surrounding the city. Trees, their tips crusted with frost, covered each inch of the bottoms of the walls, lights moving through their leaves.

Everything I could see was white and ivory, frozen in time and splendor. Even the air tasted like snow, although it was not freezing at all. I could hear sweet music filtering from the city, but couldn't make out the words just yet. From where we were riding, we also couldn't see beyond the wall, but even that was breathtaking.

"Cam? What do you want to do?" Aliyah asked.

"We came this far," I said. "We might as well keep going."

We nudged our gryphons forward on the ice; it crunched underneath their heavy weight, but did not break. It must have been magic. The magic touched something within me as well, the *Book* stirring in my chest with . . . *pleasure*?

The gate of the city opened as soon as we got close. What looked like a palace made of diamonds, rubies, and emeralds appeared at the base of the metropolis, but my attention was drawn to a hooded figure stepping outside to greet us.

"We've been waiting for you," it said as it approached. The figure removed the hood, and a dark-skinned man stood in front of us, his ears sharp and pointing toward the sky. Locs cascaded down his back like rivers, their middles and ends curled with golden clasps. Soft wings flew behind him, the color of night. He was tall, taller than an aziza should've been from what I had seen. A curved sword was hitched to the side of his clothing, which consisted of a ruby brocade vest, tight shokoto trousers, and light armor. He approached gracefully, almost as if he were floating across the ground. He stopped in front of our gryphons, his hooded coat and hair flowing in the wind. He stared at us with golden eyes, and when he smiled, his incisors were sharp and elongated.

He bowed to us. "My name is Arinze. Welcome to the Crystal City. Ala requests your presence in the palace."

Zion and Aliyah gazed at me, waiting for me to make the first move. I urged Ugo to lean down, and he bent low to the man until I was face-to-face with him. "She knew we were coming?"

"She did. She was the one who caught the boy from the other world."

"I knew it!" I said. "Well, what's next?"

Arinze's wings fluttered in the air. "You follow me, of course. I will take you to the palace."

We followed Arinze as he flew through the open gate into the coolness of the day.

The city inside was bustling with activity, aziza floating through the air, walking across the frozen grounds, or driving chariots that were drenched in flames.

"Um, this is *nothing* like I imagined," Zion said. "Aren't the aziza supposed to be smaller creatures?"

The *Book*'s pages fluttered inside me, but Arinze answered his question before I could. "We are humanlike, the aziza. However, we keep our traditions to ourselves, to be separate from humans. The aziza you saw in Ramala's palace were an offshoot of us, sprites that we created to help heal the divisions between the four clans during the time of the slave trade. When Ramala took the throne, we gave them to her as a gift."

"But also took them back," Aliyah said. "The queen told Cameron that."

"Yes, we took them back," Arinze said. "Ala's request. We are a people who strive and deserve to separate ourselves from others. We cannot allow our magic to be tainted by human hands." I remembered what the *Book* had told us, that humans had used the aziza's magic for their own gain, taking what they needed by force. No wonder they holed themselves in their city alone. I felt proud that we were able, as humans, to see it firsthand.

We arrived in a market, sprites dancing through the crowds of the aziza. The market was split into four sectors, the middle left bare for walking. Stalls rose on each side, azizan vendors selling fish, cuts of meat, jewels, goblets of drink, and exotic creatures, and calling out to passersby. Children no older than us, their wings barely sprouting from their backs, ran through the stands laughing and playing, with circlets of flowers surrounding their heads. Everywhere the children stepped, light beamed into the sky, spheres of energy releasing from the ground from the force of their feet. We must have been unexpected, humans entering a city where they were rarely seen, on the back of gryphons no less. But the aziza barely glanced our way.

We could hear snippets of conversations as we passed through. An older aziza, her hair turned gray and wrinkles lining her face, stepped out of a tent, holding flasks of light. She called out, "Selling all types of sprite magic. Magic of healing, transformation, and weather. For a price of just one year of azizan life, you can have an eternity of magic." She pulled out another flask of light as aziza swarmed around her. "Also selling bottles of enhancement. Boost your magic for short periods of time, performing godlike feats with just one sip." More encircled, clamoring for her attention.

My attention, though, was drawn to the children. They darted in and out of the market, kicking up dusts of energy. As they moved, they floated off the ground ever so slightly, falling back down seconds later. Their hands glowed with ethereal light, and orbs of elemental magic floated around them. There were balls of water crystals, flame, swirling cyclones of sand, and clouds filled with rain. One of the children extricated themselves from the crowd as we passed, staring up at me with wide eyes.

"Hold on," I called to Arinze, jumping off Ugo and bending low to the male child. He looked no more than eight years old—in human years—and his small wings fluttered weakly in the air. His hair was rough, like mine, and his dark-brown skin held a luster like fireflies had lit him from within.

Our eyes locked.

He held out his hands to me, cupping them into a bowl shape. Swirling gold appeared there, and a flower grew from the middle, extending into the air. In another second, the top of it crusted over with snow, and a small sprite was born, fluttering inside the leaves, yawning and stretching in exhaustion. I gasped at the creation as the boy smiled at me.

"What's your name?" I said, my breath leaving my mouth frosty and cold.

"He can't speak," Arinze said, flying down to me. "Not yet. He's too young."

The young aziza held out the flower to me.

Arinze chuckled. "You should probably take it. In the Crystal City, it is considered rude to not take and use what is offered for free."

"Thank you," I said to the young boy. He bowed to me, his tattered dashiki grazing the ground. I put the flower along with the buzzing sprite into my pack.

"We should hurry," Arinze said. "The crowds will only grow larger."

My mind lingered on the young boy. So much power he had, and he couldn't even speak just yet.

As we continued on, the Crystal City drew me in with its beauty. The buildings reminded me of skyscrapers from my own world, the tops of them brushing against the clouds. Aziza flew in and out of the open windows, releasing energized dust particles that floated down. Passageways filled the spaces in between the buildings, aziza on foot walking in and out, some of them pushing wagons of produce to the market, some singing to themselves, and some conversing with others. In the distance, a large crystal sea flowed from left to the right. Its waters, though, acted oddly, like they were divided by barriers. Some parts were choppy, some flowed naturally, and others were still. Plumes of scarlet and cerulean energy breached its surface.

"Wait. What is that?" Zion pointed at the water. Every time one of the plumes erupted, a skiff appeared, straight from the bottom of the sea. The skiffs were multicolored, aziza with pointed ears and fish tails crowding on them. They flowed through the water, breaking upward from the waves, and then plummeting back down underneath the crystal sea.

"It's how we travel," Arinze said as we continued. "From our city and into the mortal world. We're almost to the palace."

After we finally left the markets and buildings behind, the air warmed. The path we traveled turned to concrete, and a sweetness filled my nose. The sun shone as birds sang in the air. This new place was empty of aziza, and a large castle rose in front of us, sitting upon the greenest grass I'd ever seen. Like everything else, the palace glinted in the sun, encrusted with diamonds. Although it was huge and spanned miles, it still seemed homey, and when the chimneys blew smoke into the air, an intoxicating scent of meat wafted outward. A ruby-red door beckoned us forward.

"Welcome to the palace," Arinze said. "Ala is just on the other side of that door."

CHAPTER ELEVEN

I whispered to Ugo after we settled on the ground, telling him to rest and find food. The gryphons took off, screeching as they disappeared into the clouds.

We walked behind Arinze through the palace's entrance.

"I'm hungry," Zion said. "We didn't eat breakfast this morning."

"Shh," I said. "We're here to get Vince. We can eat afterward."

It was empty inside, a cool draft blowing through the windows. Arinze opened a large door made of iroko wood, with carvings I couldn't quite make out. I hadn't seen anything, animal or human, that looked like those images since coming to Chidani.

Aliyah clutched her chest as we were led inside. "This place is different," she said. "I've been feeling this since we walked through the market. Everything seems . . ."

"God-made?" Zion whispered.

"Exactly," she said. "Like, the entire place is magic, like it shouldn't exist at all."

"Agreed," Zion said.

The room we entered was empty, except for two figures sitting on two thrones. My breath caught as I recognized them at first sight. Zion scooted closer to me, so close that I could feel his warmth. He buried his head underneath my armpit.

"I can't," he whispered. "Not more gods. They can be *so* scary. Can I just leave?"

"It's okay," Aliyah said, joining us. "I'm not too sure about this, either, but we came here for a reason. We do this, and then we can leave. Ala is Agbala's mother, right? That means she can't be that bad."

"Um, weren't *you* the one who convinced me that Agbala didn't care about us just a few months ago? Maybe Zion is right," I pointed out.

Aliyah placed her hands on her hips. "It's what I thought *then*. Well, kinda still do. But my perception has changed. It's almost like gods are different, or something. They aren't human. So, they wouldn't care about us the way we care, right?"

I nodded as Arinze flew in the air toward the identical thrones. "I mean, Aliyah, you got a point." I grabbed Zion's face and pulled it upward. "It'll be okay, I promise. Didn't we say that everything we do, we do it together?" He nodded in response. "Good, so let's do this. I'll take the lead."

"Descendant?" Arinze called from the head of the room. "The gods would like to speak with you."

I walked up the middle of the room, Aliyah and Zion following cautiously behind me, my feet falling on and sinking in plush carpet. I noted how different this room was from Ramala's Throne Room. This one was warmer, made of deep burgundy wood. And empty, as if there were nothing else needed except for the power of the gods.

The god on the right—I noticed that her throne was positioned a few feet in front of the other one—spoke first, an expectant tone in her voice. "Arinze?"

"Of course," he said, bowing deeply, his wings folding inward. "My queen. My goddess. The Descendant and his friends are here to see you."

She leaned forward, regarding us. Her movements were almost imperceptible to the human eye. She was and then she was not. I blinked, and it seemed as if she disappeared into thin air. In another blink, she was back in front of me in all her splendor.

"Descendant?" she said to me.

"You're not like Agbala at all," I blurted out, not knowing what else to say.

"Cameron!" Aliyah said, shocked, as Zion groaned aloud.

The mother goddess's laughter filtered through the entire room, loud and all-encompassing. It was grating, like glass breaking, forcing us to clutch our heads in pain.

"I am not," she said, standing. We took a step back, stunned as she towered above us, much taller than *any* god we'd seen so far. "Humongous" was a word that came to mind, but even that didn't embody all that Ala was. I tried to avert my gaze from her to the male god behind her—who somehow was firmly asleep—but she snapped her fingers, bringing us back to attention.

"You're here for a reason, I presume? To see me and my son, Anyanwu?" she asked, as the right sleeve of her dress fell away, showing a dark arm encircled with golden bangles. Her eyes narrowed, and flames overtook her irises. She touched the sleek, ruby beads tied around her waist as she regarded us. The *Book* gave me its name: mgbaji. Thinking of the *Book* caused me to lose a bit of my confidence. I mean, Agbala had created it, and she had told me that the other gods had been angry with her about that. I wasn't sure if Ala would strike me where I stood if I mentioned it, since its creation was against her own law.

"We—we're here for someone," I said meekly. "A friend from our world. Vince is his name. He . . . well . . . ," I said, not really sure how to explain it.

I turned to Aliyah. "I got nothing."

She shrugged in response, her eyes darting back and forth. "Well, you better think of something fast," she croaked.

Zion cleared his throat. "We fought Amina the last time we were here," he began, surprising me. "We won. But that didn't mean our world was safe. The mmo had already escaped. One took over someone we know, trying to steal

Cameron's gift, *The Book of Chidani*. He fell into one of the portals, and we thought he would be here, since the aziza are known to heal those in need."

Ala snapped her fingers again, and this time, the god who sat to the right of her jolted awake, yelping. Flames erupted all over his body; we clutched one another in deep fright. Anyanwu grabbed on to his mother's hand, standing up to match her height, staring down at us. When he opened his mouth, soot and smoke drifted down to the floor and his hair caught fire.

"My son, Anyanwu," Ala began, lovingly caressing his arm as he awakened. The beads of her mgbaji clinked together as she moved. "And my sun. *He* was the one who caught your friend, the human who came barreling into Chidani without permission." Her expression turned stormy. "We saw, though, that he was harmed, that he was . . . *different* than the humans we watch."

Anyanwu moved in front of Ala and walked down the steps to us, and as he did, he grew smaller, to the size of a normal human man. It comforted me, somewhat, but he was still a god and his presence was fire, heat drifting off his orange kaftan in waves.

"You'll have to excuse my mother," he said, the voice emanating from his throat uncharacteristically soft for someone who was the literal sun. "She's not used to dealing with humans, especially not in the city she birthed. She does not mean to scare you. She only means to help."

"We only came here to find Vince," I said, shaking.

Anyanwu whispered the name and closed his eyes, as if he were tasting it, trying it out for the first time. "Vince," he said, opening his eyes. "Different. Obscure. Human." He stood there for a while, quiet as he regarded us, his body igniting with flame. We waited for a long while as Ala shifted behind her son, sitting down on her throne. The silence stretched on for what seemed like hours as I looked at Zion and Aliyah, who only shrugged in response. The sound of Arinze lifting himself in the air brought me back to the present, giving me the courage to speak again.

"If he's here, can we have him? We'd like to take him back to our world."

Anyanwu bowed to us, walking backward until he was sitting slightly behind his mother again, his visage returning to his god nature. He looked even scarier than Ala did now, with how his flames dripped down his body, engulfing his clothing, his eyes turning into pits of fire. His hair smoked, ash dropping down to the floor. In one second, it seemed that he was bald as the hair burned, but in another, it was full of luster and health.

"He is here," Ala said, smiling a bit. "But he rightfully belongs to me. And my people, the aziza."

"Why?" I said, my confidence returning just a bit.

Her smile grew wider. "Because we caught and saved him, my dear. Why not?"

Anyanwu inclined his head toward Ala. "Mother, we said

that we would help the Descendant. He needs us. You awakened me for this moment."

"We did say that," Ala said, nodding. "But, when have we ever not liked to play games with humans, or bargain with them? Our lives can be boring, living for centuries upon centuries." She cleared her throat once. "Let's make it fun. The Descendant and the heroes must acquire him themselves."

Anyanwu bowed his head. "So be it, Mother."

"Acquire?" Aliyah said to Ala. "What does that mean?"

"In order to rescue this Vince, you'll need to retrieve him on your own. And, if you cannot . . ." She snapped her fingers again, the sound deafening. Zion gasped and turned to us, his eyes full of fear.

"Please, please, please, no," he said to us.

"Zion?" I said as he gasped and choked, holding on to his neck. He fell against me; I caught him as his eyes closed, but he felt different. Light. As if all his weight had turned to nothing.

"Zion! Zion!" Aliyah called to him, doing her best to wake him up. She turned angry tears to Ala and screamed, "What did you do to him? Give him back!"

"If you cannot," Ala repeated, "then your friend, Zion, will stay with us, too."

"Why?" Aliyah yelled. "He didn't do anything!"

"As I'm sure Ramala has told you, the gods' graces always demand a bargain, my dear. We do not offer our magic for free."

Zion gasped again in his unconsciousness and floated in the air like he were a balloon, right out of my arms. I jumped up to get him back, but my hands flowed though him like water. A silver substance surrounded his body, cocooning him into an unbreakable embrace. He flew near the gods on their thrones until Ala snapped once again.

Arinze flew to us, a worried look crossing his face.

"Give him back!" I yelled, running toward them. "Give him back!"

"Cameron!" Aliyah screamed from behind me.

But it was to no avail. Ala snapped one last time, and the room's walls exploded.

CHAPTER TWELVE

The floor of the castle opened, swallowing Aliyah and me up as we fell into darkness. We screamed until we couldn't scream anymore. In another second, we hit sand, our packs softening the brunt of the force.

"Cam?" Aliyah said.

I groaned in response, spitting out blood from my mouth. The pain ratcheted across my head, my chest, and my legs.

"Cam?" Aliyah said again, scooting over to me. "What—what happened? We—we . . . how are we going to get out of here?" I groaned again, not sure if the pain I was feeling would ever end.

"You have to move," a voice said. It was Arinze, speaking to us in the darkness. As if a match had been lit, he appeared above us, his wings shining with light. Sparkles fell down upon us as he removed a flask from his pocket. "Here," he said, throwing it to Aliyah. She caught it, opened it, and snared the sparkles falling from Arinze's wings. She drank some from the flask, shivering as she did, and then she maneuvered the top of the flask to my mouth.

"Drink, Cameron, drink," she said, forcing my lips apart. I moaned as Aliyah massaged my throat, coaxing me to swallow. The taste was familiar, like ice in a freezing cold drink.

"You have to move," Arinze said again as healing took over my body and I was able to sit up. "Zion doesn't have much time, and we have to find Vince."

"He doesn't have much time?" I repeated, struggling to my feet, hugging Aliyah for her help, and then shifting my pack on my back. "What does that mean?"

"If we don't find Vince in time," Arinze said, his eyes widening, "then you forfeit Zion's life."

"But I have to save *both* of them!" I screamed.

"Then you'd better move and use me for help."

We scrambled into the darkness, Arinze's wing illumination lighting our way.

"I really *hate* these gods and the games they play," Aliyah yelled into the emptiness surrounding us.

"What do we do first?" I said as I caught my breath. "How much time do we have? Where do we find Vince?" I could barely contain all my questions and was so bewildered that I didn't notice the sharp pain in my chest at first. I groaned again as I leaned against one of the walls in the dungeon, clutching my chest.

"Cameron, it's the *Book*. It's trying to tell you something. Read it and let's figure out a plan."

Aliyah's commanding voice anchored me, and I did what I was told. I pulled the *Book* out of me and watched as it floated around the darkness, shining light on the rubble in the dungeon.

"It's not that Ala is bad," Arinze was saying as he flew in between us. "It's just how things are done here, given the pains she's taken to create the Crystal City and its inhabitants."

"Not right now, Arinze," Aliyah said as I grabbed the *Book* and we both pored over it. It grew hot in my hands, and I yelped as it floated back in the air. Its pages turned rapidly and then fell back into my hands. There was a passage, writing itself across the page. On top of it was a drawing of Vince and Zion, both encased in the same cocoon that Ala had placed Zion in earlier.

"Look!" I said, pointing as the words wrote themselves across the coarse page. Aliyah read aloud:

"The Game of Escape is a series of trials that all heroes must undertake when a human is caught in the Crystal City. As punishment for earlier encroachment into azizan land, all humans who enter are captured, healed, and then they must wait for those who love them to save them. Once a hero shows, they must find their loved ones in Ala's palace, with the help of an aziza.

If time runs out, the caught human must stay in azizan land until the day they die. The hero must leave the Crystal City, to never return. The first trial requires wit while the second requires love."

After reading the short paragraph, another etching drew itself at the bottom of the page. It was an hourglass, swirling in golden light. When I blinked, the hourglass flipped upside down and sand inside began to drop to the bottom ever so slowly.

"It would've been nice if Ala had explained this earlier," I said, rolling my eyes. "Or if the *Book* had told us this *before* we decided to come to the Crystal City."

"Well, that would be too much like right," Aliyah said. "The gods love to play games; we should've expected that before leaving the Palacia."

"That's your timer," Arinze said, pointing to the page. "Once all the hourglass's sand reaches the bottom"—he stared at us, a sadness washing over him—"Vince's soul will be lost and so will Zion's. You need to get started. Now."

I flipped the open *Book* underneath my left arm as a passageway opened in the darkness, leading deeper into the dungeons. Aliyah and I gazed at each other for a short while. The emotion on her face was a storm, an anger so deep that I couldn't quite describe it.

"We should go," I said, reaching for her hand. "We don't have much time. We do this together."

She nodded, and we started down the passageway, Arinze's wings lighting our way. I heard the sound of water in the distance, but my heartbeat was louder as I carried the *Book* underneath my arm. I wanted to look at it, to see the sand dropping to the bottom, but I kept myself from doing so. When we rounded a bend in the passage, Arinze's light dwindled to nothing as we stepped into a bright room.

A large pool spanned from left to right, deep and the color of night, surrounded by a raised portion of marble. Empty portrait frames were fastened on the walls, each one shining with golden light. The water moved within the pool at unnatural angles, its depths so black that I was too scared to even approach. But there was no other opening in the chamber, besides the passageway we had just come from that led to only rubble.

"Arinze, any ideas?" Aliyah said as we stared at the inky blackness.

"I may not interfere," Arinze said, flitting in between us. "You'll need to figure the trials out on your own."

"Okay," Aliyah said, huffing as she repositioned her pack on her back and walking toward the pool. "The *Book* said that the trials are twofold, right?"

"Right?" I said uncertainly.

She turned and winked at me. "Remember, Daddy is a game developer. I've played them all. Games are nothing but extensions of riddles, trials, and puzzles from ancient times."

I scrunched my eyebrows, trying to think. I remembered

all the times Zion and I had gone to Aliyah's house, only so he could play every game she owned. I never liked video games much, but it was good to watch. I mentally cursed myself for not paying more attention.

"Think," Aliyah said, snapping her fingers and closing her eyes. "What did the *Book* say about the Game of Escape?"

"It said that it's in two stages," I responded.

"Right," she said, opening her eyes. "It said one is a game of wit and one is a game of love." Her expression turned soft as she gazed at me. "It didn't say which, but I would think that wit is for Vince and the love trial is for Zion."

"So, what do we do first?" I said, my face growing hot. "The *Book* didn't really give us much to go on."

After creeping closer to the edge of the pool, she stared into the darkness, shaking her head and scrunching her eyebrows. "No," she said, turning to me. "I don't think our answer is in the pool. Not just yet." She pointed to the empty portrait frames. "I think if the game is about wit first, then our answer will be in the frames. How many times have you seen an empty picture frame?"

"True," I said, going to the left of the water while Aliyah went to the right. I followed her lead and started to inspect the frames, trying to calm myself down. I looked at them from the bottom and the top, running my fingers through the grooves, to see if there was something that I was missing or a latch that I needed to pull. Each of them was empty, but every time I touched one, static shocked my fingers. It wasn't painful, but it was disconcerting enough. By the time I met Aliyah in the middle at the head of the pool, I was ready to give up.

"There's nothing here," I said, touching the last portrait frame. There was no shock.

"So, we try again," Aliyah said.

"We probably just need to go in the pool," I suggested. By now the water had started to bubble ever so slightly, a stench permeating the air. Aliyah turned up her nose and shook her head.

"Think about it," she said. "It's too easy. Going into that water will do us no good. You never go with the obvious answer when you play games. *Never.* We should switch sides. Maybe something else will happen."

So we did, me positioning myself at the end of the wall where she was before, feeling each of the picture frames. Arinze flew over the water, his wings making a buzzing like flies would. I glared at him. "You could be helping us here."

"As I said, I cannot—"

"Yeah, yeah, we got it," I groaned, continuing to feel along the frames. Like the other side, I felt the static again on each frame until Aliyah and I met again. I reached out once more to touch the last frame. Again, there was no shock.

"Maybe we should—" Aliyah began.

"Wait!" I yelled, so loud that Aliyah jumped in the air. "I think I know. Each one of these felt the same, but this one,"

I said, pointing at the one that I felt nothing from, "felt different. I mean, I didn't feel anything."

"You sure?" Aliyah said, looking unconvinced. "I felt a slight shock for each of them."

"Here, touch this one and the one beside it."

She did and then gasped. "You're right. This one has a shock, but this one feels like nothing."

I grasped the frame, pulling at it. It didn't budge. I grunted, this time yanking with all my strength. The clasp at the top broke, and the wall behind it crumbled. I caught the frame as it dropped, and a large hole appeared in its place, golden light spewing from it. After taking a deep breath and setting the frame on the ground, I thrust my hand into the hole, rummaging around until I brushed against something rough. I grabbed it and saw that it was a scroll made of papyrus, an ancient type of paper. I had seen things like this many times at the Palacia.

I unrolled it and read the message written in Igbo, the magic of the *Book* aiding me. As I read, the words rearranged themselves into English:

> You have reached the Room of the Lost,
> where you will find what has been hidden. But
> first, you must answer this riddle: What binds
> is also what liberates. What destroys is also what
> heals. What breaks also has power. It is made of

precious jewels and contains the magic of creation.
Find that and you shall find what is lost.

"Is that it?" Aliyah said, pacing back and forth underneath the frames as the pool continued to bubble behind us. "Is Ala serious about this? What could she mean by that?"

I thought, trying my hardest to understand it. I read the message over and over, thinking about what it could mean. I opened the *Book*, willing it to show me something. But everything was blank, its pages swirling around in shadows. The last time I had seen shadows, it was when I was anxious, too overcome with emotion. But this felt different. Almost like there was a *greater* power at work here. And that power had to be Ala, the mother goddess.

"Wait!" I said, closing the *Book*. "I think I may know what it is." Now it was time for Aliyah to stop and for me to pace, thinking aloud. I shook the paper in the air as I spoke.

"The riddle says that what has been lost holds the magic of creation. That has to be a reference to Ala, right?"

"I mean, yeah," Aliyah said. "But this is her domain. Of course, it would have something to do with her."

"*Exactly*," I said, smiling. "Which would mean that whatever it is belongs to her." My smile turned bigger as I thought about what we had seen and heard since coming here. "And the riddle wouldn't refer to anything we haven't seen or experienced. At least I don't think so."

"Cam, explain yourself," Aliyah groaned. "Now, *you're* talking in riddles."

My eyebrow arched. "Is this the first time you haven't been the smartest one in the room?"

"Cam," she warned.

"Okay, okay," I said, holding my hands up. "Like I said, we've seen this object before. The riddle says it contains the magic of creation, that it heals as well as it destroys, that it binds as well as it liberates."

"And Ala is a goddess of healing, but she is also *the* goddess of liberation," Aliyah said, catching on. "She releases dead souls into the afterlife, those souls who are not touched by trauma like the mmo."

"Exactly!" I said, pointing at her. "And what is the symbol of that healing?" I opened the *Book* again, rustling through its pages until I got to Ala's section. I didn't read the words, didn't have to. I pointed at the goddess, as her dress moved in the wind. My attention, though, was drawn to the beads encircling her waist. "The mgbaji," I said. "It's her symbol. We saw it wrapped around her when we came into the Throne Room. It's a symbol of a rite, of a passage from one destination to another, of healing, of heritage."

"Which would explain the passageway we took from the rubble to here," Aliyah said.

"Yes," I said. "I think that's what's lost. We find it and we find Vince."

"Cam . . . ," Aliyah said, pointing to the *Book*. The

116

hourglass had appeared again, its sands washing away to the bottom. A quarter of it had disappeared.

I shook my head and put the *Book* back inside me. "The mgbaji *has* to be what we need to find."

Above us, Arinze clapped once. "Perfect answer."

Before we could respond, the water swirled underneath him, the inkiness flowing away until what remained was a bright blue, so clear that the bottom could be seen. The bubbling stopped, and smooth waves appeared, leaving behind a sweet scent. A glint of red gleamed near the bottom.

I groaned as Aliyah approached the pool, remembering when we had found the crown. "We have to go underwater. Again?"

"It's the only path," she said. "There's no other way out of here." She turned to me. "You comin'? Ala's mgbaji is down there."

"I cannot help—" Arinze began to say.

"Yeah, yeah, yeah," I said. "We heard you the first and second time."

Following Aliyah's lead, I took off my pack and handed it over to Arinze with our boots and socks placed inside.

We both took a deep breath and stood on the edge of the marble, holding each other's hands.

"I hope we are able to breathe like last time."

"It has to work the same way," Aliyah whispered, but she didn't seem so sure of herself.

After taking another deep breath, we both jumped into

the pool, the water's icy depths gripping us like cold fingers. In a few seconds, it turned warm and inviting. A light shined on my chest, threading its way through me and into Aliyah's hand, which gripped mine. She gasped as the magic of the *Book* poured into her. I expelled a breath, and sweet relief filled my lungs as I grew accustomed to the deep water. The mgbaji gleamed again in the distance, and we plunged deeper into the water's depths.

We were quiet for a while as we swam; I was unsure of what I could say. I had figured out the riddle, but what could be awaiting us at the bottom? This was no ordinary pool as we swam for a long time, going deeper and deeper.

I caught a glimpse of the glint once again, right when I thought I was falling asleep.

There, I said telepathically, pointing downward. *That has to be the mgbaji.*

But what greeted us at the pool's floor was not just the mgbaji. The pool immediately turned dark in places as a shadow blocked the light before swooshing right in front of us. A shiver of fear tickled up my arm and spine as the object came into shape.

A colossal black serpent with orange stripes, its eyes the color of the sun, flicked its tongue at us. Wrapped around its slithering tail was the mgbaji, made of cowrie shells, clay, and amber stones. The serpent swam so close to us that we barely dodged it. Our movement made slight waves and ripples in the water. The serpent should have noticed us, but it didn't; it just kept swimming in a circle.

It's asleep, Aliyah whispered.

Doesn't look like it, I said, shivering.

It can't see us, she responded as we shifted far away from the serpent. *We need to somehow get the mgbaji from around its tail.*

Sounds easier said than done.

If we go fast, it shouldn't be too hard, Aliyah said. *Remember the trickster god, Agwu?*

Dambe. It had aided us then, so maybe it would help us now? If I was being honest, I really didn't want to be eaten by a serpent, but what other choice did we have? Vince's and Zion's lives depended on it.

Okay, I said, breathing hard. *Dambe is our only choice. But it should be me. Not you. I have the magic of the* Book, *too.*

Cam, no, I don't think—

No, I said, turning to her and gripping her face. *I'm going. You stay here. If something happens, swim back to Arinze and get help.*

She nodded as I swam away from her. Going into Dambe was instant, but the music was different, deeper than anything I had ever felt before. I became one with the water, sensed its ripples over my skin that felt like soft touches. I maneuvered to the side as I slowed down, getting a glimpse of the large serpent, its eyes opening and closing as it stared at nothing.

The mgbaji beads were like a beacon, calling to me and pulling me forward.

In another second, I was swimming underneath the creature, stretching my hands upward to grasp at the mgbaji.

Come on, come on, I whispered. I grabbed it and pulled.

The serpent ratcheted upward, the mgbaji tightening against its tail, causing me to let it go. It swam forward and then turned its head around, level with its tail. It stared at me with bright yellow eyes, alert and ready to strike. I squeaked in fear, unable to scream. It flicked its tongue at me, so close that it brushed against my face.

I tried to grab the mgbaji once again, but I was too far away now. I careened backward as I swam away, but the serpent was quicker. With a swipe, it reared around and slammed its tail against my chest, sending me flying to the other side of the pool, my back striking the marble. The serpent moved quickly toward me, its unnaturally humongous mouth opening with a sickening *creak,* as if it hadn't eaten in a long while. Centuries probably. Long spiked teeth protruded from its mouth, and a loud noise erupted straight from its maw. A whirlpool was forming, swirling deep in its throat at first.

It reared upward, so close to me that I froze in fear.

Is that—

It *pushed* forward with its mouth, releasing the whirlpool with a deafening explosion. The mixture of water and air slammed into me, sending me hurtling backward, right into the marble again. This time, though, I crashed through the wall and sunk into the rock. Pain radiated through every part of my body as my head jerked from left to right. I tried to gain my bearings, but I shook so violently from dizziness that I retched all over my clothes and into the water around me.

What kinda serpent does that? I did my best to remove myself from the marble by pushing out with my hands to the side, but it was almost too heavy, encasing me like a tomb. I watched in horror as the serpent circled again on the other side of the pool and then shot toward me like a cannon. I moved from left to right, trying to wiggle out of the rock prison, but still could barely move. I pushed outward to clear the fragments that trapped me.

Ahh! Aliyah popped out of nowhere and swam downward, using the power of her body to clamp down on the serpent's huge mouth.

Aliyah! I said, struggling again. *Leave me! Get out of here and get help!*

No, she said, groaning. *Hurry up and get out here and help me with this thing. Grab the mgbaji!*

With colossal effort, I closed my eyes, calling for Dambe. In one second, fear radiated through me, and in another, a complete calm settled upon my shoulders. When I opened my eyes, I found that my body had slipped from the fissure in the marble and I was floating in the water again. Aliyah was still struggling to keep the serpent's mouth closed. I swam fast across the pool, using Dambe to aid me.

Grunting as I did, I grabbed it by the tail and clawed at

the mgbaji. It reared up, throwing Aliyah off its back. It swept around and hard teeth tore at the flesh of my arm. Pain washed across me, my vision blurring. With another swipe, I grabbed at the mgbaji with my left hand, lacing my fingers underneath the scarlet beads. I pulled with all my strength, and the large band fell away from the mottled, slippery skin.

As soon as I cradled the mgbaji in my hands, the serpent immediately let my arm go and I fell unconscious.

CHAPTER THIRTEEN

Wake up, wake up, oh, please wake up, Cam, I heard Aliyah saying. But I couldn't open my eyes, could only hear her voice. I could just make out her hands finding my mouth, thrusting it open, and emptying something icy into it. *Please wake up. This should help.*

She massaged my throat with her hand. Once I swallowed, I felt sweet relief and the pain in my arm went away. My eyelids fluttered open to see her gazing at me expectantly, holding Arinze's flask. The mgbaji curled around my hands.

This thing better be worth our lives! I said angrily, almost throwing it into the water around us.

Oh, you're awake, Aliyah said, grabbing me in a strong hug. I hugged her back, grateful for the closeness. *Once you grabbed the mgbaji, the serpent disappeared, like it had never been there!*

Of course, it did, I muttered. *We almost died . . . again.*

I know, she said, releasing me as I stuffed the mgbaji in my pocket.

Before I could respond, two glass platforms rose from the icy depths of the water and settled underneath our bodies.

What now? Aliyah asked.

Probably the next and final game, I said, shivering as the platforms rose through the water. They went so fast that we had to grasp the edges.

When we broke the surface, we were no longer in the room of portrait frames. The platforms had stopped midair in a clearing of sorts, trees encircling the entire place.

"Any idea where we are?" Aliyah said.

"Nope," I said. Our clothes had dried completely as we soared, and weak sunlight filtering through the trees washed over me. However, I didn't trust this warmth. One could never trust the gods or the sense of peace you felt when you were near them.

"You have found and captured the mgbaji," a voice said, coming from the sky. Arinze flew over the trees, his wings sparkling in the soft sunlight. A grave look passed over his face.

"That means we passed the first test?" I asked.

He nodded. "Now the most challenging one is next. As the *Book* has told you, this will be a trial of love."

As he spoke, he handed a golden bow and arrow to me, their light so bright that it blinded me for a bit. "This is the weapon you will use for the second task. It belongs to Anyanwu, so I would advise that you guard it well." He rummaged through his dashiki before handing me a weathered piece of paper. "You must read this, too."

I glanced at Aliyah once before angling my eyes downward to read off the papyrus:

Congratulations, you have completed the first trial, one that requires you to have wit and be of sound mind. This final task will require you to examine your heart and make a tough decision. One has lost, but one has gained. Death is the end, but life is the beginning. Hatred can hurt, but love can also heal. Make the decision to strike, and you will finally gain what you seek. And maybe, just maybe, death may not be the end. At least, for once.

When I finished reading, the trees shuffled in the distance. Small pillars appeared in the center of each tree, five of them in total. Different objects were placed on the top of four of them, obscured by smoke. The object on the third one in the middle floated off the pillar, before coming toward us.

The smoke drifted away as a silvery cocooned figure hovered above me like a rain cloud. I gasped when I saw Vince, his eyes closed but fitful. He didn't look peaceful at all, as if he were fighting something in his sleep.

Arinze coughed a bit before speaking. "It would seem

that you would like to keep him protected for the time being, given . . . all he has been through."

"I think that's the right approach," Aliyah said, gazing nervously at the silver cloud that contained Vince. "He doesn't look like he has been all the way healed."

"He's in process," Arinze responded. "He's asleep until the healing is complete. When you finish here, take him back to the Palacia and send him home."

"Agbala can do that," I said.

Arinze nodded before turning back to the pillars. "Now, you must make a decision, Descendant." He gestured to the air, and the hourglass appeared, its sand almost out. "For your time is almost up."

"And what is that decision?" I said.

"To get Zion back and to leave the Crystal City, you must decide which items on top of the pillars you will shoot with Anyanwu's arrow. But take heed, you only get one chance. Figure out the riddle and choose right, and you will gain him back. If you choose wrong, you forfeit them both." At Arinze's words, the smoke that obscured the objects on the pillars dissipated, revealing them to us.

"Laying on the pressure a little thick there, aren't you, Arinze?" I grumbled.

"Concentrate," Aliyah said, as her platform moved close to me. "We only get one shot at this. Now, let's think and make the right decision."

The sound from the sand dropping into the bottom of the

hourglass was starting to make me shake, my palms beginning to sweat.

"First, let's look and see what's on the pillars before we get into answering the riddle," I suggested through gritted teeth.

On the far left was a familiar riding pack. "That's Zion's," I whispered, pointing to it, about to lift my arrow to my bow.

"Wait," Aliyah said, grabbing my raised hand. "Let's keep looking. It might be a distraction. Most times, the first answer is not the best answer."

On the next pillar was Zion's armor, including knee and wrist leather pads. The middle pillar was now empty. The fourth pillar held a piece of meat. The final pillar held a flask of azizan light. They all were familiar, but I couldn't decide which one I needed to choose.

"They *all* belong to Zion," I said, frustrated, sweat beading on my brow. "This is too hard." I stood on the platform, trying to decide. But the more I racked my brain, I could still think of nothing to help me make the right decision.

"There has to be something to make this easier," Aliyah said. "Let's look at the riddle again." She took it from me, opened it, and we shared reading it.

"It's a lot like the first one," I said, thinking aloud. "A bunch of contradictions."

"And if this is a trial of love, it's obvious the person we both love is Zion."

I pointed at each of the objects on the pillars, the riding pack, the armor, the piece of meat, which I recognized was goat now, and the flask of light. "Okay, so what do they all have in common? Or how are they all different?"

"I mean . . . they all belonged to Zion, right?"

"Hmm . . . it can't be that easy, can it?" I asked.

"Well, let's take it piece by piece," Aliyah suggested, counting on her fingers. "First, it says that 'one has lost, but one has gained.' What can that mean?"

"Obviously, Zion is the one lost. Or maybe it means Vince? But can that really be about him? I mean, Zion was taken from both of us, as he means a lot to us both personally. So, we didn't really *gain* Vince in the same way that we want to gain Zion back." A grain of sand settled at the bottom of the hourglass. I threw up my hands. "I got nothing, Aliyah."

"Well, that's obviously referring to Zion, and not Vince," she said, pointing toward the sleeping Vince above our heads. "So let's take the next point. It says, 'Death is the end, but life is the beginning.' I think . . ." She closed her eyes. "What could that mean?" she whispered. "Maybe it means that . . ."

"Is it referring to my parents?" I asked. "I mean, we know Mama is still alive, and so could Daddy. Maybe . . ." Another grain of sand settled at the bottom of the hourglass.

"No," she said, shaking her head. "It can't be about them. I mean, not in that way. It has to be focused on Zion solely. Especially if this game is about love."

I thought harder, until an image came into my mind, of me being scared of Zion dying, of him leaving me like Mama and Daddy had left me. He and Grandma were the only ones

I had left now, and I remembered thinking that I didn't want him in Chidani, getting hurt because of me.

When I relayed that information to Aliyah, she nodded in response. "Right, that's all about Zion. You fear him dying. Me too, but it means something different to you. Like, Zion was there for you when your parents couldn't be."

My cheeks grew hot again, so I continued with the last part of the riddle. "The last part, 'Hatred can hurt, but love can also heal,' has nothing to do with Zion. I've never hated him. Ever. How can that apply to him?"

Aliyah smiled. "Then that would lead us back to square one."

A *whoosh* of wind brought our attentions to the pillars. The objects rose, floating in the air above them, shining in golden light. They were like beacons, drawing me closer to a decision. To the only decision we had to save Zion's life. Another grain of sand settled at the bottom of the hourglass, the top half almost empty. "You must hurry, Descendant," Arinze urged.

I shifted from foot to foot. "And square one would be?"

"What does each object have in common with each other? I mean, I think I have an idea, but I think the game of love is supposed to be about you. And not me."

"Come on, Aliyah—"

"No," she said, firmly. "Think hard. Because I can give you my opinion, but ultimately, you have to make the decision to strike, like the riddle said."

I groaned, but I thought hard as she suggested. *What do*

the objects have in common? I looked at them one by one, the riding pack, the armor, the flask, and the goat meat. Ever since coming to Chidani, Zion had changed, almost like the kingdom had become a second skin for him. He had integrated himself here, but it had taken me so long to be that same hero. It was almost like this had been his new home.

"Wait!" I yelled. "That's it!"

"What?" Aliyah said.

I turned to her, gripping her hands. "All of these objects belonged to Zion. But not *outside* of Chidani. They all are a part of him that belongs to this place. He got the riding pack after he learned how to fight."

"The armor he used when he was learning how to be a warrior," Aliyah pointed out.

I jumped in excitement. "And the goat meat . . . he *loves* that. Remember the Cave of Shadows?"

Aliyah shivered. "How could I forget that?"

"When we were there, *he* was the one who got the food. Not us. And what the fire gave him was goat meat."

"Well, that's three objects," Aliyah responded. "But what about the flask of azizan light? What's the significance of that?"

"That . . ." I grimaced. "That was when Agwu attacked him, remember? He fell on the boulder and shattered his leg."

Aliyah sighed. "And then I tried to use the azizan light to heal him, but we had to call on Agbala when it didn't work." She shifted from foot to foot. "So, we know what they all have in common, each a piece of Zion from our first trip to

Chidani. But how does that help us strike the object that will free him?"

A knowing look sprang on Aliyah's face, but then it vanished as soon as it came. She immediately settled, as though a peace had settled upon her shoulders.

I knew the answer to her question. Deep inside, I knew. And Aliyah knew, too. I remembered talking to her before we left the Palacia on the trip to find Ramala's crown. She had told me I loved Zion, but I hadn't been able to accept it then. It was deeper than that, though. At least for us. He was family just like Grandma was. In a lot of ways, he had saved me when Mama and Daddy had disappeared. He had been a lifeline for me, making me laugh when I didn't want to laugh, smile when I didn't want to smile. No, Zion wasn't just my friend.

"I know which object we have to strike," I said, calm and collected. "It's the flask of azizan light. It was when Zion needed me the most, lying there on the ground with his leg broken. It was when I realized I loved him like family, like how I had loved Mama and Daddy. Like I love Grandma. But also, even more than that."

"I know." That was all she said. But those two words gave me more strength than she could ever know. I raised the arrow to my bow and lifted it to my shoulder, nocking it into place. As I exhaled, I took aim and released it in the direction of the flask of light. It flew across the open space with sharp precision, connecting against the flask at lightning speed.

"It is done," Arinze announced.

The flask exploded, and the light inside burst through, bathing the clearing in multicolored illumination. I covered my eyes for a second, not able to take it all in.

"Cam?" a weak voice said.

A figure walked through the light, floating on air with its eyes fluttering open. Its curled hair was tussled, and its clothes were wrinkled. It looked as if it had been asleep for centuries, but it was familiar. A rush of joy spread through my body as I eased my platform forward. I caught Zion in my arms and crushed him against my chest.

"We won," I said, breathless, as I dropped Anyanwu's bow and arrow. "I got you back. We won."

CHAPTER FOURTEEN

The scene dissipated, as if someone had taken a bottle and shaken it up. We found ourselves standing back in Ala's Throne Room, both her and Anyanwu in the same place we had left them. Vince still floated above us in the silver cloud.

They made no movement.

I just kept hugging Zion, unwilling to let him go again.

"What happened?" he groaned, wrapping his arms around me and squeezing me back. "My head hurts so bad."

"A lot," I said, laughing a bit.

He groaned again before looking around at the gods on their thrones. His eyes turned to slits, like a snake's. "It's all coming back now. You tried to kill me!"

"Not so," Ala replied, shaking her head. "That's just how we do things here."

Zion started forward, breaking free of my hug. "I oughta—"

"But did you die?" Ala said.

I grabbed Zion immediately.

"Can we just leave?" I asked the gods. "We did the trials. We got both of our friends back. We can go now, right?"

"You can," Ala said. "A god's words are binding." She waved her hand in a dismissive motion toward the entrance doors. "You may leave now, and you may take your wards with you."

Arinze bowed, and we shuffled away from them as far as we could, Zion throwing nasty glances their way.

"Wait!" Anyanwu barked from behind us.

We froze in place at how loud he was. I turned to him, anger beginning to take over. "What now?!" I cowered almost immediately, though. He was walking, no, *gliding* over to us like he had become part of the air.

He was still tall as a giant, glaring with fiery eyes. Smoke and ash rained down on us from his mouth as he spoke. I coughed a bit as he rummaged through his kaftan.

"You left something," he said, handing out his golden bow and arrow to me. He inclined his head my way and squinted. "I expect you will need it in the conflict ahead."

"I don't want them," I said. "I don't need them."

"I think you will," he said. "Take them. You've earned them. You will also notice a . . . change in your gryphons when you mount them. They won't hurt you. Now that you've saved Vince, everything else should fall into place." *The same thing Mmiri had said.*

In his huge hands, they were nothing more than toys. But as I grasped them, they seemed to weigh a ton. I didn't remember them weighing so much in the trials.

"Um . . . well, thanks?"

He nodded before striding back to the throne, but not before I noticed anger in his stormy face. *What was that expression all about?*

"He will need to be sent home," Ala mentioned, gesturing at the floating Vince. "I am sure that Agbala will be able to do so. The evil attached to him was deeper than any of us had imagined, which is why he must now sleep and recover."

"We know, we know," I said.

That was the last thing they said to us.

"We should leave," Arinze whispered, beginning to make his way to the doors. "Our time here is done."

Aliyah and Zion bickered the entire time as we made our way to the desert.

He stamped his feet. "Why is it always me? Why am I always the one hurt?"

Aliyah rolled her eyes as she and I put back on our socks and boots. "It could have easily been me, Zion. Or Cameron for that matter."

"It's never Cameron," Zion was saying as we followed Arinze. "He's the 'chosen one' who has to save the world."

I stopped in my tracks. "You want my spot? You want to

be the Descendant? Because I would give you the *Book* in exchange for my parents if you really wanted it."

Zion's face turned red as he fidgeted with the curls in his hair. "You're right. I—I didn't mean . . ." He paused for a moment before speaking again. "I'm sorry."

The arguing stopped then, and we continued on until we returned to the desert. Arinze floated around us for a while, his magic falling down as dust from the sky. Aliyah and Zion unscrewed their flasks, refilling them to the top; I opened my pack, placing Anyanwu's gift inside while I coaxed my sprite awake, using his magic to fill mine. After, Arinze flew next to Vince.

I called Ugo from the sky before speaking. "I think we need to get the ring now. Anyanwu gave me his bow and arrow, and he said he changed the gryphons, whatever that means. He wouldn't do that for no reason. He also said the same thing Mmiri said about saving Vince. We find that ring, and that'll get us closer to getting Mama back. I don't want to go back to the Palacia, because Agbala and Ramala might make us rest and train for days before trying to talk us out of it. We should go now. And then all three gifts will have been found."

"I can take your friend Vince back to the Palacia if you want," Arinze offered. "I'll give him directly to Agbala, and she can send him home, his memory erased."

"Good," I said, before watching Arinze grab Vince's hand through the cocoon and zipping away into the far distance.

"We're going to the Sun Kingdom?" Zion asked, grinning a bit.

"We sure are." I nodded. "Anyanwu wouldn't have given me his bow and arrow if he didn't know that something was there, that the ring might be there."

"Well, we already know what the *Book* said about the ring, or at least what it showed us," Aliyah pointed out.

"Exactly," I said, as I gazed at the Crystal City, whose form had already seemed to waver in the heat, like it was disappearing from view. "The Sun Kingdom, huh? I'm kinda done with the gods and their domains. But that's where the ring is."

"Then let's go," Zion said.

I grabbed his hand and Aliyah's before the gryphons thudded on the sand. When I wrapped my fingers through Ugo's feathers, they burst into flames at my touch.

"Whoa!" Zion said. "Some kinda change. Anyanwu was right."

Mounting Ugo felt different, but not in a bad way. He was warm, not hot, and his breath came out in streams of smoke, almost like Anyanwu's. His snow-white color had turned the color of flame, a mixture of different shades of oranges and reds. Connecting to him felt familiar, though, as if we were one. By the time I was done marveling at Ugo, Aliyah and Zion had jumped on Odum and Ike. Flames covered our entire area of the desert for miles, the gryphons' wingspans so large that they encompassed everything.

We flew into the air, leaving a stream of smoke and ash behind us.

The last thing I saw before we disappeared into the clouds was the Crystal City in the distance, dwindling away to nothing.

CHAPTER FIFTEEN

We broke through the cloud cover, our clothes and packs soaking wet. We flew toward the sun, watching it grow larger and larger as we went, drying us almost immediately. However, it was cut in half, the right side of it dark and the left side of it brimming with yellow.

"The barrier," I murmured, digging my feet ever so slightly into Ugo's side. We flew closer and closer, a pressure pushing on my chest growing heavier the higher we climbed. In another second, we burst through an atmospheric layer, appearing near the top of a mountain that I hadn't seen earlier. Which could only mean we were close to or actually in the Sun Kingdom. The view was absolutely breathtaking, as if we were the only ones in the world. A peace settled upon me, as if nothing had happened to us the past few days.

A wooden bridge was attached to the top of the mountain. It stretched all the way into the distance, past clouds that obscured the rest of the kingdom from view. The gryphons touched us down on the bridge with a *thunk*, pawing at the ground as they did. There was a knowingness as I touched Ugo.

"We'll have to take the rest of the journey alone," I said.

We jumped off the gryphons, giving them small pats and rubs as they chirped. They looked different, but they were still the same loveable yet fierce creatures we had come to know. After a while, they chirped a bit more, and then flew into the air, fire still consuming them.

"What a sight," Zion said.

We stood on the bridge, none of us really knowing what to do.

"Any ideas?" Aliyah said.

"Hold on," I said, raising my hands up and cupping my ears. "I hear something." The sound was like wagon wheels on a dirt road. From the cloud cover came a carriage, so large that it barely fit on the bridge. It came to us slowly, led by what looked like battle horses. But these horses were different; wings of fire spread along their backs, smoke released from their nostrils, their bodies covered in armor. They stopped in front of us, the carriage empty and driverless.

"I think we have to ride this," I said, going around to the side of the carriage, opening the door. Inside, the area was plush, filled with cushions and velvety fabric the color of the sun. The carriage was so large that I was sure that this had to be Anyanwu's. We were nothing more than ants compared to this thing.

"Look," Aliyah said, pointing to the seat. A letter in a worn envelope sat there, a red-blood seal with wax still dripping from it.

We got in, but not before hustling Zion inside. "I'm so tired of these gods," he protested. "What if it's a trap. What if something tries to take *me* again." He tried to run, but where was he really going without the gryphons to help him? I grabbed him to keep him still.

We settled inside, our backs resting in pure luxury, before opening the letter. It was humongous, fit for a god. The paper inside was so long that it fell to the floor as we read the large letters inside:

> Welcome to the Sun Kingdom. As you are guests of Anyanwu, the god of the sky, who pulls the sun from left to right, no harm shall befall you here. As humans, you may not stay here for long. Make haste on your business so that you may return to your rightful land.

"Well, *that* doesn't sound ominous," Zion muttered.

"It reads like a form letter," I said, rolling the letter back up and sticking it in its envelope.

"What's a form letter?" Zion asked.

"It's a letter that everyone gets, no matter who they are," Aliyah said.

"And from how worn it looks," I said, "I don't think anyone but Anyanwu has been here for a long while."

After I spoke, with a jerk, the carriage rose in the air and then turned to face the cloud cover. I held on to the seat as Zion screamed. Aliyah reached out and closed the huge side door, just in time as the carriage jerked again. The horses snorted, and then we shot forward. We moved so fast that it was meaningless to even try to look out the open windows. Zion continued screaming as the vehicle shifted once and started to climb through the air. After a while of climbing, it shifted again, flying forward now. When it slowed down, I snatched a glance out of the window opening, but I only saw a mixture of reds, oranges, and yellow streaking past my eyes. My heart froze in my chest as we flew, panic settling in. After a while, I noticed that I hadn't taken a breath. I expelled air as we continued.

After a few moments, the carriage slowed to the point where I felt my stomach's contents weren't going to come up anymore. I looked out the opening on the left again and gasped.

"Look!" I said, pointing downward. Aliyah did as I said, while Zion kept his face in his hands.

The Sun Kingdom was glorious to behold, much more awe-inspiring than the Palacia had been the first time we came to Chidani. Everything seemed to drip in a mixture of gold and flame. Birds made of fire screeched in the air, flying near the carriage and all around the city. When I looked down, I noticed that the ground was covered in soot and sand, diamonds glittering from its depths. Geysers opened in random places in the ground, releasing hot water into the sky. Zion peeked out from the middle of his fingers.

We soared over the kingdom, my eyes drawn to one of the most magnificent structures I had ever seen. It was a statue of Anyanwu, rising from the ground like a sentinel tower. His arms were raised in the air, and his left hand held a blazing ball of fire, meant to represent the sun, while the right was empty. Anklets covered both of his legs, the left pointing downward while the right was lifted with his knee bent, slanted to the right. Jackalberry and marula trees rose from the sand, encircling his legs.

"What is that wrapped around him?" Zion said, finally getting over his fear and scooting over to Aliyah to look out.

As I looked closer, I noticed a giant double-headed serpent wrapped around the statue's body, curling from the ground all the way to the stomach and up to Anyanwu's head. A dangling necklace encircled his neck, heavy and dripping down his chest. He wore a kufi fused with diamonds, rubies, and emeralds on top of his head. But it was the statue's eyes that drew me in; they were white and blazing, staring into nothingness. The face was the exact image of Anyanwu, with cheeks sunken in a bit, deep and warm like sand, eyebrows arched, mouth full. I had never seen anything like it, and probably never would again.

Streets of gold encircled the statue and stretched into different directions as far as the eye could see. Magnificent homes rose from the sand, the same color of the streets, their facades glistening in the warm air. A smell of newness wafted to my nose as I took it all in, the tightly packed homes, the alleyways in between them, and the wagons and stores that littered the roads. However, there was no sound of people bustling through, of them talking and yelling to one another, of merriment and cheer. The entire kingdom was empty, at least from what I could see from where we were flying. I wondered about that, how and why Anyanwu lived by himself. Surely a god wouldn't want to be alone? The wagons, homes, and tools told me that there had been people here before, but everything seemed new, as if no one had lived there before or in centuries.

"It's quiet," I whispered. "Too quiet. I wonder why that is."

Zion snorted. "From the way the gods act, you would think Anyanwu would have people worshipping him here. Ala has the aziza in the Crystal City."

"Very curious," Aliyah said.

I pointed. "We're coming up on Anyanwu's home, I think."

A humongous palace was directly behind the statue. The carriage dipped down and settled on the soot and sand, giving us a better view of it. Another bridge, this one made of steel, stretched from the sand all the way to Anyanwu's home. I got out of the carriage. I sunk a bit and felt a warm breeze riffle through my dashiki and shokoto trousers. Rising smoke clogged my throat a bit, making me cough to clear it. Aliyah and Zion joined me right in front of the bridge.

What looked like water streamed from left to right underneath the structure.

"Wait," Zion said, pointing down. "That's not water."

"That's definitely not water," Aliyah said. "That's lava." Molten rock flowed underneath the bridge, every so often releasing small geysers into the air. The bridge shook where we stood. I took a step forward, and when it steadied, I kept moving, Zion and Aliyah following behind me.

The palace was just as splendorous as Anyanwu's statue. It reminded me of the Palacia, but was bigger, built from sandstone, with structures larger than human proportion. I was getting that "ant" feeling once again. Those same firebirds we had seen on the way into the kingdom screeched and flew around the tops of the turrets and towers. The palace stretched for miles in each direction, covered in flames. The area around it was barren, as though the fire had burned everything in existence. A large door was set in the middle, made of brass and iron. Fit for a king and a god.

"From what we read in the *Book*, the ring would be in Anyanwu's Throne Room," I mused aloud as we continued to walk on the bridge, getting closer and closer to his palace.

"I'm still in awe of even being here," Zion said.

"Where was it again?" Aliyah whispered, her eyes widening. "It seems like we looked at it so long ago now."

She was right. We had only been back in Chidani for probably a couple of days, but it had felt like months after everything we had been through. But I remembered exactly where the ring was. "It's on his throne," I said, breathing in the hot air. "The back of it."

"Remember the crown, though?" Zion said.

Who couldn't?

"There was dark magic around it," Aliyah said.

I pulled out my jewel-encrusted sword from my pack. "And how much you wanna bet that there is more here, too? Remember we saw that dark figure in the *Book*."

"How could Anyanwu not know his ring was placed here?" Aliyah asked, shivering a bit as she pulled out her sword, too.

"Have you seen him?" I joked, staring at Zion. "He looks like he sleeps more than he's awake. Just like Zion."

"Whatever," Zion said, rolling his eyes as we approached the palace's door. "He didn't seem sleepy enough when we were in the Crystal City. He just sat there and watched as his mother kidnapped me. I will admit, though, that sleep was one of the best I've had in a while."

"Zion," Aliyah groaned. "Let's keep our thoughts on the task at hand, please. We need to get that ring for Cameron."

"No," I corrected her, as the door opened while we approached. "We need to get that ring to close the barrier for good." I thought about Grandma again as we went into the sun-lit chamber. I wondered if she was okay, if she was think-ing about me. She was probably freaking out, especially given how time worked here and in my world. By now, she was either waiting for me and Zion at home, standing behind her screen door, or, if we hadn't shown up, she was making her way down to the bus stop to wait for us. When she didn't see us getting off the bus, she would know that something wrong had happened, that we were somehow in Chidani. She had watched us like a hawk after we came back the first time; who would have thought that we'd open a portal from school instead of from home?

Although it was warm outside, inside the entrance was cool. A wall of rock stopped us from going forward, an iron door fixed in the middle of it, a keyhole situated on the right side. I stepped up and foolishly knocked.

"Really, Cam?" Zion asked.

I shrugged. "What else are we supposed to do?"

"Hmm," Aliyah said, bending over and peering at the rock, running her free hand along the bottom of it. "I'm try-ing to see if there's a key here."

"You mean how our parents always leave a key underneath the floor mat outside of our houses?" Zion asked, arching his left eyebrow. "I mean, I don't think it works like that here, either."

"Then what do we do?" Aliyah said, repeating my words. "We didn't come here for nothing. We can't get the ring unless we know how to get through this door."

"Want me to try my Summoner magic?" I asked. "Maybe I can try it here." I placed a hand gently against the rock and closed my eyes. I concentrated hard, willing the shadows to swirl around my fingers, Summoning the key to the entrance.

"Cam?" I heard Zion say.

I gasped as pain lanced across my chest, so deep that I almost screamed. I opened my eyes once, and then they slammed shut, thrusting me into darkness.

I became lost in that night.

CHAPTER SIXTEEN

Soft chuckles brushed past my ears first before vision returned to my eyes.

I lay on warm sand, its grittiness pushing against my legs. Anyanwu stood above me, holding a hand out to me, his eyes ablaze. That same anger I had seen last time crossed his face, while his mouth lifted in a small smirk.

"Descendant?" he said derisively, as if he cared nothing for me, as if my presence were funny to him.

I refused his hand, sitting up in the near darkness, resting against the sand.

"What happened?" I asked.

Anyanwu shrugged at my refusal and stood back. He had changed his appearance again, his gigantic nature of earlier now human size. But, even looking at him now, he was nothing resembling normal. An emerald agbada flowed from his neck to his feet, while his hair spilled down his back, golden beads drawn through it. He produced flame out of thin air before walking around the small room, lighting the candles hanging on the ancient sconces in the wall.

"You Summoned me, I presume," he said in that ever-present soft voice.

"I wasn't really trying to Summon you," I replied, still resting on the sand. "I was trying to get the key, to open the door to your Throne Room."

His smirk changed to a blazing full smile. "How do you like my kingdom, my Burning Palace?"

"I would like them more if you would give me the key," I said. "But the temperature's a little warm. Hot even."

"You must not lie to a god."

I sighed. "Fine. It's nice. I guess. Warm. Just right."

"Of course it would be for the 'Descendant' and his friends."

I frowned. "That's why I'm here? For you to mock me?"

A fake pity appeared in Anyanwu's expression. "Such anger from such a small, insignificant human. Especially to one who has only wanted to help you."

"It was helping me to kidnap my friend and then make it so he would die if I was not fast enough to save him?" I said, anger blooming in my chest. "I don't think help works that way."

"Ah, ah, ah," he said, shaking a finger in my direction. "That was not me. I do not own, create, or control the Crystal City. That was Mother's decision to take your friends. But you were successful, as I knew you would be." He inclined his head in my direction in a bow, releasing his arms to fall to the sand in false supplication. "I mean, I would think a game like that would be just a mere annoyance for such a strong human. You are the Descendant after all."

"Just give me the key," I said, standing up. "I Summoned it, so it is mine. At least for as long as I need it. Agbala said—"

"Do not *dare* speak of her!" Anyanwu said, his appearance shifting a bit, growing taller, until he gained his bearings and fell back to normal. "Agbala is of no importance to me, the sister that betrayed us."

I thought back to what Agbala had said about the *Book*'s creation, and an understanding started to dawn on me. "She created the *Book*," I responded. "Which would mean . . . she created the Descendants, the ones with the powers of the gods."

Anger seethed from Anyanwu, so hot and deep that the sand began to smoke underneath my feet and the candles along the wall began to melt ever so slightly. "She did."

"Which means . . . ," I said, stepping forward. "You *have* to give me the key. Because I Summoned it. Because it's *my* magic as the Descendant, which is just as powerful as your god magic. You don't like that you can be controlled by a human. That sounds much like what Agwu said when I retrieved Amadioha's scepter."

He said nothing, which meant that I was onto the truth.

"You can't intervene in human affairs," I said, smiling, repeating what the gods had said to me over and over again. "Well, you can, but Agbala said that there are consequences for doing that."

"You think you are so smart," Anyanwu said, pacing up and down the chamber. "You know nothing, Descendant."

"I know you loved Queen Ramala." The words came out my mouth so fast that I could barely stop them. By the time I realized what I had done, the sentence couldn't be taken back. I shut my mouth, though, hoping he wouldn't harm me as much as I feared.

To my surprise, Anyanwu looked small and defeated, his shoulders slumping and powers seeming to wane. He spoke to me softly this time, croaking. "You know nothing about me and Ramala. Don't mention that."

I did as I was told. We stood in silence for a long while, me not willing to say anything else to anger him. I wanted to, but Anyanwu didn't look happy to be controlled by the Descendant, that a human had the powers of a god. And to be honest, I didn't care about his happiness, even though he had given me his bow and arrow. Zion had almost died, again. And that I couldn't forgive.

"You play with us," I finally whispered. "Gods do. You play with us like toys."

Anyanwu shrugged. "That is our nature. And has been that way for centuries."

"Rules are rules, I guess," I said snidely, holding out my hand. "Give me the key. You have to."

Anyanwu sighed, jerking a bit, like he was trying to fight the inevitable. He snapped his fingers much like Ala had, the sound so loud that the candles blew out before flickering back to life a second later. "You shall have it as decreed."

"Good," I said, sitting down and resting my back on the sand. "Now send me back to my friends."

Kneeling down, he placed a warm hand on my forehead.

His demeanor softened, the flame in his eyes reducing to nothing. It was the first time I had seen them; they were the color of sweetgrass. "Find my ring. And then bring it back to the queen."

Something in his voice gave me pause; a deep sadness settled in his gaze.

I offered a question. "Why is your kingdom empty?"

"Oh, Descendant," he said, tears leaking from his eyes, tinged with fire, releasing smoke into the air. "If you have to ask, then you already know the answer."

"Ramala," I said. "You loved her. When she rejected you . . ."

"My kingdom was populated because I willed it so. The people were extensions of myself. When Ramala rejected me, my loneliness birthed desolation. Emptiness. And so it shall be until the end of time."

"But—"

"Go back, Descendant. And do what I wish."

"I will," I said, closing my eyes. "Give me the key."

"I did."

The grittiness of the sand was replaced with such a softness that I thought I was either back in my own bed or back in the Descendant's chambers in the Palacia.

I kept my eyes closed for a while, wrapping myself in the heavy bedding. I rolled over once and then bumped into something hard. I opened my eyes now, seeing Zion curled up next to me, sleeping. When I looked around the room, nothing seemed familiar. Reaching out, I shook Zion awake, my heart beating.

"Zion. Zion. Wake up."

He groaned once, opened his eyes, and then fell back asleep. I pushed him again. He moaned and rubbed at his eyes. "What, Cam?"

"What happened? Last thing I remember was passing out."

"You did," he said groggily. His hair was tangled and stuck out in impossible directions. I reached out and ran my fingers through his tight coils, trying to get them back in place. "We tried to wake you up, but you wouldn't. We didn't panic this time, though. We thought Agbala had called you back or something."

"No, she didn't," I said, remembering what Anyanwu had said. "I'm . . . cloaking us from her. The gods don't seem to like her very much, though."

"Oh, yeah, they still mad because she created the *Book* without their permission."

"Well, what happened?"

Someone stood up at the head of the room, and I jumped straight up, trying to grab at my sword, but it wasn't sitting by me anymore.

"It's me!" Aliyah said, dropping her covers on the cushion she was just lying on.

"What happened?" I repeated.

"You wouldn't wake up, so we just waited," Aliyah began. "Then a side door magically appeared out of nowhere, leading upward to a tower. So we picked you up, hustled you inside, and this was here." She gestured to the room around us. "We decided to just sit here and wait until you came back. Didn't know it would take hours, though."

"Wait. I've been gone for hours? It didn't seem that long!"

Aliyah nodded. "Where did you go?"

A smell brushed past my nose. A nice smell. It made me ravenous, and I realized we hadn't eaten or slept in a long while. "Wait. What's that?"

They both shrugged. I went to go investigate. When I stepped out of the bedroom, I found myself in a sitting room, much like the one we used in the Palacia, but different. Windows lined the area on each side. When I looked closer, though, I realized that they weren't windows at all; they were large, carved holes in the walls, opening to the sky around us.

"Whoa," Zion said, coming to stand by me. "This wasn't here yesterday. The only thing that was here was the bedroom."

"Anyanwu," I whispered, taking in the view. Large firebirds swept past the openings in the walls, their wings covered in flame, sending warmth and air blowing through the room. A golden table was set in the middle of the floor, piled with plates of food. There were bread sandwiches made with boiled goose eggs and beef, mackerel in geisha sauce, akara made from bean paste, steamed pudding topped with custard powder, ewa agoyin served with soft chewy bread, and fried plantain with a side of egg stew. The *Book*'s pages flipped inside me as the words for the food came.

"I'm so hungry," Zion said, patting his stomach. I noticed that he was dressed in a robe that swept the floor as he walked. "I'm going to go eat." He went to the table and sat down while I went back in the bedroom and bathing area. Aliyah was rummaging through her pack; she was wearing a sleeping robe, too.

"So we just got comfortable in the night, not knowing what was going to happen?"

She shrugged. "I mean, you were unconscious and wouldn't

wake up. We couldn't exactly carry you back to Anyanwu's carriage when we had come so close to getting the ring. I'm going to go outside and eat with Zion. Hurry up."

I stepped into the bathing room, where another robe had been placed on a cushion in the middle. I took off my tattered clothing, washed as best as I could, and then put on the robe. When I got back into the sitting area, Aliyah and Zion had sat down and prepared their plates. I made one, too, piling it so high that I wasn't sure if I could eat it all. But I definitely would try.

"So, where did you go?" Zion said, stuffing his face. He paused, looking at the food with suspicion. "Wait. Anyanwu wouldn't poison this or something, would he?"

"To Anyanwu. I Summoned him." I shook my head. "And, no, I don't think so. He . . . respects me, I think. He wants us to win. He told me to find the ring and give it back to Ramala. He loves her still, even after all of these centuries."

"I thought you were trying to Summon the key?" Aliyah asked, taking a drink from a steaming goblet.

"He said he gave it to me," I replied, confused as I ate. "He was angry that I had magic, that I had the power of the gods. But the Descendant's powers come from a god. He didn't have a choice but to give me the key." I looked around the room again. "It's got to be in here somewhere, or he wouldn't have allowed us in his palace."

We ate in silence, finally calming down from everything that had happened. I thought about Grandma again, and how she must have been pulling her hair out at us being gone. I thought about Vince, hopefully being sent home right now. I also thought about what Makai and the others were thinking about our absence; at least Vince's appearance would tell them that we were safe for now.

After we finished eating, the plates and food in front of us vanished into thin air, as if they'd never existed. I looked out one of the openings in the wall. Although it was a kingdom, the city below was still empty. The statue of Anyanwu stood in the hazy distance, so tall that its head almost came up to the top of the tower we were in. The buildings held a golden glint to them, shiny and new. I wondered what it felt like to Anyanwu to be in a place alone for so long. No wonder he chose to sleep, monitoring the sun instead of living. I knew a lot about grief, too.

The twinge of sadness for Anyanwu was replaced with deep anger, though, just thinking about what had happened to Zion. The gods did things on their own whims with little care for anyone else. They had scorned Agbala for extending sanctuary to the Igbo people all those years ago because it conflicted with their timing and their rules.

The sounds of rummaging behind me told me that Zion and Aliyah had started to search for the key to the Throne Room. I wasn't itching to join them, not right now when we finally had some semblance of peace. So, I pulled up one of the chairs from the table and sat near one of the openings, watching the empty kingdom below as the firebirds passed back and forth.

After a while, Aliyah and Zion joined me, too, and I told them about the vision. Time passed, but here, the light never went dark and the breeze continued, as if we were sitting on a tropical island and not actually inside a roiling ball of fire. It was peaceful here, as if the passage of time couldn't reach us.

"I could stay here forever," I whispered, but then realized that that wasn't true. There would be no peace until I had my mama and daddy back. Even if I had to kill Amina for it. "We saved Vince, just like Mmiri said that we should do. And we saved him in record time."

"Time passes differently here," Aliyah pointed out. "Did we make it to him before the two-moon time period was up?"

"Yeah," Zion agreed. "Who knows how long we were in the Crystal City? I was knocked out for most of it, but it definitely felt like a long time."

I closed my eyes, hoping that the *Book* would provide me with an answer. I saw it all in my mind, Arinze returning Vince to the Palacia, Agbala's look of surprise when Arinze asked her to send him home, and the number of times the sun and moon had risen and fallen. I even saw drawings of us flying on our gryphons from the Palacia all the way to the Crystal City. Time was a fickle thing, but it presented itself as another hourglass, larger than the one we used in the Game of Escape. Every time the sun sank, the hourglass's sand would diminish to nothing. I counted fourteen diminishings.

"We've been gone for two weeks," I said, smiling wide as I opened my eyes. "We did what we needed to do."

"The *Book* gave you all of that?" Zion whispered.

I nodded. "It's beautiful, seeing it all, seeing history unfold. The *Book* isn't stagnant; as history changes, so does it."

"The next step?" Aliyah asked.

"We find that key, find that ring, and get back to the Palacia and get my parents back. Just like Mmiri alluded to."

"But how does saving Vince lead to your parents?" Zion asked.

I shook my head, a sadness filtering through me. "I don't know. She wouldn't have said it, though, if it weren't true."

A soft pressure fell into my robe with a *thunk*.

"What was that?" Aliyah asked.

My forehead scrunched as I riffled through the pockets of my robe, feeling a roughness underneath my hands. I pulled out a huge golden key, its light shining even in the constant morning of the sun.

"Whoa," Zion said, staring at it. "How did you get that?"

"I don't know," I said. "It just fell into my lap, I guess."

I sat there for a while, marveling at it, thinking about what it meant. In a few minutes, we would be inside Anyanwu's Throne Room, and the ring would be ours. That meant that

Ramala would finally be safe, and the kingdom would be, too, once again.

And I could devote my time to getting my mama and daddy back.

I stared at them both.

"Let's go get that ring."

CHAPTER SEVENTEEN

When we returned to our chambers, we found our clothing had been magically repaired and washed. We put them on, attaching our armor, and then slinging our packs over our backs.

I closed my eyes as I gripped my sword and the bow and arrow, breathing in and out. We made our way to the chambers' entrance and walked down a flight of stairs before coming back to the stone wall that encircled the Throne Room.

"Here goes nothing," I said, thrusting the key inside the keyhole. Electricity spread from my fingers to my forearm, making me gasp. I yelped when the key disappeared from my hand and smoke filtered from underneath the door.

We took a step back as the smoke filled the antechamber. After a while, the door *creaked* as it pushed against the floor, moving forward. With a heavy yawn, it opened to the right, slamming against the opposite wall with an unpleasant *crunch*.

"Let's do this," I said, gripping my sword even tighter as the smoke cleared. We moved forward into the Throne Room, fear gripping me like a vise.

The floor was a deep black sandstone, with swirls of gold painted into it. Although the room was empty, I sensed a heavy presence, as if it were the most powerful place in the universe. A magnificent throne sat in the middle of the room, raised on a silver dais of multiple steps. Like the floor, the throne was black, though I suspected that it was made of marble instead of sandstone. Multicolored cushions were laid out on the large seat that I imagined could fit several people comfortably.

"It's just as we saw it in the *Book*," Zion whispered in awe.

When I looked up, I saw an opening in the top of the room. There it was, the sun that Anyanwu watched from day to day, night to night. It shimmered in the space beyond the room, pulsating with oranges, reds, and yellows. Even from where we were standing, we could see sun flares bouncing off it.

I took a cautious step forward, my boots making a *clacking* sound. We made our way around the throne, and there it was: the ring, shimmering, and turning, affixed to the back as if it always belonged there. Here, though, the ring looked more like a hoop, as large as Anyanwu's giant fingers.

"Be careful, Cam," Aliyah said as I moved closer with my sword raised.

"I need that ring," I said, throwing caution to the wind. With every step I took, a pain built in my chest so fierce that it almost made me cry out. But I kept going, knowing that I was closer to my parents. I hooked my sword in the middle of the ring and pulled with all my strength. It dropped from the throne, encircling my weapon and falling down to touch its hilt. Even through the pain, I managed to smile.

"Yes, I got you," I said, taking the ring and clasping it on a hook on the side of my pack.

A cry pierced through the Throne Room, so loud that I almost dropped my sword. Shadows appeared next, surrounding us, darkening the room. We ran around the throne to stand in front of it, our backs to one another, our swords raised. The shadows continued to circle us, crying out in unmistakable agony. I knew what they were before they even materialized. A deep part of me *knew* they would be here, because dark magic was the only thing that could protect the gods' gifts.

"They're coming!" I screamed. "Get ready!"

The mmo stepped out from the shadows, some falling to the floor, and some suspended in the air. They were dark-and-gray creatures, their eyes a deep scarlet, their skin the color of stone. Cloaks of darkness shrouded their shoulders as they materialized. However, these mmo were different from those we had encountered before; their bodies blazed with fire, flames reaching to the sky in place of their hair. Skeletal arms reached out toward us, mixed with gristle and marrow. A dank, swampy smell filled the Throne Room, and every time they got closer, flames burst from their unclothed feet. Their mouths opened in screams, hanging in inhuman angles as blood spattered the floor.

"Use Dambe. Fight them off. And let's get out of here!" I yelled to Aliyah and Zion. They both nodded and disappeared into thin air. I called for Dambe, a warm blast surrounding my body as I went forward with my sword, screaming as I did. I connected with two mmo almost immediately, the thought of seeing my parents again guiding my movements. When I slashed my sword down, I cut them both at the same time, slicing them right across the chest. They screamed, and when they died, they burst open, magma falling to the sandstone.

I sidestepped it and kept going, this time jumping in the air to meet one that was falling from the opening in the sky. We struggled in the air. I sent it flying with a kick, chasing after it and slicing through its throat before we hit the sandstone. I stumbled to the floor, rolled over twice, and then stood.

"*Book, book, book,*" three of them were saying, running over toward me, magma falling from them as they did.

"Ahh!" I screamed, going forward and crashing into one of them. As we fell, fire and smoke surrounded us, and the only thing I could see were the mmo's red eyes and the gray, slack skin of its face. Another grabbed me from behind, but not before I slashed the fallen one in the heart. The other mmo picked me up, but I swung around and wrapped my leg around its chest, bringing it to the floor. I stabbed it and stood, facing the third one now.

A sinister smile wrapped its face as it came closer and closer. It dropped its cloak on the sandstone, and my stomach clenched at the sight of the skeletal body. I slashed out, but it disappeared into thin air, instantly appearing again, this time right in front of me. I slashed once more, but it grabbed my sword and threw it to the floor. I watched its feet, like I had done with Makai, and saw them shift in the flames ever so slightly. I was gone the next second, circling around it before kicking it in the back. It fell, which gave me the chance to retrieve my sword.

By the time it was in my hand, the mmo had grabbed me by the neck, squeezing hard so that I couldn't breathe. It screamed, "Book!" in my face before throwing me across the room. My back smashed against the marble side of the throne, and I crumpled to the floor, groaning in pain. When I stood, it closed the distance between us, pinning me by the throat once again. I beat at its back, but couldn't gain purchase to slice it through the chest.

"Cameron!" Aliyah said, falling from the sky. She wrapped her legs around its chest; it screamed, reached up, and raked her face with its long nails, but she held on. I slashed at its chest and Aliyah fell. I caught her, and we both jumped to the middle of the Throne Room where Zion was finishing off a group of three.

We stood together, fighting back-to-back. Every time we struck one down, another one seemed to appear out of thin air, out of the shadows, or down from the opening in the sky. There were so many that they drowned out the sunlight, leaving us in near darkness except for the flames and magma emanating from the mmo. Every time we advanced forward to leave the Throne Room, more of them materialized, driving us back to the throne.

One grabbed me away from Aliyah and Zion and hurled me into the throng of swirling mmo.

"Aliyah, we have to get Cameron!" Zion said. I flew into spinning shadows, my shoulder smashing painfully against the sandstone. The mmo that threw me reached out with skeletal hands. It grabbed the ring attached to my pack and threw the gift across the room. It smiled before a group of them jumped on me, wrenching my sword from my hands. They pummeled me to the point of near unconsciousness.

Blood filled my mouth as they hit me; I placed my hands over my chest to protect the *Book* there, but that left my face exposed. A sickening *crunch* filled my ears as one of them punched my nose. I cried out and pushed forward with my own hand, my palm clipping the mmo in the face. It stumbled backward, and I used that opportunity to stand up. I called for Dambe, and with swift precision, I removed my pack from my back and lifted off the floor, slamming it into each one of them. They weren't dead, but it gave me a chance to run across the room to where my sword had landed. I grabbed it up and nearly ran into Zion and Aliyah.

"There's too many of them! We can't win!" Zion said, a deep gash burrowed in his forehead.

"They stole the ring," I said as more snarls erupted in the room. By now I couldn't even see the entrance we had come through. "I need to get it back. Fight them and try to clear a path for me." A plan was starting to form in my mind on using Anyanwu's bow and arrow, but I didn't have enough time to put it into words. Zion and Aliyah both nodded as I jumped in the air again, this time floating above the throng of swirling bodies.

The sight below me made my stomach churn even with the magic of Dambe aiding me. Blood, bile, and piles of skeletal parts littered the entire Throne Room, Anyanwu's throne the only thing still intact. Its dais was cracked, steps leaning to the side. Zion and Aliyah fought together, unwilling to break apart this time, their eyes filled with determination. I twirled in the air, trying to find the ring.

Come on, come on, I thought as I began to descend. *There it is.* A sliver of silver glinted past my eyes as I caught a glimpse of the ring on the steps of the dais. When I touched the floor, I held my sword tightly in my hand and ran forward, blasting through a swirling smoke of mmo before they could fully materialize. My lips opened in a scream as I ran faster than I ever had in my life.

One mmo reached out from the floor—in the midst of dying—and grabbed my feet, tripping me up. I slipped, my face hitting the sandstone. I stood and cut it down before running again, this time my eyes on the mmo instead of the ring. I burst through the crowd of mmo, leaving nothing but flame and black blood in my wake. And then there it was again, the ring resting on the top step of the dais. I walked up the steps, doing my best to ignore the pain radiating through my entire body. I wasn't even sure if it was caused by the mmo or the *Book*.

Smoke and shadow dropped right in front of me as soon as I reached for the ring. A single mmo stood in my way, a sick smile slicing across its face, showing nothing but rotted teeth. It raised its foot and kicked me in the stomach, sending me flying off the dais. I grunted and stood, doing my best not to let the pain take over.

I raised my sword. "Get. Out. Of. My. Way," I managed to say through gritted teeth. I hunched over and prepared. It matched my movement. It roared and made its way quickly down the steps and toward me. The scream was so loud, like a horror movie come to life. Its mouth elongated in such a way that it made my skin crawl. The plan came back to me again, and I continued forward as well, moving faster and faster. We crashed into each other, but I had the upper hand. I flipped the mmo over my head and entered Dambe, time slowing down. The mmo flew into the air, continuing to scream, staring at me with surprised eyes.

With one swift movement, I grabbed the ring and hooked it on my pack again. I unzipped my pack as the mmo slammed into the sandstone, leaving a crater in the floor. I grabbed Anyanwu's bow and arrow and aimed into what I thought was the center of the Throne Room, right in front of the entrance.

"Anyanwu," I whispered. "You gave me this bow and arrow as a gift. And for a reason. I hope that you are listening to me right now. I'm choosing to believe that you knew something like this would happen."

The mmo I had just thrown extricated itself from the sandstone and came for me again, right in my line of sight. "Come on, come on, just a bit closer.

"Aliyah! Zion!" I screamed. They appeared next to me almost immediately, seemingly out of thin air.

I pulled the arrow back as the mmo was mere steps away.

"Cam, whatever you're gonna do, you need to do it now," Aliyah said, agitation clear in her voice.

"Just a few more steps," I whispered. The arrow began to glow with flame, and a pressure built in my hands, my arms, all the way to my chest. "This thing is gonna blow!"

The mmo took one more step, and that was all I needed.

I released the arrow, and it slammed into the mmo, caving its chest in. The mmo, with a surprised look on its face, flew back into the crowd of demons. As soon as it hit them, the arrow blew up, the flames ricocheting off the walls.

The entire Throne Room exploded.

CHAPTER EIGHTEEN

"Run!" I screamed, grabbing Aliyah and Zion close to me as rubble, body parts, and flames rolled all around us. Our legs pumped as we swept through the Throne Room, every last mmo dead and scattered throughout the space in horrible positions. Just like when we came into the Sun Kingdom, the fire didn't touch us, didn't harm us.

The stone wall in front of us crumbled, blasted into pieces, leaving us only a small hole to jump through. I called for the gryphons as we went.

"Cameron, what did you do?" Aliyah screamed as we ran.

"Watch out!" Zion yelled as a blast rocked the bridge, aftershocks of the Throne Room explosion reverberating throughout the entire kingdom. It sent us careening to the side, and we clung on to the metal and rope as best as we could, but another blast shook the space, sending us falling down toward the magma.

I couldn't even scream, couldn't even form my mouth to say anything. Death flashed before my vision as we hurtled closer and closer to the river of lava. I closed my eyes, awaiting my final moments.

Swoop. Large wings encircled me as I slammed into a soft back. I opened my eyes to see Ugo carrying me into the sky, his feathers still engulfed with fire. I held on with all my strength, pulling my feet into the stirrups and holding on to his reins. The only things that came out of my mouth were streams of breaths as I hyperventilated, my heart pounding in my chest like a battering ram. I scanned the sky to make out the fuzzy outlines of Zion and Aliyah soaring along with me.

That was too close! Zion was yelling.

I closed my eyes again as I hooked an arm through the hoop ring attached to my pack. Aliyah was screaming, too, making it hard for me to gain my bearings.

Another explosion sounded; I gasped and turned around. Anyanwu's palace was literally combusting from the inside out, the force of the cataclysm sending fire and smoke higher and higher into the air. Ugo screeched once, and the gryphons soared above the fire and into the clouds.

The last thing I saw was the entirety of Anyanwu's palace falling into the lake of magma below, the black of his throne leading the way.

The gryphons teemed with exhaustion hours later, sending messages through our mental link.

We settled on the grounds of an unknown shore with a small lake, the sun giving away to night. I shivered at the cool air, so different from the Sun Kingdom. Who knew how long we had been there?

The gryphons lapped at the water as we jumped off them, no longer fiery. The adrenaline was replaced with exhaustion as I fell to the soft grass, trying to catch my breath. I wiped the mountains of sweat dripping down my brow, turning to my friends as they lay in similar positions beside me.

"Listen, y'all, let me just . . . ," I was beginning to say, but Aliyah and Zion stalked away from me. I went to follow them, but I knew that it was futile. So I just stopped and let them get some space from me for a while. They were probably tired of me; to be honest, I was kinda getting tired of it all, too. But we had gotten the ring, finally. We had saved the last of the gifts, and Amina wasn't even around to try to get them back.

I settled along the shore, taking off my boots and flexing my toes for a while before the pain of my injuries returned. My shoulder was bent out of shape, likely dislocated. When I looked into the lake, my face was almost unrecognizable; my hair was misshapen and stuck out in horrible angles. Wounds marred my face, my left eye turning black and bulging, my nose broken. The clothes that Anyanwu had repaired were completely ruined once again, mixed with dirt, magma, and mmo blood.

I groaned as I opened my pack, removing Anyanwu's bow and arrow. I nearly threw both in the rushing water in disgust but didn't. There was an unnatural power to them, something that drew me in, making the *Book* in my chest stir.

With a sigh, I rummaged in the pack again, removing the still-sleeping sprite.

"I wish I could sleep, too, little one," I said, opening a flask and shaking the magic from its wings inside. "You're so lucky."

I tipped the flask into my mouth, feeling the ice rush through my organs, healing everything. I sighed, contentment flowing through me as I put the sprite back in my pack. By the time I was done, Aliyah and Zion had returned from the trees, completely healed as well, dragging a dead deer with them. A soft breeze crept through the area as they spoke.

"I can't believe we almost died. Again," Zion said.

"I know—"

"No," Zion responded. "We understand your situation, we do. But this trip, you have been making most of the decisions for us."

"We've stuck by you, as that's what friends are supposed to do," Aliyah added. "But we didn't know what you were going to do before you did it. Plus, you get angry so quickly that it's been hard to talk to you. You went off on Zion back at the Crystal City when he didn't really deserve it."

I bowed my head in shame. "I know, I know. It was wrong and I . . . I'm sorry. Especially to you, Zion. There's just so much on my mind ever since I found out what happened to Mama. And I still don't know what happened to Daddy. I just want my parents."

"Cam, you don't even have to apologize," Zion said, coming to sit beside me, wrapping his arms around me. "You don't have to explain. We know you did what you had to do. Plus, you saved us. We just want you to understand that we are here for you and always have been. I know I can't replace your parents, but I love you just the same as they did. We both do. Just include us next time. And be a bit nicer."

I hugged him back. "I know. And I will."

I unhooked the hoop ring, and it immediately became ablaze with fire, shrinking down to normal human size. "I can't wait until we're able to give this back to the queen."

"And then after that . . . ?" Zion asked.

"We have to figure out how to save Mama and find Daddy," I said, slipping the ring on my ring finger.

"Again. I can't believe we almost just died," Zion repeated.

"I know, I know, Zion," I said, sighing again. "We had to get that ring."

He pointed to the bow and arrow. "You think Anyanwu knew that mmo were protecting it? And, dang, did Amina have to leave *so* many behind when she planted it there? I've never seen so many!"

"And the mmo were so . . . different. Scarier even," I said, shivering. "And I don't know what Anyanwu knew. The gods and their fickle ways . . ."

"I thought they couldn't intervene?" Aliyah asked.

I shrugged. "But they can freely give people gifts," I responded. "They gave Ramala the ring, the scepter, and the crown."

Zion snorted. "Sounds like interference to me. And knowing the gods, they have ways around it. Like you told us, they can *indirectly* intervene however they want."

"And I wonder how being the Descendant plays into it," Aliyah mused. "You have god status; at least you're as close to being one on a human level. Maybe they can with you."

"That's actually what I was thinking," I said. "You weren't there when I saw Anyanwu in the vision when I Summoned the key. He was so *angry* that he had to do what I told him to do, that I controlled him. He didn't have a choice but to give it to me."

"Let's go get the rest of the stuff, Zion," Aliyah said to him, leaving me alone once again with my thoughts. When they returned, they carried a log between them along with sticks. I turned my head while they prepared the deer for cooking, scraping together rocks to create a fire. It would have taken them forever, but they used Dambe to move faster.

A sweet aroma reached me after a while, and I joined them by the fire. The coolness washed away as we ate before the flames, cutting off the meat with our swords. We ate in silence; I enjoyed finally not having to be on "go," not having to always be in a position to save something or someone. At least, for now, we could relax.

After, I helped Zion and Aliyah take out and pitch our tent, and then we burned the rest of the deer carcass. We settled in the darkness when we finished, Ugo, Ike, and Odum protecting us with their wings. We could hear them screeching and shuffling a bit outside. Their presence was warm, our mental link with them strong.

Zion wiggled closer to me. "You think Ramala and the others are angry with us?"

"Probably so," I whispered, looking down at the ring on my hand. "But once they see that Ramala's ring has been returned, I don't think the anger will last long."

Aliyah placed her head on my shoulder. "Who would've known that we would have come back here, but this time with Vince in tow? I wonder if Agbala has sent him home, yet."

I probably could have found out by connecting with Agbala, but I was much too tired. Plus, it was good to be with my friends, alone, at least for a while before we had to return to the Palacia.

When I closed my eyes, the *Book*'s pages swirled behind my eyelids, a calming presence in a time of much strife. I closed its pages, dimming its lights.

"Good night," I said.

———————————

"Wake up," Zion said, tugging on my shoulders.

I yawned, opening my eyes just a bit to see him over me. "What?" I groaned. "I feel like I haven't been asleep that long."

Zion shrugged. "I think we should train a bit."

"Train?" I moaned, flipping over. "For what?"

"You're a Summoner, right? We need to return to the Palacia with something."

"We have the ring," I said, closing my eyes. "Go to sleep, Zion."

Plop. The punch against my back was so painful it made me catch my breath.

"Zion," I coughed.

"Wake up. Now," he said, pulling me to my feet. "And don't wake up Aliyah."

"Jeez," I whispered, stepping out of the tent with him in the near darkness. "The sound of you hitting me will probably wake her up."

"Aliyah told me that Bakari told you that you should train in Summoning magic. Is that right?" he said, staring into my eyes. "He's going to be angry when we return, so we might as well practice now so that you can master it."

"I just want sleep," I said.

"Practice and I'll let you sleep."

"Whatever." I turned to go back in the tent.

In a split second, Zion was in front of me, his feet stomping the ground. A smile appeared on his face as he raised his hand, the ring in his palm.

"Wait, how did you get that?" I said, searching my fingers. "Give that back, Zion."

"Nope," he said, raising it higher in the air. His figure blurred a bit as the sand shifted. The next thing I saw was him appearing right next to the lake.

"Zion," I warned, gritting my teeth, elongating his name like a song.

"Summon the ring, Cameron," he said. "I refuse to let you go into fighting Amina without having a power that can rival hers. She's too strong." He raised the ring again, his figure blurring.

"Wait!" I said, but he blasted off so fast that I could barely see him. He ran across the water with such force that it almost seemed like he was flying. I closed my eyes, concentrating hard, until the wind picked up around me, Dambe catching me in its magic. My feet blurred as they touched the water, liquid sloshing over me as I ran after Zion. My eyes moved quickly, and came into focus, showing Zion just ahead of me. I gasped as he turned toward me, adventure unfolding in his expression. A smile—no, a mischievous smirk—widened across his face as he lifted his hand again and threw the ring far into the air and outward.

"Catch!" he screamed as he stopped and halted in front of me, sending a wave of water my way.

"No!" I yelled, fear flooding my heart. *I can't lose that ring.* When I thrust my hands forward, they became drowned in shadow and gold, and in the next second, the ring was back in my hands. "I did it!" I screamed.

The wave Zion sent crashed into me then, plunging me in the lake's water. I sputtered and coughed, swimming back to land. As my feet squelched into the sand, Zion shimmered in front of me, sand swirling around him.

"What's wrong with you?!" I said, spitting water out of my mouth and squeezing it out of my clothes.

"Hmm," Zion said, his eyes sparkling. "You know, this reminds me of when Mama taught me how to swim. She just threw me in the water and told me to float. Granted, probably not the best thing for her to do." He winked at me. "But it worked."

"Don't *do* that again," I said, removing my wet socks. "We can't lose the ring."

"We won't," Zion said. "You're a Summoner. Use your power." In another blast of sand, Zion disappeared.

"Wait—" I managed to say before he grabbed the ring

from me once again, spinning off into the distance. I followed him, close behind this time, but never really catching up with him. I emptied my mind, focusing on the task at hand. A panic settled in my chest, though, making my heartbeat faster. If Zion managed to lose that ring . . .

That fear spurred me on, causing me to run faster. We blasted into the woods surrounding the lake. I jumped high, feeling as if I were flying at first, before crashing into Zion. We dropped to the ground, but as soon as I made to straddle him, he was gone again, yelling into the air, "Summon the ring, Cameron. Stop trying to fight me."

I stood and closed my eyes, willing the frustration to leave me like Makai and Agbala had taught me all those months ago. The *Book* appeared in my mind, and I mentally flipped through its pages until it showed me the ring, circling over Anyanwu's throne. However, the page shifted until a picture of me surfaced, with a smile shining on my face, holding the ring triumphantly.

When I opened my eyes, determination gripped me now, shadows and gold swirling around my hands once again. First, the fear had made me Summon the ring, but now, it was *mine*; I had captured it from Amina's hiding place. *Swooshes* of wind passed by me as Zion continued to run back and forth. I knew what to do now, but I waited until I felt him move farther and farther away from me, miles away from me before I *pulled* him.

I heard a loud gasp, and then there he was, floating in front of me, his hair standing on end, swirling in that same shadow and gold that encircled my fingertips. A look of fear passed through his face as he stared at me, his right hand holding the ring.

"Cameron, let me down," he said, his voice coated in a supernatural volume that I couldn't quite understand, almost as if he were underwater.

"But why?" I said, cocking my head, laughing a bit. "You stole the ring from me."

"I was just trying to help," he said, a nervous smile curling his mouth.

"Were you?" I said innocently.

"Ye-yeah," he stuttered. "We need you to be ready for any and everything. Mastering your Summoning power will help you with that."

"I can understand that," I said. I took a step forward and grasped the ring, taking it from him. After I put it in my pocket, I walked away from him back to the tent. "Thank you for helping me master my Summoning magic."

"Wait!" he yelled after me. "You can't just leave me here!"

"Oh, I don't know," I said, stomping through the woods. "Maybe you just need to sleep there for the rest of the night."

"Cameron!" he called after me. "Cameron! Let me go!"

I strode back into the tent and placed Anyanwu's gift on my ring finger again, and it immediately shrunk so that it was fixed to my skin like a second glove. When I closed my eyes to sleep, I saw Zion again, struggling in his prison of shadow and gold. I *pulled* again, and he burst in front of me, huffing and puffing.

"That wasn't funny, Cameron," he said.

"Good night, Zion," I said, laughing myself to sleep.

CHAPTER NINETEEN

We took the long way back to the Palacia, flying slowly and disembarking on the ground whenever we felt like it. During that time, Zion and Aliyah took turns practicing Summoning with me, but the night in the woods with Zion helped me to master it. Zion was still mad at me for imprisoning him, and I still thought it was funny.

When we returned to the Palacia days later, Agbala stood in the crowded Throne Room in her constant position beside Ramala, who sat on her throne. Vince floated above her, still covered in the silver cocoon.

I couldn't quite read the expression in the queen's eyes, but Agbala was clearly furious with us. Her aura, usually a white light that encircled her, was now an angry red, pulsating every time she took a breath.

"Just give her the ring and you will be fine," Makai had

said to us when we had swooped down into the Palacia's courtyard.

Even now, Agbala was trying to parse through my thoughts, but it was easy to keep her out now. I clamped down on her consciousness, driving her out. She might have created the *Book*, but she didn't have permission to my mind.

"Step forward," Ramala said to us quietly.

We did as we were told, Makai gently pushing us from behind. I stepped in front of Zion and Aliyah, nervously playing with the shoulder strap of my pack.

"You've been gone a long while," she said as the audience parted for us. Curious eyes glanced over us, but I tried my best not to stare back, keeping my gaze on Ramala and Agbala.

"How long?" I croaked.

Agbala raised one finger. "A moon."

"Agbala," Ramala warned. "Let me do the talking."

"A moon," I repeated. "That is a long time."

Zion snickered behind me.

"I've erased the intruder's memory," Agbala said, pointing to Vince. "He will not be a problem for us or you in the future."

"Then send him home," I said.

"We will," Ramala said.

We stepped up the stairs of the dais and stood right before Ramala. Agbala gasped when we did, the aura surrounding her turning to an ivory white, her emotions changing quickly.

I thrust out my hand and showed the ring to them. The

onlookers who stood nearest to the throne cried out, whispering to one another, the message spreading until the entire room erupted in shouts and cheers.

"*The final gift has returned!*"

I smiled a bit, before taking it off my ring finger. "We found it. It was in Anyanwu's palace, in the Sun Kingdom. Amina put it there."

"Not before we almost died, though," Zion said bitterly.

"The last gift," Ramala whispered, sitting up straighter. "I never thought anyone would find it again, bringing me back to full power."

"I want my mother back," I said, my voice shaking. "I want Amina to give her back. And that's it."

"Think about this—" Agbala started to say.

"No!" I said, just loud enough for them to hear. "I don't care if she's the queen's sister. She killed my mother and turned her into a mmo. I want her back, even if I have to kill her myself."

Agbala whispered to Ramala, who had grown stony as I spoke.

"Do you know what you're asking me for?" Ramala said.

"I do," I said, simmering. "I know she's your sister, but she's harmed so many. Killed so many. Hundreds of soldiers, dead. Hundreds of them turned to mmo. Including my mother."

"Cameron, you must understand," Agbala said, walking toward me. "Amina's magic is tied to Ekwensu's. There's a link between the two."

"I saw that in the vision I had when I touched the crown."

"Which means that *blood* connects them, a deep magic that is hard to understand. A human who connects with a god in that way . . . can be unstoppable. Amina controls the mmo because, by extension, Ekwensu controls them. You would have to sever the link between Amina and Ekwensu in order to sever her link to the mmo."

"To get my mother back, I'd have to kill the princess," I responded. It wasn't a question.

Agbala nodded. "Yes, she'd either have to give her to you willingly, or you'd have to kill her to release your mother's soul."

"And she's never going to give my mother back willingly, not after I've recovered all three gifts for the queen."

"She's not," Ramala said. "And I cannot allow you to kill my sister, no matter the vendetta you have against her."

"I DON'T CARE WHAT YOU CAN OR CAN-NOT ALLOW!" I screamed so loud that the Throne Room quieted.

"Cam—" Zion said, his hand squeezing my shoulder.

"No!" I said, shrugging him off, the tears finally coming now after so long being away. "I want my mother. Now. We have risked our lives, multiple times, for these gifts! My own mother and father risked their lives, too! And for what? To die? To suffer in death as a mmo? That's not fair!" I was so heated that I continued, not allowing any of them to stop me.

"Amina sent her *demons* to my world, and they attacked

people, all to get at me! What if they had grabbed Aliyah or Zion? Or my grandmother? More of my family would be lost because you can't seem to keep your belongings safe," I said through gritted teeth, my anger so hot that I felt that I would catch on fire. "And then when we get here, Ala almost killed Zion in her twisted game just so we could get Vince back.

"Yes, your own mother," I spat at Agbala before she could speak, "tried to kill my friend, one of the only family I still have left! And then when we got to Anyanwu's kingdom, we were almost outnumbered and outmatched. All for this!" I threw the ring down on the floor; everyone in the room gasped. Ramala reached out, and it flew from the floor, fashioning itself around her finger.

But I wasn't done.

"I am so tired of almost dying because of something that wasn't even my fault." The tears streamed down to my ruined clothes, soaking the collar of my dashiki. "Like I said, I want my mama back, and I want her back now!"

When I had finished, I just stood there, breathing in and out at the exertion of screaming at the top of my lungs. The room stayed quiet. I was *done* being their puppet, being the person they needed when I got nothing in return. I didn't think it should work that way; if the queen could bargain with the gods for her people's freedom from enslavers, then I should be able to bargain, too.

Ramala snapped her fingers, her scepter blazing with

lightning. When she pointed it at Vince, a blue portal appeared above him. She thrust out with her scepter, and Vince flew into the portal, disappearing inside.

"I've done what you asked," Ramala said.

"Now, give me Amina."

A strong arm clamped on my shoulder, squeezing so hard that I yelped. A hard, deep voice spoke to me then. "Cameron, let's go. Now."

I tried to shrug off the person, but he was much too strong for me.

"Cameron, let's go. Now," he repeated. When I looked up, it was Bakari, staring at me with intense eyes, the scar on his cheek standing out in the honey-colored light of the Throne Room.

"No, Bakari—"

With a swift movement, he picked me up and threw me over his shoulder, carrying me out of the Throne Room and into the courtyard.

"Let me down! Let me down! Let me down!" I screamed as Bakari continued to carry me through the night, holding me in such a tight grip that it was hard to move. I knew I looked foolish being carried like a little child, but at this point, all the care in the world had left me.

Bakari didn't let me go until his boots scraped against soft grass, and a familiar stone sculpture reached my eyes, the Ikenga that stood at the front of his hut.

He set me down on the grass and strode inside his home, pulling me with him. I paced up and down the entrance, the anger continuing like the rolling magma in Anyanwu's kingdom. "They can't do this, Bakari," I said as he stared at me with impassive eyes. "They can't just make a decision about *my* mama's life after everything I did for them!"

"I know, Cameron," Bakari said in a soft voice.

"No, you don't understand, I—" I stopped when I realized that Bakari had essentially agreed with me. "Wait, what?" I had been so used to everyone treating me like a child, like I couldn't make my own decisions, that his agreeing with me seemed weird.

"I know how you feel," he said, rummaging around in his kitchen area for a while, before returning with mangoes, offering me one. "I lost my family and friends, too. In those days, I was so angry, especially when the barrier was created. I knew I couldn't see them ever again. I can imagine your pain because I've *been* through your pain."

I took a bite of the mango, settling on one of the cushions in his living area. He continued to stand.

"I just don't understand why everything has to be so hard," I whispered. "Ramala can't just keep Mama away from me. It's not fair. Amina has to pay for what she did."

"Then make her pay."

I stared at him, marveling again at how we looked so much alike. The lack of emotion in his eyes had been replaced with passion, an emotion I couldn't quite read. It was also the first time he had gone against Ramala's words. I thought about the time he, Makai, and Halifa had led me, Zion, and Aliyah back to our chambers on her orders when the mmo had broken through the Palacia. This was a different Bakari, though, someone who wanted revenge. Not just for himself, but for me, too.

"How, Bakari?" I asked, sighing. "Ramala won't let me anywhere near Amina to even try."

He came over and sat down on the cushion in front of me, smiling a bit. "Aren't you the Descendant?"

"Yeah, I—"

"And aren't you supposed to be a Summoner?" he asked, his eyebrows arching.

I nodded, thinking about all I had done since returning to Chidani. "I am."

"The same as Nneka?"

I had Summoned Nneka's soul just a few months ago, not knowing I was using my magic. I had never told Agbala about our meeting, and even she didn't know what my power was before she found out when I almost killed Amina.

"Yes," I answered. "But what does that have to do with me?"

Bakari grabbed my hands, squeezing them. "Cameron,

think. You have great power, a great magic that only you understand."

I did think now, trying to figure out yet another riddle. I remembered what I had seen in Amina's vision, how she had sold her soul to Ekwensu for a blood price. I remembered how I called Nneka forth without realizing it. I also remembered something recent that had happened, Ramala and Agbala talking about Amina's bargain with Ekwensu. She had bargained her soul, gaining control of the mmo in the process. They were connected to her in a way that meant that if she died, they were released from servitude. I also remembered Mmiri's words, about everything falling into place for me when I saved Vince. Maybe she hadn't meant that saving Vince would save my mother; maybe she meant the *knowledge* I gained from saving him would somehow give me enough knowledge to save her. *Wait . . . all of this has the soul connected to it.*

Amina sold her soul, Mama's soul was lost, and the mmo almost took Vince's soul.

"Wait," I said, putting the mango down. "Is it possible to . . . ?"

Bakari nodded, encouraging me on. "Yes?"

"But that would take so much magic," I whispered, before gazing into Bakari's eyes.

"Yes?"

"I have to Summon Mama's soul from Amina. I mean, if

I can Summon Nneka and weapons, then surely I can do the same with a soul," I said, my mind whirring with the possibilities. "That way, Ramala can get what she wants and keep her sister alive, and I can get Mama back."

"Then that's what you will do," Bakari responded.

"But . . ." I raised my hands and then let them fall. "I don't know how to Summon a soul! An entire soul! How am I supposed to get Mama back if the only practice I've had is with small things?"

Bakari smiled before engulfing me in a hug. "Do not worry, Cameron Battle. We will figure it out. Together." He stood before rummaging around in a closet in his short hallway. After he threw a bundle of bedsheets my way, which hit me in the face, I fell down on the cushions.

"Sleep well," he said, laughing a bit. "We will figure this out tomorrow."

CHAPTER TWENTY

"Um . . . do you even know what you're doing?" I asked Bakari the next morning, standing in the small yard in the back of his hut. A gate made of iroko wood surrounded his home, giving us some privacy from prying eyes.

"Nope," he said. "I don't know anything about Summoning magic, but I do know you shouldn't have to learn this on your own." He paced back and forth in front of me while I felt foolish.

"Now, tell me something about this magic. When do you use it? What do you feel?"

"Um . . . ," I said, thinking, scratching my scalp. "It usually happens in moments of stress, I think. When I couldn't use the *Book*, I called Nneka without realizing it; it was at a moment where I thought I would give up. And when Zion took the ring from me, I feared I would lose it."

"And why did you think you needed to give up?"

I opened my mouth, not really knowing how to say it. "Cameron?"

"It was when . . . when I thought Zion would die." My face grew hot as I thought about Zion shattering his leg. "It was the first time I realized I loved him like my own family."

"Good," he said, continuing to pace. "That's good information to know." Something passed through his expression, but I couldn't quite catch it.

"What else?" he said. "Did it happen before that?"

"Hmm." I thought again. "Wait! Yes, it did!"

"When? And what happened?"

It was another memory that I didn't like talking about, a memory that didn't belong to me. It was when I had finally learned to face my fear and fight.

Tears burned in my eyes as I began to talk. "It was when we went to the Cave of Shadows and saw Nsi. I saw . . . Amina defeat Mama and Daddy. I had Summoned a sword and broken the image because I was so furious, so angry, Bakari. Because she took something away from me that I loved."

Bakari snapped his fingers. "So love and fear are some of your triggers."

"I guess," I said, shrugging.

"So you have to think about what you love whenever you start Summoning. That would make the most sense considering those moments are the most emotional for you."

"We're talking about a soul, here, Bakari," I said, growing

frustrated. "I can't just Summon something like that. At least, not on purpose."

"Why not?" he said, stopping in front of me. "You've done more than *any* person should do at such a young age."

I didn't say anything to the truth in that. Bakari left me for a moment, rummaging at the side of his hut. When he came back, carrying a heavy training mat, I had made a decision. It either was the worst idea I had ever had, or it would be my best.

"What?" Bakari asked.

"I need to Summon your soul."

He sat on the mat, closing his eyes.

"Then Summon my soul."

I laughed. "Wait. That's all it took?"

He opened his eyes, gazing at me so intently that I shivered. This was no joke.

"Maybe we shouldn't," I suggested.

"Why not?"

"Because . . . like I said when I first came here . . . I can't lose you, too. You're my family. I've lost too much."

He smiled. "So that means you love me, or close to it?"

"Yeah, I guess."

"Good," he said, closing his eyes again and lying down on the mat. "That's your anchor. Now, try to take my soul. It's the only way you'll be able to practice getting your mother back."

I trembled a bit as I walked over and sat next to him. He looked peaceful, almost as if he were asleep in the morning

sun. After taking a deep breath, I closed my eyes, feeling foolish. We sat there in silence for a while. It was easy to think,
though. About how I had lost my mama and daddy. About
how I had met Bakari when I got to Chidani, after thinking I
only had Grandma left. About how emotional I had gotten
when he had shown me that we were related.

My hand shot out, not of my own volition.

Bakari gasped, and my eyes opened wide. My right hand
glowed with shadows and golden light as it hovered over his
chest. He croaked aloud and then grunted in pain. I removed
my hand immediately, and the light disappeared.

His eyes fluttered open.

"Maybe I made the wrong decision."

"I think it was working," Bakari said, holding his hand
over his chest. "My heart is beating so fast. It felt like my life
was . . . slipping away."

My eyes widened. "I don't think that's a good thing."

"We have to finish it."

"I don't know."

"You have to. Do you want your mother back or not?"

I sighed, marching away while he closed his eyes again.
I stood at his back entrance, trying to gain my bearings. This
was dangerous magic, magic that could have disastrous results
if done wrong. I wanted Mama back; she probably could have
trained me through it all, showing me how to use it to help
and not harm. The thought of her buoyed me forward, though.

Thinking about that last instant I had seen her—when Amina had shown her to me and then taken her once again—was enough to keep me moving even though I didn't want to hurt Bakari.

I went back over and sat next to him. I sighed once, and then closed my eyes, thinking of seeing Mama again and how that would feel.

My right hand thrust out again, and the shadows and golden light returned as I opened my eyes. Bakari gasped again, and I tried my best to ignore the sound. I had to keep going or I would lose my nerve all over again.

A grunt escaped Bakari's mouth as it fell open. A white, filmy substance floated out, flying toward my hand. I grasped it, caressing it, as it flitted in and out of my hands. I marveled at it, feeling *life* teem within me. It took much effort to control it, but it was Bakari's soul. When I looked down at him, I noticed that the substance was still attached to his mouth as he stared at me, the life in his eyes mostly gone.

I panicked then, a realization settling on my shoulders. All I had to do was to pull, to *tug*, and his soul would be mine, untethered from him. And Bakari would be dead. There was an excitement, too. That I could manipulate someone in this way, that I could get my mama back.

A pain so sharp beat against my head, and then my chest felt like it was exploding as Bakari gasped underneath me.

"Let him go!" a voice screamed from inside me.

The effort to sit back up was colossal, like someone had squeezed a boulder inside me and was trying to extract it. The pain was so monumental that I almost passed out from it.

There was that voice again, loud and familiar. "Let him go! Now!"

I thrust the soul back downward, where it settled into Bakari's mouth.

"Cameron?" he said, coughing. "Did it work?"

Gray swirls swam across my vision, and I fell forward.

"Wake up!" The voice was urgent.

I did, opening my eyes. I sat on a dry, sandy plain staring into a set of large, frantic, brown eyes.

"Nneka?" I groaned, sitting up. "What happened?"

The same multicolored cowrie beads shaped her braided hair; she was just as young as when I had seen her the first time. This time, though, the river that spread in front of us had begun to dry up, the shore showing in places it hadn't before. Smoke rose from its depths, and a rank smell reached my nose.

"You are what happened," she said, gesturing to the river.

"I did this?" I asked.

"You did," she said, nodding before reaching out to touch my chest. "You are the keeper of the *Book*, Cameron. There are things that Agbala hasn't told you, or maybe she didn't realize them."

I rolled my eyes. "I am sure that Agbala knows *exactly* what she is keeping or not keeping from me."

If Nneka's eyes could have gotten bigger, they probably would have. "Listen to me!"

"What?"

"The *Book* isn't just yours, Cameron," she said, pressing her hands against me harder. "It's *all* of ours."

"What does that mean?"

Nneka closed her eyes now, shaking her head. "When a Descendant dies, they become one with the *Book*. They become one of its pages. They live within it. Which is why you can see me. I'm dead, yes, but my soul exists within the *Book*, within you. All of the Descendants do."

"Which means . . ."

"Look," she said, pointing all around her. It wasn't just the river that looked contaminated; the sand had also begun to look brittle, and in some places, darkness blanketed the area. Almost like how the barrier looked. Even the sky had turned from a deep blue to a night with no stars. Like we were sitting in a void or a dark hole. "The entire fabric of reality is changing. You were using too much magic, and that magic was going against what nature intended. You cannot manipulate life and death, as that is not what the Descendant's magic is supposed to be used for. A Summoner can only use a certain amount of magic before the *Book* will be destroyed. And with it, we will be, too."

I stood up, anger filtering through me so hard that I was

sweating. "Wait, what? I was trying to save my mama! I should be able to Summon what I want!"

"And you can," Nneka reassured me. "But at what costs? The Descendants depend on the magic of the *Book* to help the next one complete their duty. Do you think Princess Amina is the only one who wants to hurt Queen Ramala? There have been others out there who have plotted against the queen, and we have stood in their way each time."

"I was just practicing," I whispered, feeling defeated. "Amina has Mama's soul and won't return her. It's not fair, Nneka."

She caressed my cheek from her short height. "I know, Cameron. But sometimes, death is death. We cannot all control what happens to us."

Something needled at my brain, but I couldn't quite put it into words just yet. "I want Mama back."

"You'll have to figure out some other way," Nneka said, tears starting to swim in her eyes. "I used to be a Summoner, too."

"I know," I said, sitting back down. "I read about it."

"You have the same magic I had."

"What magic did Mama have?"

Nneka smiled, wiping the tears away. "You've seen her in action. She could fight, but more adeptly than anyone in history. She didn't even have to use Dambe when she was in Chidani; she could move so fast that almost no one could beat her."

But Amina managed to.

"As I said, I was a Summoner when I was alive. As the first Descendant, I made it my mission to find what I had lost."

"What did you lose?"

The tears fell from her eyes now, sliding down her dark-brown face. "My family. I lost them all to the slave trade at such a young age." She shook her head as she remembered. "It's why as a soul, I choose to exist as a child. To honor their memory."

"You tried to get them back."

Nneka nodded. "I did. After I escaped slavery, I went to Chidani alone. When I grew older, I tried to Summon my family through the barrier, to bring them back to me after years of being the Descendant. I almost destroyed the *Book* in the process. And I lost my life. You see, if I had succeeded, that which gives us power would be no more, the barrier would cease to exist, and the mmo would take over everything."

I didn't say anything, *couldn't* say anything at this point. I knew what she was feeling; I was trying to Summon my own mother back. And the bigger picture was greater than my own emotions.

As we sat in silence, the river began to roar back to life, flowing from side to side, the putrid scent leaving. The dark parts of the sand began to shift and move away, a warm heat returning to the ground. The shore receded as the water covered it, and the inky blackness of the sky began to turn a bright blue. Birds screeched in the sky as they flew past.

"What's happening?" I asked, looking around.

"Healing," Nneka said. "The *Book* is healing itself. It has the same magic that Agbala has, the magic of healing."

"Because you stopped me in enough time?"

"Yes."

"Are you telling me that I should never try to Summon souls because the *Book* will be destroyed and so will Chidani's protectors?"

"Yes," Nneka said. She inclined her head to the left.

"There has to be another way to get Mama back," I said, frustration settling upon my shoulders like boulders. "I have to get her back somehow."

Nneka shook her head, and I could feel her frustration matching mine. "Not unless Amina freely gives her back or you kill her." She placed her hand on my chest again. "And let me tell you, Ramala is even more powerful than you could ever be now that you have returned the three gifts. She will never allow you to get close to her sister. And now that she's strong and able to rule the way she used to, you can't stop her or change her opinion."

"I will find a way," I demanded. "No one is keeping me from Mama."

"Ramala will," Nneka said, sadly. "She will ensure that her kingdom stays intact by any means necessary. And to do that, she has to keep Amina alive and bound so that she can never get the gifts ever again."

I sighed, thinking about everything I had lost. I had only

wanted to regain what was fair for all my work up to this point, and that was to save my parents. Amina had taken everything from me, and now, so would Ramala. I had to come up with a plan to get them back.

I just had to.

"I want to go back to Bakari," I said softly. "Let me just go back."

Hurt appeared on Nneka's face, but then she nodded. She placed warm hands on my forehead. "Then you shall go back, Cameron. Remember what I said. Protect the Descendants at all costs. I know you miss your mother, but all heroes have to make sacrifices."

I closed my eyes, shutting myself away from her. "Just send me back."

"Wait," she said, pointing at the sky, a shower of energy leaving her index finger as I opened my eyes. "You can't get your mother back, but I want you to leave here with something. I don't want you sad. And I know I should let you find this out on your own, but you've been through so much. I have seen so much throughout the centuries, and I can no longer be neutral in this."

I watched as something appeared in the sky, translucent, covered in gold. Nneka wrapped her hands around it and circled it around her fingers before handing it over to me.

"What's this?" I asked.

"Something that you must see. I saw it years ago, around a goddess's neck. It's only fair that you see it now."

"Why would I care about a goddess's trinket?"

"Your mother's soul is gone, Cameron. Gone, and never coming back. But there may be one more soul you can save. Just think."

I did, marveling at the necklace, an opal stone affixed to its center. If I looked closely, I thought I could make out . . . *something* shifting inside the stone, like it was a living thing.

"What in the . . . ?" I said, but then my mind began to whir with the possibilities. If Mama was supposedly dead, then that meant that—

"I have to go," I said hurriedly as the necklace disappeared. "I've seen this necklace before. Send me back, Nneka."

Nneka whispered to me as I felt myself floating away.

"The Descendants belong in the *Book*, living and dead. It's what they deserve. Now, do what you have to do."

CHAPTER TWENTY-ONE

"I need to be alone, Bakari," I said to him after I awakened.

"Wait, where did you go?" he asked me. "Did the magic work?"

"Something like that," I said, walking away. "Just give me a few moments."

I turned my back and went alone, thinking about all that had happened. I could feel the magic brewing underneath the surface, and every time I looked at my hands, shadows and gold swirled around my fingers. Every time I thought of Mama and Daddy, or Zion and Grandma, magic flowed through me in a way that I had never felt before. It was like a well opened inside me, connecting with the *Book*. I had found my destiny and my magic, but I couldn't even use it to bring my mama back. If I did, the Descendants would cease to exist. And it would be all my fault.

Maybe death *was* the end of the road. I was foolish to believe that I could bring Mama back.

But I *could* bring someone else back, especially if Nneka was right. I had seen that necklace before, around the neck of Idemmili, the sea goddess, when she came to us the first time in Onitsha. It was when we had gone there with Bakari, Makai, and Halifa to search its waters for Ramala's crown.

By the time I had gotten to my chambers in the Palacia, I had made my decision.

"What have y'all been doing since I've been gone?" I asked Zion and Aliyah when I returned. They both were eating in our sitting room.

"After Bakari took you away, no one went to look for you. Agbala told us that you would be safe with him, so we just rested," Zion said.

"And ate," Aliyah said, shading her eyes to glare at Zion. "You already know your best friend ate everything in sight."

"What?" Zion asked, rolling his eyes. "We had been gone for a long time. I figure, we just saved the kingdom, right? Might as well be treated like kings. I almost *died* for this. That's the least they could do."

"And that he did," Aliyah said. "Zion's been walking around in ceremonial clothes ever since you left, meeting the nobles, shaking hands, and eating to his heart's content. You would think *he* was the Descendant."

"*Anyway*," Zion said.

"I need to see Idemmili," I said, interrupting their story.

"Huh?" Aliyah said.

"Just come with me," I said, taking them both by the hands and leading them outside of the Palacia, telling them everything that had happened since Bakari had taken me— well, everything except Summoning his soul.

"What do you mean about Idemmili having your father?" Zion asked.

"Nneka showed me something in the vision I had, something that belonged to the goddess," I said. "I just know Idemmili has him."

A rock formation rose from the deep water of the lake as we approached, shadows of the mondao lying across its face.

"What's your plan?" Zion said, sitting on the sand. "You know we are with you, but we need more."

Aliyah sat on one of the boulders near the edge of the lake while Zion created his own version of the Palacia in the sand, which didn't look too good. I went silent for a while, just thinking about everything we had been through together. I was glad to see them being able to take a break from constant, endless danger. They deserved that; I was sad that I was about to shatter that happiness.

"I'm going to Summon Idemmili to get Daddy back," I said. Zion stood and took a step back from his sandcastle, a shocked expression appearing on his face.

"You're going to do what?" Aliyah said from her perch on top of the boulder. I thrust my hand out, commanding my magic forward, pointing shadowy and gold fingers toward the water. I watched as it bubbled.

I didn't answer the question at first, but I did make a show of smashing Zion's sandcastle with my boot. Just because.

"Hey!" he protested, but I silenced him by explaining everything.

"Nneka showed me her necklace when I tried to Summon Bakari's soul."

"You tried to what?!" Aliyah screamed.

"Just listen," I said. "She told me that I couldn't Summon Mama's soul without the Descendants who live in the *Book* being destroyed. But she also said that another soul could be living and showed me Idemmili's necklace. It has to be Idemmili. It has to."

"Explain more," Aliyah said.

"In my vision in the Cave of Shadows, I saw Mama and Daddy get defeated. Daddy fell into the water. Nneka showed me Idemmili's necklace to show me that the goddess has Daddy, that she saved him, somehow."

"Whoa," Zion said.

"I know," I responded.

"Cam," Aliyah said, jumping from the boulder and coming toward me. "Can I give you a hug? I am so sorry about all of this."

I nodded in response, and they both held me for a long while. I breathed them in, closing my eyes, feeling the magic fill every part of my skin to the point where I felt like I was overflowing with it once again. Their love permeated everything within me. In this moment, I felt one with them, as if I didn't need any family but them. But I also felt something, too, a slight tug as I called for Idemmili with my magic, Summoning her to me.

The bubbling of the lake's water brought me back to the present, and the same empty sadness filled me again. I opened my eyes to see the rock formation empty, the colorful mondao on top of it disappearing. The water was churning in a huge circle, like a black hole, spinning and spinning.

"Um, what's going on?" Zion asked, pointing at the lake.

They both let me go and we stared.

"I don't think that's a good thing?" Aliyah said.

I showed them my hands, and they gasped. "I'm calling Idemmili," I said. "Now that I've figured it out, I demand she come." *Please let my thoughts be true.*

"You're calling a *god*?" Zion asked, incredulously.

The water swirled faster and faster until a tall figure rose from its depths, a golden trident in its hand. Idemmili stood on the lake, her feet standing on top of the surface. A crown rested on her head. Her iro wrapped tight around her waist, the color of diamonds. She stared at us with impassive eyes, changing from dark brown to the deepest blue. A smell of honey reached my nose.

"Idemmili?" I said.

"You dare Summon me, boy?" she said.

"It is my right as the Descendant," I said. But then my confidence dissipated to the point where my shoulders sagged, and I dropped my eyes to the sand. I still had my courage, but Idemmili hadn't wronged me like some of the other gods had. "I mean, it is my right, but you are the only one who can help me with my problem. So I'm asking nicely for you to help us." I raised my gaze.

She nodded at me, as if she were acknowledging my power. "You are correct. It is your right to command me. But I do appreciate your humbleness. I couldn't intervene when you were here last, but I am glad that you have found out the secrets the waters hold." Then, she pointed a finger at Zion. "Are you ready for your reward?"

Zion squeaked in fear. I remembered it all now, how she had shown up in the village of Onitsha, offering us the ocean to find the queen's crown. In that moment, she had singled out Zion for his help, but she hadn't elaborated further.

"Reward?" he asked.

"What does that mean?" Aliyah said.

She thrust her trident forward. "It's time for him to help you."

"I knew it," I whispered.

"You're a god," Aliyah pointed out. "You're not supposed to intervene."

"I'm not intervening," Idemmili said, smiling a bit, the first time I had ever seen her show any emotion. She thrust her trident in Zion's direction again. "But he can."

"Um . . . ," Zion said.

"Take it, hero." She held it high in her right hand.

"Wait, no!" Zion said, but Idemmili didn't listen. She threw the trident like a javelin in his direction. He jumped high in the air, screaming as he did. He grasped the weapon and landed on the sand. His entire body shone with light, his hair standing up on end as what seemed like lightning rolled all around him. Aliyah and I took a step back, gasping as the earth crumbled underneath his feet. A huge crater opened up underneath him, and the illuminated current that surrounded him was like a barrier, keeping us from him. He also grew just a bit taller, and his eyes took on that same impassive look that Idemmili's had.

I directed my fury at her. "What did you do to him?" I screamed.

"I gave him his destiny," she said, before she leaped into the churning water's depths, disappearing underneath.

"Zion?" I said, taking a step toward him.

"We need to go," he said. Even his voice had changed, becoming an uncomfortable mixture of Idemmili's and his own.

"Go where?" Aliyah said. "What are you talking about?"

As Zion moved, the electric current surrounding him did, too.

"We need to go," he repeated, stepping into the lake. "He's awaiting you."

"Daddy," I said.

Zion continued to wade into the water.

"We have to go with him," I said to Aliyah, making my decision, taking off my boots. "We can't just leave him. I know Daddy is down there."

Aliyah nodded, following my lead. By the time we got into the water, Zion towered above us now to the point where he looked like a god. He grasped both of our arms, and the electric current surrounded us, too.

"Zion—" Aliyah started to say, but he tightened his hold on us and jumped right in the churning water, straight into the sinking hole.

———————

Mondao tails encircled us as we swam through the lake's depths, myriads of colors bursting through my eyesight. A deep fear bit at me, and that same fear showed in Aliyah's eyes. I could barely see her, though, considering how large Zion had grown in just a few minutes.

His hands caressed mine ever so slightly, and the feeling of Zion was familiar, telling me that although Idemmili had turned him into a godlike creature, he was still the same Zion

I knew and loved. The trident's handle struck me in the side, which brought me out of my reverie. When I breathed, it felt like air, Zion's current protecting us.

Cameron? Where are we going? Is the Book *telling you anything?* Aliyah said from Zion's other side as we were pulled through the water.

I couldn't say anything but shake my head. Surprisingly, the *Book* told me nothing, as if Idemmili's magic was so strong that it was counteracting it somehow. She had said, through Zion, that "he" was waiting for me. That had to have meant Daddy.

We continued to swim alongside the large Zion, the mondao tails and the current leading us on. The mondao's domain was like a kingdom within the palace grounds. Huge rock structures rose in the lake's depths, their faces and sides struck through with burrowed holes. Mondao heads stuck out of them, their hair long and braided down their green skin. They came out, swimming around and around in a circle, so fast that I could barely see them. They were of all ages and sizes, some of them appearing like children with long, sparkling tails.

The water was a light blue, like the sky had looked before we had gone into the Sun Kingdom for the ring. After a while, the mondao swarmed above us in an astounding circle formation, swimming fast. The beads they wore in their hair shined in different shades of golds, reds, greens, and diamonds.

We're almost there, Zion said, tightening his grip on us as he swam faster through the water, deeper and deeper. The deeper we went, the bluer the water became.

Look! Aliyah said, pointing. We had reached the floor of the lake, which seemed more like an ocean given how long it took to swim down. Warm sand settled against our feet as we stepped onto the floor.

But my attention was on a large, glistening cave built into the lake's ground, its entire structure infused with diamonds that glinted so brightly that I could barely see. It shimmered in my eyesight, as though a haze of heat were in front of it.

Zion let us go at this moment, floating forward, leaving some of his electric current with us.

I grabbed Aliyah, both of us treading water, too afraid to follow Zion.

We watched as he thrust his trident forward, right through the cloudy water. It struck through, a large sound clanging in the area like glass breaking. He reoriented himself, his feet settling upon the ground. With what looked like immense effort, he took a strong step forward through the haze. After, he turned to us, his hair settling down, his clothes no longer rippling, the current surrounding him was gone.

"You may come now," he said, gesturing toward us. "The barrier is down."

"Thoughts?" Aliyah asked me.

"Why is it always Zion?" I groaned, taking a step forward. "Idemmili has something for me to see. I need to see it."

Aliyah and I both swam through the mist, and found ourselves standing on the sand, as if we were walking on land, air surrounding us now instead of water.

I gasped as my clothing dried, and my toes sunk through the sand, feeling its brittleness.

Zion stood in front of us, smiling, returned to his normal height. The trident looked massive in his hands now.

"Zion? Or . . . are you Idemmili? Or . . . a mixture?" Aliyah asked.

He laughed. "It's me! It was me the entire time!"

"Was it?" I said, raising my left eyebrow.

Zion shrugged, holding on to the trident. "I mean, I think so. When I caught this, I automatically knew what I had to do." He turned around in the direction of the large cave.

"The first piece of the puzzle awaits us inside," Zion said, strolling in.

"'Awaits'?" I said, as we watched him leave. "What kid uses words like that?"

"Gods who turn kids into gods," Aliyah said.

"We still need to follow him," I said, going forward.

I went inside the dark cave, Aliyah right behind me.

I bumped into Zion, but he didn't move. I grabbed his hand and waited for Aliyah to catch up. We couldn't see in the darkness, but a light, tinged with gold, came into focus almost immediately.

A figure stepped through the light, speaking in an unmistakably low, fiery, and deep voice.

"Cameron."

A lump appeared in my throat, and tears burned my eyes as I took him in.

"Dad?"

CHAPTER TWENTY-TWO

I ran into his arms, smashing into his bare chest, not caring if this was a trick or not, not caring if the gods were playing with me.

"Oh!" I gasped when I realized that I didn't pass through him as if he were smoke, that everything about him was real. *Felt* real. The tears fell as soon as I smelled him, as his beard tickled my cheek as he bent over me to hold me close. It was the scent of sandalwood, of the woods surrounding Grandma's house, of the minty smell of his aftershave. Of the air after a summer storm. But these weren't angry or sad tears; no, these were the emotions I had been carrying with me for so long, as if an ocean inside me had finally broken free. He held me like a baby, cradling me in his arms, squeezing me so tightly that I was sure he wanted to keep me with him forever. And I wanted to never let him go.

"Dad," I said again, not knowing what else to say.

The sounds of Aliyah and Zion crying, too, brought me out of my jumbled thoughts.

"What?" I said, as Daddy gently placed me on the ground. "How?"

"Idemmili," Daddy said, holding me away from him, taking me in. "Cameron, you have grown . . . so much since I last saw you." His voice caught in his throat. "You're a young man now. Hardened. A soldier. I . . . we didn't want this life for you." His calloused hands ran through my coarse hair before they fell on my ripped dashiki. He shook his head. "No, no, we didn't want this. The fact that you're here tells me everything I need to know. You're the Descendant now."

I stood there, staring at him. He was still Daddy, but he was much changed. His skin held a luster about it, as if the stars shone through it. It was the color of a mixture of greens and dark browns, as if he existed in two places at once. When I looked down, I noticed that he only had one foot. A mondao tail snaked to the sand in place of his left one, corded with diamonds and rubies. But when I blinked, it changed into a human foot as Daddy took a step forward. While a beautiful necklace surrounded his neck, a deep wound marred his bare chest, right in the middle.

I reflected on what I had seen in the Cave of Shadows, how Amina had seemingly killed him; yet he had slipped into the creek, not to be seen again until now.

"What happened?" I whispered as tears continued to leak

from my eyes. "What happened to you? How are you even here; how are you alive?"

Zion and Aliyah came to stand by me, offering me support by touching my shoulders.

Daddy held out a strong hand to us.

"I'll tell you everything you need to know."

———

The cave was like a museum, situated in the middle of a palace. We sat around a large oval-shaped golden table, me sitting right next to Daddy. I was still in awe that he was here, that he was alive, that he was with me again. And I was *never* going to let him out of my sight this time.

Daddy's eyes flashed yellow, his necklace glowed with an ethereal light, and a fire bloomed in the fireplace located at the head of the room we sat in. Our bare feet settled on plush rugs, seemingly appearing out of thin air. The cave rock walls held large paintings of Idemmili in various poses; in each one, her trident that Zion now carried was ever present. Daddy folded his hands on the table, speaking in a low, familiar, controlled voice.

"Princess Amina happened to me."

"I know," I said, gulping. "I saw you in the Cave of Shadows. I thought she had killed you."

He sighed, rubbing his beard, shaking his head. "I didn't want any of this for you. You shouldn't have seen that; no child should."

Zion cleared his throat before speaking. "You're literally sitting in front of us, Mr. Lonnie." He shrugged when Aliyah sent him a mean look. "We thought you were . . . gone for so long."

"When I dropped into the creek," Daddy began, grabbing my hand, "I thought I was dead. A deep darkness settled upon me, and I gave myself up, thinking that everything I knew was lost. That we had lost against Amina. But, it wasn't the end for me. At least, not in the way I thought. It was more of a beginning."

"Idemmili saved you?" Aliyah asked.

He shook his head, his long beard almost brushing the table. "No, not Idemmili. At least not in a direct way."

"The gods and their games," I muttered.

When Daddy chuckled, the room shook.

"Whoa," I said, holding on to the table. He was different, in more ways than one.

He grasped the necklace, caressing it lovingly. "I opened my eyes one last time in that creek, as the breath almost left my body. I wanted to *live*, Cameron, more than anything in this world." He turned somber eyes to me. "I wanted to live for you, to be there for you. To help turn you into the man I grew to be. That's when this necklace appeared around my neck."

Zion held up his trident while I thought about receiving Anyanwu's bow and arrow. It was clear to me that over the centuries, the gods had found their own little ways to intervene in human affairs, always one step ahead.

"Why would she save you, though?" I asked.

Daddy shrugged. "I don't see her much, at least not in person. I see her in visions and dreams, mostly. When I awakened and grabbed the necklace, I was reborn into what you see now." He shuddered a bit, his skin continuing to glow. "It was painful, much more painful than the wound Amina gave me. It was like I was ripped into multiple pieces, just to be put back together again. I lost consciousness a number of times, and when I finally came to, I was in this new body. I could breathe and swim underwater, and the mondao responded to me as if I were their king."

"And you've been living here the entire time?" I asked.

He nodded. "Yes, I have. It was like my mind changed, too, after the transformation. All I wanted to do was swim around and live here." He stared into my eyes with his fiery ones. "Yes, I wanted to see you and your mother for so long, but every time the thought came to my head, my mind was wrenched back here, in this place. I can only imagine that it was because I accepted Idemmili's bargain with me: my life for her help. After a while, years passed and I still wasn't able to get back to you."

"It's been two years since you've been gone," I whispered, grabbing his hand. "Mama is . . . Mama is . . ." I couldn't force myself to say it, couldn't bring myself to tell him the awful truth of everything that had happened.

"You don't have to say it," Daddy said, squeezing my hand hard. "The fact that you're even here . . . that you're older than when I last saw you, tells me what I need to know. I just don't know why your friends are here with you." He eyed Aliyah. "And I don't think I even know who you are."

We explained everything that had happened since I touched the *Book* with Zion and Aliyah now, telling him that we had found all three of Ramala's gifts and what our plans were going forward.

Pride washed over Daddy's face as he heard our story. "You did what me and your mama couldn't. We didn't last long before . . ."

"She's not dead, though," I blurted out.

"Cameron . . . ," Zion warned.

"No, he needs to know the full truth," I said, taking a deep breath before speaking again. "Amina didn't kill Mama, at least not in the way that you think. She turned her into a mmo."

Although Daddy gasped in horror, I continued on. "I saw it all in the vision Nsi gave me. And in the battle against Amina, she showed me that Mama was still alive. That probably would have happened to you, too, if you hadn't fallen into the water."

"Cameron, you shouldn't give him false hope," Aliyah whispered. "Remember what Nneka said."

"No," I said, burning with rage before I admitted the full truth to Daddy. "I'm a Summoner."

He sat quietly as I explained everything to him.

"I can't come back to land with you," he said sadly when

I finished. "I can't help you even if I wanted to. This new body begins to break apart if I am on land for too long. But I . . . I want to see your mother again."

"Why can't you?" I asked, sadness replacing my fury. "I just got you back. I can't leave you now. I don't want to leave you behind."

Daddy's eyes filled with tears. "It was part of the bargain I made, I think. As you probably know, the gods don't act unless an exchange has been struck. I wanted to live, so Idemmili presented me that option. But it came with this body, this mondao-human body, that gives me life, but doesn't let me walk on land for long. I am free, but only in her seas. To control it as a king."

"He's right," Aliyah whispered. "We know everything about the gods, Cameron, and how they can be."

I stood, pushing the table; it was so heavy that it didn't even budge. "No! I want my parents back! *Both* of them!"

"Cam, calm down—" Dad started to say, still holding my hand. I snatched it away from him.

"I'm so tired of this. There's no point in trying to save Mama if I can't save you, too."

"But you can't save your mama—" Aliyah began to say.

"Just leave me alone!" I yelled, cutting her off, walking out of the room and into the cave's entrance, angry, hot tears leaking from my eyes. I went outside to stare at the lake and the mondao continuing to swirl around us like thunderstorm clouds. I felt at a loss, especially after everything I had gone through up to this point. Now, I couldn't even save Daddy, the one who had cuddled with me at night, brushing his beard across my cheeks as he read the *Book* to me? The one who was my model for what a man should be? It was all too much. I had already gotten bad news about Summoning Mama's soul, and now I had to put up with losing Daddy once again?

Someone kissed the tears on my cheek. It was Daddy, coming to comfort me.

"It's okay, Cam."

"It's not okay," I mumbled, crushing my face into his chest. He rubbed his hands in my hair. "I need you here, with me, on land."

"Can I show you something?" he asked.

I nodded. "Yes, you can."

He pulled away from me, wiping away the rest of my tears before smiling. "I'm more alive here than I have ever been."

"What does that mean?"

"Let me show you."

In a swift movement, he grabbed me by the waist with strong arms and jumped forward. The lake's water, which was suspended above us, met and caught us immediately—me screaming along the way.

Daddy transformed as soon as the water splashed into us, his tail appearing as his legs disappeared. The light emanating from him turned brighter and warmer, as if he were the sun underneath the sea. When it surrounded me, I was able to breathe deeply.

"Hold on!" he said in his familiar, thunderous voice, laughing a bit.

I screamed again as we careened through the water, going so fast that I could barely catch my breath. I closed my eyes, hoping that it would be over soon.

CHAPTER TWENTY-THREE

"You can look now," Daddy said much later. We had settled on a small, abandoned island, deep in the middle of an ocean. Daddy's tail remained in the water.

"Wow," I said. No land could be seen anywhere, which meant we had to be far away from where we had left Zion and Aliyah.

"This is all my domain, Cam," he said. "The Atlantic Ocean."

"This is all yours?" I asked.

He shrugged. "I would think so. The mondao can't swim this far, and I can get here in a blink of an eye. With that being said . . ." He grabbed me around the waist once again as his body glowed golden. "This is how it looks above. Let me take you underneath?"

When I nodded, Daddy and I jumped back into the

ocean. This time, however, I kept my eyes open, wanting to see everything. There was nothing at first, except for the deep blueness of the water. After a short while, we came close to the ocean floor, Daddy's tail moving so fast that I could barely see it.

A huge shipwreck rose in front of us, so large that it looked more like a mountain than anything else. Its rotted wood crumbled like dust when I touched it. We sped through it, Daddy showing me everything inside. His mood turned somber when we went to the deck underneath. He didn't say anything, but I knew what it was the moment I saw the bloodstains and the chains. We quickly went to another area, which held chests filled with lost gold and jewels. It was disconcerting to see the riches displayed here when we had just seen the rooms where our enslaved ancestors were held through no fault of their own.

"Hypocrisy," Daddy said, reading the expression on my face. "They took us, and then stole our riches from us."

"And our history," I responded.

"But now, both have returned to us."

He then went through all the chests, showing me the gold and jewels; there was no need for him to say anything else. As he did, I thought about Amina and how she wanted revenge for everyone who had been lost. All in the service of gold. Their lives meant nothing to their enslavers. As he showed me, I almost couldn't blame her, but deeper in me was a realization that no one deserved for her to take over both worlds, killing everyone who wasn't an Igbo descendent. I would survive if she won, yes, but would my friends? Would their families? There was a legacy that enslavement created, and my friends were part of it.

After, we continued on. It was good we were going so fast because fear was always at the forefront of the experience, especially as the creatures we saw grew weirder. An octopus-shaped monster rose from the underwater sand, the color of night. A tentacle, covered with what seemed like lights, stretched out and wrapped around Daddy's body, pulling him close. I screamed, preparing to fight, but Daddy's laughter stopped me. The monster wrapped Daddy tighter, and he placed a kiss on its head before it dropped him to the ground.

He grabbed me again, and we were off, swimming along the ocean floor once more. A large city rose in the water, so large that it rivaled the Palacia's size. I gasped as we swam nearer and then redirected upward to hover over it. Down below, sea creatures whisked in and out of its crowded depths. Mondao of all shapes and sizes—some of them with human faces and some of them unrecognizable—either swam or floated upright along its streets. Buildings grew from the sand, stretching upward, gleaming with rubies, emeralds, and diamonds. If I hadn't peered closer, and if we weren't underwater, I would have thought that I was looking at a human city.

The roar from the city was deafening and incomprehensible. As soon as Daddy stepped into one of the golden streets, though, his tail turning into legs, everything quieted. As if he were a king who had come back from a long mission. And I was right because everything seemed to bow in his presence, not completely, but enough to make it clear that he was Idemmili's representative in some way.

We swept through the city in silence, Daddy only pointing at things that he wanted me to see. A group of mondao children were playing with sticks, kicking a ball in between them in a large courtyard before a tall palace, completely ignoring us. Markets were packed with stalls and makeshift wagons, sea creatures selling their wares, speaking in tongues I could not recognize. The entire time, I was willing the *Book* to tell or show me something, anything, but just like when Zion brought us underwater, its magic seemed blocked.

We floated up to the top of the palace, watching the citizens below. At this height, I could see statues of Idemmili resplendent in her ever-present, colorful iros rising upward. They were so realistic that if I hadn't squinted closer, I would've thought she had truly appeared before us. Her outstretched hands held torches, firelight beaming down onto the city despite the fact that we were underwater.

"This is absolutely beautiful," I breathed.

"It is." Daddy nodded. "There are hundreds of them in

the ocean, cities built from Idemmili's blood. I come to them often, and they see me as her symbol when she's not here. They treat me like a god."

I stared at the light surrounding his body like sunbeams. "Are you, you know, a god?"

Daddy sighed, staring at the sunbeams on his greenish-brown hands. "Something like that. Or something between human and god. I don't really know, Cam. I can't really answer that question."

"Why did you show me all of this?" I asked.

He was quiet for a long while, pulling at his long beard as we watched the sea creatures below. Sitting with him felt familiar, like the times he would pick me up from school on the days he got off work early. The times he would cook breakfast for me on the weekends if Mama wanted to sleep in. Or our fishing trips where Daddy didn't know how to use the fishing lines and lures; in those times, it was just me and him, the journey being the fun part instead of the destination. Or those times when I threw tantrums or got really angry at something—he'd grab me and sit with me on the couch as I calmed down, talking to me in soft tones, showing me the perfect way to handle my emotions.

"Because I wanted to show you that I'll always be here for you, Cameron." He turned his gaze to mine, lingering there for a long while before speaking again. "I am alive, in every sense of the word. I'm not dead, and I'm not going anywhere."

He gestured to the city, spreading both of his hands over it in the shape of a bowl. "The oceans and the waters are mine to travel, whenever and wherever I see fit."

He moved his hands to my chest, thumping it with an index finger. "The *Book* is inside you?" Ruby light spread across that area and then down to my stomach.

I nodded.

"I remember when your mama had the *Book*, right after your grandma passed it down to her. I didn't know that months after Agbala shoved it into her chest she would die . . ."

"*She's not dead*," I said through gritted teeth.

"But she is, Cam," he said, enfolding me in his arms and placing his head above mine. "And that's okay. If you use your magic, then you'll die, too. She would want you to live. I am telling you this because *I'm* here, and I'll always be your father. You have to remember that."

"But I want her back, too."

"I know you do," he sighed. "I want her back as well. But even if she came back, I couldn't be with her. I'm telling you and showing you all of this because I am here and will always be. You're the Descendant, so that means you can see me any and every time you want. You can open the barrier at will. And, gods have free reign, so Idemmili's magic will allow me to go anywhere, inside and outside of the barrier. I . . . I just can't go on land with you for long, can't return to you like I was before all of this happened."

He had a point, and a good one at that. I held him tighter in this moment, glad that he would never let me go and that I'd always be able to be near him, even though he couldn't be the father he used to be. When Grandma told me my parents had died, my heart had broken into two, both Mama and Daddy holding an equal share. I didn't have that language to explain it until now, because one side of my heart was healing, being filled up with Daddy's presence. He had returned to me and so had half of my heart.

But I couldn't deny that the other half, the one that belonged to Mama, still lay dormant. When Nneka told me I couldn't bring her back without risking the *Book* and my own life, that half had almost broken into pieces.

I wanted both halves to connect again. Daddy alone wouldn't do it.

"Are you ready to keep going?" he asked softly.

"Yes," I responded.

We floated upward, Daddy's legs turning back into a tail thrashing about, causing waves to crash against the top of the palace. We swam forward like a cannon, so fast that it almost gave me whiplash. I wasn't sure how much time had passed, but he showed me everything: deep seas with such monstrous creatures that I blanked them out of my mind as soon as I saw them, caves that held long-lost treasures, underwater volcanoes that threatened to erupt at any time, and newly formed islands. We settled upon warm sand a number of times, right in front of waterfalls. He laughed when the water splashed over me, drenching me. We swam along beaches, poking our heads out, seeing different tribes of people making their way to the water.

But that wasn't the most impressive. We swam in small lakes, ponds, and creeks, swimming next to schools of tiny fish. Daddy would hold them in his hands, speaking to them in soft whispers. And though I could never prove it, I could have sworn that they were whispering back to him. He told me that the water held secrets, that everything had a pulse, even the smallest creatures to ever exist and that he could communicate with it all. He said that he could feel it all, feel the control he had over water.

At the end of our trip, the barrier stretched as far as the eye could see, rising from the ocean as a black wall, reaching all the way to the heavens. When he touched it, though, his hands did not burn; they only shone with a light the color of diamonds that spread across his entire body until his hair stood on end. It provided much-needed illumination as the day had finally turned to night.

"We have to return to your friends," he said.

"I don't want to leave you."

"You have to, though," he said. "As I said, you'll always have access to me, you and your friends, through the world's waters."

With a grunt, he thrust both of his hands into the water, and a whirlpool formed. It swarmed with bright cerulean and cobalt. He grabbed my hand and smiled.

"Once we go through this, we will be back at the Palacia's lake. Are you ready?"

I nodded and smiled back. "Yep."

"You might want to take a deep breath, as it is a bumpy ride."

"Wait—"

A soft laugh escaped his mouth as he jumped into the whirlpool with me.

CHAPTER TWENTY-FOUR

After returning to Aliyah and Zion—who had found cushions to sleep on in Daddy's sprawling cave—we returned to the Palacia's lake's surface the next morning. His tail swept underneath us, lifting us upward until it thrust us high into the air. We collapsed on the shore, our clothes marred with wet dirt as the sun shone on our backs.

"Cameron!" a familiar voice screamed. Wheels rolled over the ground as a battle chariot burst into view from the side of the Palacia.

"Uh-oh," Zion said while I sighed and Aliyah rolled her eyes. I took one last look at the lake and could just make out Daddy below the surface, watching us with those same bright eyes.

"Cameron!" that voice screamed again. It was Makai. When the chariot came to a stop near us, he jumped out of it, Bakari and Halifa following right behind him.

"Listen," I said.

"No!" Makai said, strolling up to us. Bakari and Halifa helped us to our feet while Makai regarded us with pure anger. "Where have you been?" he yelled.

We said nothing, just stood there trembling as the lake's water dripped off us in droves and our clothes stuck to our bodies.

"You've been gone for *days*!" he screamed, pacing back and forth in front of us. "There's a time difference in the land of the Palacia and the world of the lake. With no warning, you decided to leave the Palacia, on your own accord, without telling us! Again! How can you keep doing this? Not to mention, you look terrible! No soldier should look this way!"

"Well, *technically*," Zion started to say, holding his trident forward.

"Zion," I warned.

"Technically," Zion continued, "we didn't actually *leave* the Palacia, so we weren't really missing."

Bakari put his hand over his mouth, hiding his laughter. When Makai tossed him a harsh look, Bakari coughed to stop himself from laughing.

"Not funny, Zion," Halifa said.

"Where. Have. You. Been?!"

Zion held his trident higher and explained everything that had happened.

Makai's anger seeped out of his face, and his shoulders sagged, as if a heavy burden had been placed on his shoulders. Halifa and Bakari gasped in surprise when Zion had finished.

"You're saying that Lonnie, the one who helped the last Descendant, is alive?" Makai asked.

"He is," I said, smiling a bit. "My daddy is alive." Saying those words brought a sense of peace to me, especially after Dad had shown me everything Idemmili had given him in exchange to keep him alive.

After speaking for a while, Makai led us back to the Palacia in the chariot. When we got to our chambers, Zion went off to the pool in our room to bathe.

"I need to eat. I feel like I haven't done that in a while," he said.

"I'll be right behind you," I said before grabbing Aliyah's hand. "I can't believe he's alive."

"He is," she said, grinning before giving me a wet hug. "I'm glad for you. You deserve that after everything you've done for Chidani. I wouldn't choose anyone else to be the Descendant."

After Aliyah had gone into her bedroom, Bakari and Halifa walked in, settling in the hard chairs that surrounded the sitting area, their seats furnished with multi-colored cushions. I thought for a while before I began to speak aloud. I knew Bakari would want to hear more about

Daddy, as he was the closest thing Bakari would ever get to family besides me.

"The bargain he made with Idemmili doesn't make him weak," I said, scrunching my eyebrows, thinking aloud. "I . . . I thank him for it."

"Of course not," Halifa whispered.

"We're soldiers, Cameron," Bakari said, scratching the scar on his cheek. "That doesn't mean we're not human; the body will always try to preserve itself, to live."

I shook my head. "It's not just that, though. It's something else he told me. He said he wanted to live, not because he was afraid to die; he wanted to live for me, for Mama, to show me what a true man should be. He wanted to get home to me."

A mixture of happy and sad tears fell down my face now, as I thought about everything I had seen and done. Although he wasn't here, I still felt his presence, and I took comfort in knowing that I could see him whenever I wanted, now that I knew he was all right.

"I want Mama," I whispered, the tears flowing from me like the flowing waterfalls Daddy had shown me. Halifa and Bakari came over to me now, engulfing me in their arms. I stayed there for a long while, breathing them in.

Even though I knew they were trying to comfort me, nothing could replace the half of my heart that was broken, shrouded in shadows.

Zion whipped a towel at me, smacking my back.

"Zion, can you stop playing and leave me alone?" I yelled as I entered the bathing room. The hot water swirled around, steam lifting from its surface. Zion stood near me, doing a dance for me, naked, of course.

"And can you put some clothes on?!"

"Sorry!" he yelled, leaving the room, cackling as he did.

Sighing, I took off my wet clothes and threw them against the marble floor. When they landed, they disappeared into thin air. Probably getting washed and repaired.

I settled into the hot water, drifting to the middle of the humongous pool. I swam on my back, treading water as I stayed afloat. Soap suds came next, engulfing my body.

I narrowed my eyes. "Can we not use magic this time when cleaning me? I'd like to do it myself." A sponge, soap, a comb, and other cleaning utensils appeared out of thin air at my words, floating over my head in circles. The sight didn't surprise me; I was just glad that they didn't attack me like they did the first time I came to Chidani.

I reached up and grabbed the rattail comb first, gliding it through my tangled hair, careful at first. My thoughts floated away in the breeze, helping to make the hot pool experience more of a routine than anything else. When I dipped the sponge in the water, suds were automatically created, and I washed my body. As soon as I dropped below the surface, the heat wrapped around me like a warm hug.

When I finished bathing, a familiar, motherly presence

settled around me, caressing my heart. Agbala. After I dried off and put a clean, white robe around me, I found her in the sitting area, Bakari and Halifa gone.

"Hello, Descendant."

She appraised me with concerned eyes. "I'm still connected to you, through the *Book*. You've learned to keep me out of your mind, though. I wish you wouldn't do that."

She snapped her fingers and light exploded in my eyes. When I opened them, everything seemed different—slower, more methodical, like everything had been drowned in quicksand. A haze rose from the floor, like the sun's rays had found themselves in the Palacia.

"What happened?"

"I slowed down time," she said. "And time is of the essence. I want to tell you a little about me before we consult the *Book* together."

I narrowed my eyes. "Leave me alone," I said, walking out of the sitting room and into the bedroom. I heard snores and saw Zion sound asleep in our bed, his head on one of the huge pillows while a foot dangled over the side. I sighed, pivoting back toward the sitting room, where the table was piled with food.

Agbala stared at me while I picked up a plate and started placing food on top of it.

"Cameron, we must speak—"

"I said, leave me alone!" I stamped over to one of the large, cushioned chairs and sat down. My eyes gazed at the Ikenga in the corner next to my bedroom, reminding me of Mama. The person Agbala and Ramala were keeping away from me.

"I wish you would start acting like the Descendant, someone with a mission to help save us all."

I shoveled goat meat into my mouth and stared at her, saying nothing. She was right, but after everything I had been through, I felt I had a *right* to act the way I was now. Agbala's presence settled upon me, familiar, like a warm embrace, like the sun. I opened my mind to her so she could see exactly how I was feeling. She jolted back, surprised when I gave her access, but also probably startled by my thoughts.

"Bakari told me that you found your father," she said, switching tactics.

"We did," I responded curtly.

"You know, the gods are the reason that he is still alive. Without Idemmili—"

"Stop," I said, angrily placing my food in my lap. "She didn't do it for me. Or for him. She did it because she had a job for him, wanting him to control the seas in her absence."

She inclined her head. "You know that is not the truth. She would have not given Zion her trident if she had not meant for you to find him. She did it because she knew you would need him. I may not agree with her ways, and I may be . . . *different* . . . now that I am not wholly in the gods' favor, but I know Idemmili. More than you could ever know."

Of course she was right, but I wouldn't give her the satisfaction of telling her she was. But then, what she just said made me think about what she told me not so long ago.

"You're not the only one who has lost something. I almost died creating the *Book* and protecting the humans. I've lost something, too . . . There were consequences for my actions . . . ," she had told me after Agwu had hurt Zion.

"What did you mean by that?" I asked. "You know, when you say you're different now? That there were consequences for your actions?"

Agbala sat still for a while, the aura around her changing from white to blue. I imagined her to be thinking, but who knows what gods did when they grew quiet?

"When I created the *Book*," Agbala began, sighing as she did, "I did something unforgivable. Even my own mother couldn't save me from the consequences." She closed her eyes as she remembered, turning her face from me as if she were ashamed of her actions.

"I wanted to find a way to save everyone, so that our people would no longer know the pains of slavery. The gods demand that there is always an even exchange of power, a bargain struck to keep the sides equal." She opened her eyes now, gazing into mine. "No human should ever gain the powers of a god."

"Yet, you gave them to me."

"It was the only way to save the people," Agbala said. "I did it because . . . I do not know. I awakened into something else, my consciousness rising above the petty arguments of the gods. I did something that they could never do, that they didn't think they even had the power to do; I gave the Descendants and you the potential to be great. The potential to be gods."

"And you suffered for that?"

She nodded and clutched her chest. "Oh, a great deal. I think Chukwu—my father—made a mistake when he made me the goddess of healing and justice. I saw what my mother and my siblings had done with Ramala and the barrier, and I just *had* to act. I couldn't allow our people, the ones who gave us life, to suffer in another world without us. Without a Descendant. If it weren't for the people, we wouldn't continue to exist. Without their prayers, we are nothing."

Pity started to creep through me, but I did my best not to show it. "Well, what happened? You created the *Book* and then what?"

"Pain is what happened." She shook her head. "A pain so severe that I thought I would cease to exist. I went away, alone, and pooled all my magic together to create the *Book*. I then gave it to the Igbo people as they crossed the Atlantic, hoping it would find the first Descendant. When it did, an agony so great settled upon me that I thought all was lost for me." She stared at me so hard that I grew uncomfortable, beginning to shift in my seat. "You don't *ever* want to experience pain like a god can. There's no cure."

"What else?" I whispered.

"The other gods found me, sensing the magic in every corner of the world. They came to the cave I had hidden in, and saw me prostrate on the ground, curled in a ball."

Pity leaked from me like a faucet now, and I was sure she could feel it. "And they didn't help you."

Agbala shook her head. "No, they didn't. They admonished me for what I had done, inflicting more pain on me with their words, and taking most of my power from me. But I knew the costs of my actions, so I knew what was coming next." She took a deep breath before continuing. "They used their own magic on me, banishing me from the land of gods."

My forehead furrowed in confusion. "What does that mean?"

"They created a fissure between me and them. Did you ever wonder why I can seem human at times?"

"Aliyah mentioned it a while back."

"It's because of what they did to me, as punishment. They destroyed all my palaces, my temples, and took away most of my remaining magic. They left me with nothing, made me only a little better than a human. Ramala found me days later, her magic sensing mine. She gave me a home in the

Palacia, and I promised her I would always protect her, the Descendants, and the gifts. When they were stolen, I did everything I could to find them, supporting the Descendants along the way."

"I'm sorry that happened to you."

"There's still pain for what they did to me, my mother included. Physical and mental pain. You see, I am more like you than anything else, a humanlike figure with godlike powers. Like you, the magic takes its toll on me, too."

"You did all of that for my people?"

Her gaze was so fierce as she stared at me, her mouth curling in a snarl. "I did, and I would do it all over again. And again. And again. The gods were *wrong*, Cameron. They left your people, our people, to chains and whips. I raised the Descendants because I *wanted* to, to save you. And I did that. And . . . I don't regret that at all. So, you can be angry with me for everything I have done. I am not all the way innocent in this, that I know for sure. But I did what I had to, to save your people."

She came to me, then, pointing at my chest. "I did this because it was the only way."

I nodded, unsure if I should apologize. She laughed softly, then caressed my cheeks. "You don't have to say anything. I *feel* your remorse. Our connection runs deep, for centuries before you were even born."

"What now? I just don't know what else to do. I found

Daddy, but what about Mama? What if Amina is just too powerful to beat?"

Her aura surrounded me as she snapped her fingers once more. I gasped as coldness seeped into every part of me, pulling inside. In a flash of light, the *Book* pushed itself out of me, swirling in the air before Agbala caught it.

"Oh, we don't give up. We fight back. The *Book* has never led us wrong, has it? I think it's time to pay my brother a visit."

"Ekwensu?" I said.

"Yes," she said, sitting next to me and opening the *Book*. When she placed her hand over its pages, they fluttered and turned at her command. "Cameron, you'll need to help me with this. I fear that your magic is greater than mine at this point."

When I placed my hand on top of hers, shadows and gold intertwined between our fingers and the pages turned even faster. I could sense a calming settle on Agbala's shoulders as she helped me to my feet to stand beside her, my magic aiding hers. Possibly healing the pain she was still feeling.

"Why are we doing this?" I whispered.

"Amina is still too powerful," Agbala said, muttering underneath her breath as her eyes darted back and forth. "I can sense it from her prison. Her magic is starting to overpower the chains I placed around her. We need to see what she's planning and need to see it now."

When her eyes found mine again, a pain ratcheted through

my body, and my stomach muscles constricted. Nausea roiled in my gut, and saliva rose in my throat. The *Book*'s pages stopped on a picture of Ekwensu, his skeletal frame taking up the entire page.

She grasped my hand, hard, as the shadows grew.

"We need to get to Shukti. Now."

CHAPTER TWENTY-FIVE

We settled in blackness for a while, still holding hands, our feet resting on a hard surface.

"You have failed me, Amina," a voice said.

When my eyes adjusted to the darkness, I saw that we were standing on a familiar mountain. The moon stretched across the sky, so close to us that I felt I could touch it. I knew exactly where we were.

"Let's go forward, Cameron," Agbala said, tightening her hand around mine. "Don't let go."

I saw his throne first, made of bone. The top of it stretched high into the air.

"I did not fail you," someone else said in a strained voice. Amina. But how was she here if she was in chains back at the Palacia?

I saw the back of Ekwensu's head second, nothing more

than a skull. The death god raised a skeletal hand in the air, and a figure rose from the ground. It was Amina, still shrouded in shadows, lightning, and chains that seemed to be made from the sun.

What in the . . . ?

"How am I here?" she said, straining hard against Agbala's chains. "Let me out of these, Ekwensu."

"You have failed me, Princess," Ekwensu reiterated, his voice still reminding me of slithering snakes. "But you also forget that you are only powerful because *I* will it so."

"My soul," she sputtered.

Ekwensu nodded. "Yes, your soul. You gave it to me in exchange for my magic. This is why you are here. I can pull you to me at any time I would like."

Amina struggled again, but she could not break the chains. "Let me go, Ekwensu," she repeated, pleading now. "I can help you. I did not fail you; all you have to do is give me one more . . ."

Ekwensu raised his hand again, his agbada sleeves falling down to reveal his skeletal arms, coated over with blackness. He brought his fingers into a fist, squeezing hard. Amina cried out as her body contorted inside the chains, screamed in such agony that even I was fearful for her. I tried to turn around, to run with Agbala, to escape Amina's vision, but an invisible barrier stopped me. I was tied to her in more ways than I ever wanted to be.

"It's all right, Cameron," Agbala said. "They can't harm you here. They cannot see us."

Amina continued to howl as Ekwensu laughed wickedly.

"Ekwensu, please!" Amina shrieked. He opened his hand again, his palm facing the sky. She breathed hard, her braided hair falling into her eyes.

"As I have said, you have been nothing but a failure to me. You asked me for my magic so that you could steal the gifts and kill the Descendant once and for all. So that I could become one with the world again, so that I could help you usher in a new legacy on both planes."

"I tried," Amina said, tears leaking from her eyes. "I tried, Ekwensu. Just give me one more chance. I can do this. I know I can."

"I don't think you can," Ekwensu said, closing his fist again. I shut my eyes as Amina yelped again, hoping that all of this would be over, soon.

"I . . . I know what I can do," Amina said between cries.

"Yes?" Ekwensu said. "You may speak." I imagined him opening his fist.

"I can kill the Descendant once and for all," Amina breathed, her voice tortured. "You just need to leave Shukti to help me."

I opened my eyes now, curious as to what Ekwensu would say. We stepped around the throne and watched him. Ekwensu inclined his head to the side, as if he were thinking on her words.

"You would have me leave Shukti . . . and completely destroy Chidani? *Against* the rules the gods have made? That would leave me with more consequences, Princess."

"Not Chidani," Amina said. "Just the Palacia and its soldiers. That would give me enough time to steal the gifts from Ramala again, and then I'll have control of the barrier once and for all. And if we win, you wouldn't have to worry about the gods' rules."

"She knows we found the ring?" I whispered.

"Her connection to the mmo is still strong," Agbala said. "She sees everything they see."

"You couldn't kill the Descendant the first time," Ekwensu said. "How would you do that now?"

My blood began to boil as Amina negotiated with Ekwensu. I *knew* it. If only Ramala had killed her or allowed me to at least *try*, none of this would be happening. Zion and Aliyah and Grandma would be safe. But no, Ramala had decreed that I couldn't touch Amina, that I couldn't even try to get Mama back. And now, Amina would try to kill me once again, just so that the death god could rule both worlds, while she ruled at his side.

"You have my soul," Amina began, her body shuddering at what she would say next. "You're also a god. I . . . I . . ."

"Continue," Ekwensu said, smiling a horrible smile. "I need to hear you say it."

She gulped once before continuing. "Use me. Use my

body and soul. Fuse yourself with me to directly intervene in the quest to kill the Descendant, Ramala, and take the barrier for ourselves. The pain would be great, but the victory would be greater. I admit I couldn't do it the first time on my own; if you help me, we can and will win. Just think, if we are able to successfully kill the Descendant *and* steal the gifts . . ."

"We'd be unstoppable," Ekwensu mused, the fire in his eyes blazing. "And my brothers and sisters could never harm me. Agbala, that . . . *child* . . . who created the *Book* in the first place, would be completely destroyed."

"Yes, yes, yes," Amina said, nodding. "Think of the possibilities."

"You have made your case, Princess," Ekwensu said, rising, his body *creaking* as he did. He rose in the air, his agbada flowing in nonexistent wind as she flew to him. He caressed her face; everywhere he touched, she winced in response as if his fingers burned.

"You have not served me well," Ekwensu admitted. "But you have given me something that none of my other servants have not; you have survived. And that says a lot about you. I will consider your proposal."

"How will I know if you have decided for my side?"

He floated backward, rising higher in the air, his arms stretched wide.

"Oh . . . you will know." He regarded her figure as though

he were hungry. "I have your soul, which means I have your life. You will know . . . when you feel a searing pain, much deeper than anything you have felt before. Only then you will know that we are one, in more ways than you could have ever thought possible."

CHAPTER TWENTY-SIX

"No," I said, as Agbala pulled me through the darkness, back to my chambers.

"The *Book* will always give you guidance," Agbala said to me, releasing my hand. "Remember that."

"We need to fight," I said.

"We fight for what I almost died for and what your mother died for," Agbala said. "Wake up your friends, and I will get Makai and the others. Prepare yourselves, for Amina is coming."

With a renewed sense of purpose, I told Aliyah and Zion everything that had happened as we walked to the dungeons right behind Ramala, Makai, and Agbala. I wanted to fight, this last time, for the world Agbala had created at the expense of herself.

"That's a lot going on," Zion said.

Aliyah snorted. "I have to agree with that one."

We were dressed in our soldiers' uniforms; my hands grasped my weapons, feeling the magic pulsate within them. I remembered being emotional the first time I fought Amina, but as we continued in the darkness, calm was the only thing I felt. The thought of Ekwensu showing up made my skin crawl, but I wasn't even scared of him at this point.

Amina's moans could be heard as we approached her cell, nothing but pure agony. She floated inside, sunlight and shadows surrounding her.

"What's wrong with her?" Aliyah asked.

"Probably still planning with Ekwensu," Zion mumbled.

Another feeling crept in, something different, like an anticipation.

"Um, Ramala—"

"Quiet," she said, stepping forward.

"It's much too late, sister," Amina was saying from inside her cell, her voice deep and haunting. Different. "He's coming. Everything you know will be destroyed, and everyone you protect will perish."

"Ekwensu comes for the gifts," Ramala said to Makai. "Get the soldiers and prepare for the Palacia for another attack."

"Let's go," I whispered to Aliyah and Zion, grabbing both of their hands. "I need to fight this time." We ran through the dungeons, climbing through the hole in the ground. Amina's haunted voice continued, but I knew it was all too late now. I had a feeling Amina wouldn't be in chains for too much longer.

We crashed into Bakari as he was coming inside the Palacia.

"The sky darkens," he said, fear plain in his eyes. "Something's happening."

"Ekwensu," I said. "He's coming for the gifts and to destroy everything with Amina." We tried to walk past him, but he grabbed my arms.

"Then we have no choice but to fight."

I cast a glance at Aliyah and Zion. "I refuse to let what happened to Mama happen to you all. Not on my watch."

He nodded. "You've grown and protected us. I will rally the soldiers to fight by your side."

We stepped outside in the darkness, the force of the wind almost throwing us back inside.

"Are we sure this is a good idea?" Zion asked, jumping from foot to foot.

"There's no choice but to fight." I grabbed both of their hands again. "We do this together."

After they nodded, we leaped into action, calling for our gryphons. We raced to the edge of the mountain, launching ourselves in the air. It was calming and freeing for a while, falling down into open air. It was a time where the danger of the moment wasn't present. I tried to soak it all in as I fell, but Ugo's screech brought me out of my reverie.

I crashed into him, falling over to his side, but grabbing his reins at the same time. His icy wingspan pierced the night, providing much-needed light. I held on, pulling myself on Ugo's saddle, touching my fingers to his back. His conscious-ness merged with mine, a warm feeling settling upon my shoulders, and we were off, flying over the Palacia, back and forth. There was nothing at first, nothing but grays mixed with black as the moon vanished. We flew and flew over everything, but nothing presented itself yet. However, the pain in my chest became constant, biting, like I had sustained an injury, unable to heal. I sat on Ugo's back, looking around me for a few moments.

Everything after that happened fast. There was a shout. The sound of running feet. Another shout. A crash. A *boom*.

And then the Palacia's roof exploded.

Fire roiled in the sky as I pulled on Ugo's reins, careening upward.

Whoa! Zion said telepathically as we converged upon each other, staring downward. *What's going on?*

Shadows appeared in the roof first, flying out of the hole and into the sky like birds.

Mmo! Aliyah said, pointing.

I narrowed my eyes, waiting for the right moment to strike. I unstrapped the sword from my waist. A figure appeared from the hole next, surrounded by a white light, blasting through and flying into the sky.

Ugo, down! I screamed.

Cameron, no! Aliyah yelled from behind.

Fight the mmo! I screamed back at them as I fell toward the flames. *Ekwensu is here, connected to Amina. Defend the Palacia!*

I continued to urge Ugo downward, faster and faster as I flew closer to Amina, who was no longer held with chains. The anger built in me as I stood on top of Ugo, my boots resting firmly on his saddle. There was one thing I was sure of right now; Amina would die today at my hand, and I would get my mama back. I wasn't quite sure how I would save the Descendants at the same time—Nneka had said that if I tried to Summon a soul, the *Book* and the Descendants inside would cease to exist—but I had abandoned all reason at this point. I would not allow Mama's and Agbala's sacrifice to be in vain.

Amina's eyes found mine as her arms outstretched in the air.

"Descendant," she said, her voice surprisingly soft. "I'm much more powerful now. I shall have the *Book* once and for all."

"No!" I screamed, launching myself off Ugo and heading toward her. We crashed into each other midair, her magic holding me up.

Her face came forward, knocking into mine. Blood washed into my eyes, temporarily blinding me as I fell. My sword spun out of my hand. I wiped my eyes as Ugo caught me before I could crash into the side of the Palacia. My hands swirled with shadows as I Summoned my sword back into my palm.

"Come and get me, Descendant," Amina said, falling to the blasted-open roof. I urged Ugo in the direction of the roof, and he settled on it with his huge lion feet.

I jumped off almost immediately, smashing into the hot wood. She stood in front of me, a sinister smile widening on her face. She stared at my retrieved sword.

"I see you have mastered your Summoning ability. Too bad you will not have those powers for long."

"I don't think you know as much as you think you do," I said, arching my right eyebrow.

She growled and came for me, blasting through the smoke like a fast bullet. As soon as she moved, I calmed my nerves, closing my eyes and listening to the music of nature, entering Dambe. When I opened them, everything had slowed down; the flames looked almost beautiful as they surrounded me, touching the air like fireflies. I saw her sword swing down, and I met it with my own. They clashed together, and we both gritted our teeth before I pushed her back with my arms, so hard that she stumbled.

Before she could recover, I jumped into the air, landing right next to the hole in the roof, behind her. I grabbed her, pinning her down to the ground. But she was much too strong for me; she growled again, and her body was surrounded by a ruby aura before she screamed in my face.

"Mmo!"

She pushed me away then, and I flew across the roof, slamming into the edge. Shadows dropped from the sky, covered in black smoke. They materialized into mmo, dark, gray skeletal figures, black blood spewing from their decaying mouths. Amina stood, smiling as they surrounded her.

"Give me my mother back," I said.

She swung her sword in a complicated arch and narrowed her eyes. "Make me."

We both jumped back into the action at the same time, struggling against each other. But I was no match for her and the mmo at the same time. Two of them wrapped hard arms around my stomach and threw me back. The sword slipped out of my hand once again, and the bow and arrow fell out of my bag, skittering off the edge of the roof. But, as soon as I fell, I was up, fighting the mmo off me with my bare hands.

I couldn't see Amina through the swirling bodies, but I knew she was close by if she was trying to get the *Book*. My hands churned with shadows until the sword appeared again, and I slashed out with so much fury and strength that the mmo were no match for me. Black blood surrounded me as I tore through them. Amina stood right in front of me now, mmo standing around her.

I raised my bloody sword her way. "Are you going to hide behind your demons, Amina, or will you face me like the coward you are?"

"You will die for your insolence!" she yelled.

We engaged in battle again, an equal match. When I grabbed her by the shoulders, a look of surprise crossed her face. I pushed us upward as the mmo slashed at me with gnarled nails, lifting us into the sky to escape them.

She punched me multiple times, but I continued to hold her.

"Give me my mother back!" I yelled through the pain.

"Give me the *Book*!" she screamed.

We fell to the roof now, time returning back to normal, loud, garbled voices greeting us. Amina reached out with her boot, kicking me in the chest as we sprawled onto the ground. Shadows exploded from the sky, descending down upon me, materializing as demons. I was grabbed by a mmo as soon as I stood, holding me up high. I beat against its back, trying my hardest to get free, but two more grasped me. They led me to the opposite wall, where the roof door met the inside of the Palacia.

They tore my sword from me, then pinned both of my hands down so I couldn't Summon it again. A deep, evil laughter met my ears as the sky opened and rain pounded down.

"You shall never defeat me, Descendant." That voice was familiar, fear creeping up my spine. It was Ekwensu's voice, merging with Amina's in a way that made my skin crawl.

"Let me go," I managed to say, but the mmo holding me only gripped my neck tighter so that I could barely speak. The mmo crowded around me, speaking in their disembodied language as I heard boots shuffle on the concrete.

"You foolishly thought that you could kill me to obtain

your mother. Well, you thought wrong." The group of mmo not holding me stepped back and to the side. Amina appeared where they stood, her cloak swinging in the wind and rain. I hadn't landed a single hit on her, although she had on me.

When she stepped forward, a smirk lighted her face as she raised her sword, pointing it straight at my chest.

"I wonder where Agbala put the *Book*?" she said, smiling wider, showing pure white teeth. "Did she put it here?" She moved the sword to my left shoulder and pressed, slicing straight through the skin. I gasped, not giving her the satisfaction of my screams. "Hmm," she said, removing the sword and watching the blood wash away in the roaring thunder and rain. She moved the sword to my right shoulder now, pressing gently. "I wonder if she put it here?" She pushed the sword in again, this time with more vigor than the last time.

I cried out now, unable to stand the pain. I stared at them all, the skeletal demon faces with red eyes and the diabolical princess standing in front of me, doing as much damage as possible to me before she ripped the *Book* out of my chest, killing me for good.

"You really thought that Ekwensu wouldn't come for me, wouldn't give me the power to escape Agbala's chains?" Amina spat, digging the sword so deep that it pierced my back and clanged against the wall behind me. "You should have killed me when you had the chance." She removed the sword again and slashed it across my chest; I heard a sickening *crunch* as Amina moved the sword from left to right.

The pain was beyond anything I had felt before, reaching deep within. I screamed so loud that I was sure the entire kingdom could hear me.

Amina laughed wickedly. "As I said when you came here last time, the *Book* shall be mine."

I started to give up; everything I had done seemed to be for nothing, and all the progress I made would be cut short by the princess. Mama's sacrifice for me and the world would be for nothing. A certain peace settled inside me, as I thought about the Descendant's world inside the *Book*, about Nneka living on as a soul within it. Maybe it was time for me to go, to let it all go? I wanted to join them all, wanted to finally stop having to work so *hard* to achieve so little. I closed my eyes, willing for death to grab me. I knew that taking the *Book* out of my chest would be extremely painful, but I also knew that there was a blissful place awaiting me, one where I could be one with my ancestors once again.

When a white light blasted behind my eyelids, I thought it was all over, thought that death had finally reached me. I could hear angry screams and garbled voices, and then the mmo let me go, where I fell to the roof's concrete floor, Amina's sword still lodged in my chest.

When I opened my eyes, Queen Ramala stood at the edge of the roof, anger burning in her eyes, Amadioha's scepter held in her hand, tinged with lightning. Amina lay on the ground, barely unconscious, her eyelids already beginning to flutter. She lay in blasted mmo parts, blood spilling all over the concrete.

"Excuse my delay, sister," Ramala said. "You broke through your chains in the dungeons, almost killing me in the process. But I'm here now, to ensure you won't win."

She turned to me. "Descendant, you have a habit of trying to get yourself killed. I don't think I appreciate that." Ramala bounded over to me, shuffling through her chest armor. She kneeled down in front of me and shoved a flask of azizan light my way. "Here, drink this while I pull this sword out of you. It was foolish of you to take on Amina on your own."

I did as I was told, drinking deeply while Ramala pulled the sword from me; a sigh of relief escaped me when I didn't feel any pain.

"You must hurry," she said as she helped me to my feet. "Ekwensu is merged with Amina—she won't be unconscious for long."

"You are correct, sister," a voice said. It was Amina, groaning as she stood. She stared at Ramala's gifts, the scepter under her arm, the crown on her head, and the ring around her finger. "I see that you are completely healed now." And Ramala was; she stood up straighter than I had ever seen her, towering over me and her sister. Her face was unlined, the color of dark sand. Her hair, though, was what drew me in. This entire time, it had been streaked with gray, a striking color. But with the ring returned to her, it flowed down her back in a deep, tight black braid.

"Cameron, you need to leave," Ramala said in a firm voice. "Go find Aliyah and Zion. Protect the Palacia."

"No," I said, standing in front of Ramala as I finished healing. "She just tried to kill me. She will need to kill me, too, if she tries to come for the gifts."

"Killing children is not what I would like to do," Amina said, moving forward. She licked the tip of her sword, which then became ablaze with flame as she walked toward us. "But I do need the *Book* and the gifts to open the barrier for good. So Ekwensu and I can reign supreme. It's best and easiest if I kill you both, now that you are in the same place."

"Do your worst—" I started to say before Ramala grabbed my shoulders.

"I'm sorry, Cameron," she whispered in my ear. "But I can't allow the Descendant to die. Protect yourself, your friends, and the Palacia."

"Ramala, what—" My words were cut off as time slowed down.

"No!" I said, as Ramala gripped me by the waist, so tight that there was no way I could break free. With a strong push, Ramala threw me into the air, sending me flying over the Palacia's roof and straight down to the ground.

CHAPTER TWENTY-SEVEN

I screamed as I fell, flipping over and over in the air. The wind whipped around me ferociously, drowning out all sound.

"Oof!" I had flipped over one last time, my backside resting against Ugo's back as he screeched. I gathered my bearings and looked upward to see a flash of light coming from the roof of the Palacia.

"Cameron!" someone was saying as Ugo settled on the cobblestones.

"Aliyah!" I called as I jumped down, running to her. Zion came out of the darkness, too, limping a bit, carrying his trident. I gave him the flask of azizan light.

"Thank you," he breathed after swallowing it. "We thought you were . . ."

"I thought so, too," I said, hugging them both. "Amina almost killed me, but Ramala saved me."

Aliyah pushed me. "You know she's way too strong for even you!"

"I know, I know," I said, looking at the courtyard. "What happened?"

Zion shook his head. "The mmo. There were too many of them. They got into the palace, while we were trying to stop them. Amina's blasting into the roof did the most damage, though."

The courtyard was a complete mess, much more than it had been in the first battle. The entire rock wall at the edge of the mountain was destroyed, rubble falling onto the ground. The grass had been razed, with large holes bored into it. When I looked at the Palacia, my heart sank. Muffled sounds came from inside, but the outside had been decimated, its beautiful iroko doors shattered and torn from their hinges, gold leaf sprinkling down to the ground. The place I had come to know as a refuge for me and my friends was no more; a sadness twinged in my chest as I thought about everything the Palacia had represented to us. Then, I got angry thinking about our chambers, how it had belonged to Mama and Daddy when they were here.

"Watch out!" Zion screamed, pulling me back. A piece of plaster from the roof of the Palacia fell to the ground, engulfed in flame.

"The palace is on fire," Aliyah said. "It's going to all come down, soon."

"Then we need to get everyone out," I said, darting toward the ruined doorway.

"Cameron," Zion said, reaching out. "If Ramala saved you, then that means she wants to fight Amina alone."

"I don't care," I seethed, pulling away. "This is *my* home, too. I refuse to let Amina win. Are you gonna help me, or not?"

Zion and Aliyah nodded.

I grabbed Aliyah's hand. "Here, you come with me." I looked at Zion's trident. "Is that thing magical?"

Zion nodded and pointed it toward the ground. A blast of hot water emitted from it.

"Idemmili gave you that for a reason. Use it and put the flames out, as best you can. Aliyah and I are going inside. To fight back."

Aliyah and I jumped over ruined wood and plaster and into the great hall. It was empty, but I could hear moans of pain from every direction. I stuck my arm out and Summoned my sword.

"We should find Makai and the others," Aliyah said.

"Good idea," I replied as we walked through the darkness. "Careful," I said, looking at the shadows and dust in the great hall, leading to the Throne Room. "The mmo hide in the shadows."

The paintings on the wall were smashed, splayed out on the floor like dead things. The doors leading to the Throne Room had been broken, both laid out like open mouths. Holes bored into all the walls, the statues falling over to the side and destroyed, rubble everywhere. Noise was coming from the Throne Room, a mixture of shuffling, grunts, voices, and screams. When we looked inside, soldiers milled about, trying to protect Ramala's throne.

Shadows and blood marred every surface as the soldiers cut down the last mmo. But it was still a sad sight, exhaustion on all the guards' faces, and I diverted my eyes when I saw human bodies mixed in with the mmo corpses.

"Let's keep going," I urged Aliyah.

We crept up the stairs, holding hands as we used Dambe to go as fast as possible without being seen. By the time we got to our chambers, we were both exhausted. My heart sank further when I realized that our doors were smashed open, too, destroyed and hanging off the hinges. Familiar voices could be heard from inside.

"Makai!" I yelled, jumping over the wreckage. He was standing inside as fire burned from everywhere, fighting groups of mmo along with Halifa and Bakari.

"Cameron!" he yelled, cutting down a mmo in a blast of blood. "Help!"

Aliyah and I jumped into action, and I fell right next to Bakari. Another slice cut down the other side of his face, bleeding a little bit. I grabbed his hand and squeezed it once, before we both faced down a group of mmo slithering along the walls as shadows first. A large explosion sounded from above, shaking the entire room.

"It's Amina and Ramala," I said, gripping my sword tighter. "They are fighting each other."

"We need to bring all of the soldiers to the roof," Makai said, starting to run out of our chambers. "If Amina kills Ramala . . ." His voice trailed away as he stumbled out.

By this time the shadows slithering along the walls had dropped to the floor, materializing into demons. A pungent smell reached my nose before chaos ensued. One of them fell right next to Mama's Ikenga, and my sword came up automatically. I rushed ahead, slicing through a large group of them before turning around. We fought and fought, more demons sliding down from the ceilings. I refused to allow them to break any of Mama's things, or to get closer to the roof.

One grabbed me by the throat and threw me into the air. I fell against Halifa, and we both tumbled to the floor, groaning.

"Nice of you to show up," Halifa moaned before we were back into the fight. I took my sword and jumped, blasting through the demon that had thrown me and then two more. I wrapped my legs around the last one's body, smashing its head against the floor. Another crash sounded, but I was too busy fighting to pay attention to it. Aliyah appeared in a hush of air in front of me, pointing to my bedroom.

"They've got inside!" she screamed. "They're heading to the roof!"

"Not if I have something to say about it!" Zion careened into the room, his trident shining with a light the color of pearls and rubies, us following close behind. There, the battle continued, but the mmo badly outmatched us. A mmo threw me, and I crashed into the opposite wall, creating a crater in the plaster, my head swimming with pain. Bakari killed it and helped me to my feet, and we continued to fight. I watched as Aliyah pulled one of the sconces off the wall and fought with two weapons. Zion used his trident, striking back and forth, up and down.

A mmo released from the ceiling, falling down upon me as I was fighting alongside Bakari. I slipped on the carpet, my leg twisting as I stumbled. The mmo grabbed me, pinning me against the wall.

"Let. Me. Go!" I said, beating at its chest with the pommel of my sword. It grunted, its stomach hardening at every thrust, and then smirked at me. Blood fell from its gums as it threw me to the floor. I groaned, rolling over to the right as one of its feet came down with a thud, creating a small hole in the floor. The sounds around me rose in my ears as I kept moving, rolling and rolling until I reached the window on the other side of the bedroom. The mmo smashed down with its feet again, kicking me in the side. I flew out of the open door, into the sitting room, and then into the hallway, crashing against the wall.

"Ugh," I moaned, my mind registering a cacophony of sounds, grunts, and screams before I blacked out from the intense pain.

———————

I came to with a flask near my lips, cold liquid falling down my throat.

"There you go," Bakari was saying, wiping my brow with a tattered cloth. "He's waking up," he said. A group of people crowded around me as I healed.

"What happened?" I said.

"We are outnumbered," Bakari responded. "There's too many of them." Makai returned at this point, running into our chambers.

"We have to get to the roof," I said. "Amina and Ramala are there."

"Well, we can't get there through your chambers," Halifa said, gesturing toward the chamber doors, which were engulfed in shadows so thick that I could only see blackness and hear slithering noises. The sight and sound sent tremors through my shoulders.

Bakari asked, "Is there another way to get to the roof?"

"We can go down and fly up," Halifa suggested.

"No," Makai said. "That will take too much time, and the palace is overrun. We'd all die before we got there."

"Is there no other way to the roof from this floor?" Aliyah asked.

"The queen's chambers?" Zion said. We all eyed him. He shrugged. "What? I might have done some searching around the palace when you were visiting with Bakari a few days ago. I haven't seen the inside, but I know it's close to us."

"Her chambers are off-limits, except for dire circumstances," Makai said. He pulled out his sword. "And these are dire times. Follow me."

He led us down the hallway and into a hidden alcove that I hadn't seen before. He pressed a latch on the wall, and a door slid to the side, locking us in. With a flourish, he opened a door that led to a hidden hallway, which we all raced down, sounds of fighting following us.

Just then, an explosion rocked the walls, and we all fell backward, plaster filling the air. Although we coughed, we kept moving. With full force, Makai kicked through an iroko wood door at the end of the hallway, breaking it with his boot. Dust enveloped Ramala's chambers as we entered, obscuring my sight. I followed by feel to an opening in the wall where Makai stood in the darkness.

"Here," he said, pulling a strong rope from his pack, a grappling hook tied to it. So fast I could barely see it, he swung it outside and up to the roof, where it settled with a *clank*. He tied the other side to a large, sturdy, tall chair near the window. "We climb up."

With a grunt, he helped Bakari, Halifa, Zion, and Aliyah on the rope, hoisting them up and over. He turned eyes to me now.

"You are ready to do this on your own, Cameron," he said, thrusting the rope to me.

"I know," I said, grasping it.

He pressed my shoulder with his huge hands. "I can't protect you anymore. I'm so proud of you."

"Thanks, Makai," I said, standing on the windowsill.

"If you get close to Amina," he said as he pushed my legs upward, "kill her."

Swirls of shadow and white sparkles danced across my vision like static as I climbed. When they cleared, I saw the epic battle before me. Ramala and Amina moved so quickly that I could barely see them. Everywhere they touched, flames leaped into the air. And then, there was Agbala, falling down to the ground, her iro flowing around her like a weapon of its own. She stood calm, facing the two fighting sisters, expressionless. Amina paused as Ramala joined Agbala. Amina's smile widened and she closed her eyes.

"Where have you been?" Ramala asked.

"I'm the goddess of healing and justice," she responded. "I've been healing the soldiers as best as I can if they can be helped."

Ramala gestured toward her sister. "A little help here?"

An ethereal red light encircled Amina's body, way too bright to remind me of blood; she grew taller, as tall as Agbala. Boils rose on her skin, but she did not scream.

When she opened her eyes, she was two people, the merging complete—the collected soldier who looked like her sister, and then when she stared at Agbala, her features grew skeletal.

"Ekwensu?" Agbala said.

CHAPTER TWENTY-EIGHT

"Amina!" I screamed, not paying attention to the crowds of people around. It was time to finally face her and Ekwensu. She had killed my mother, and I would die trying to kill her if that was what it came to. Not only had she taken my mama and daddy away from me, but she also had the audacity to bring Ekwensu into our world, to destroy everything we had come to know.

Her eyes found mine now, turning into pillars of flame before reverting to her dark brown.

"Descendant," she said in a cold, bitter voice before she disappeared into shadows. Everything after that seemed to happen all at once. The shadows washed over the soldiers climbing to the roof behind me. Agbala and Ramala ran over to me, Aliyah, and Zion. Soon after, Halifa and Bakari joined us. Makai ran over to us, too, holding his fist in the air as the soldiers got into position, most of them holding swords while others held bows and arrows.

Chaos ensued. Clouds opened above, and a thunderous rain started up again, pummeling down, reducing the fire to almost nothing but a few embers that provided light. Mmo jumped from the swirling shadows, materializing into solid bone. Their gray skin stood out against the flame's light in sickening ways. Their mouths opened into monstrous snarls, their teeth elongated, brittle, and an orange-green color. Amina stood in front of them, regarding us all with nothing but hatred.

She gestured toward the large group of soldiers standing behind us. "These are all who are left?" she asked derisively. She was a cross between herself and Ekwensu; the boils on her skin had begun to leak fluid, and her face looked more like a skeleton than anything else with her flattened nose and fiery eyes. With a grunt, she threw off her robe and tossed it into the flame, holding tightly on to her sword.

"I thought gods couldn't intervene without consequences?" Aliyah whispered.

"We are forbidden to do so," Agbala said. "That doesn't mean we can't. He must face consequences now."

Makai raised his fist again, his voice shaking a bit. "Then we fight her until she dies."

I chanced a glance at Ramala, wanting to see if she would go against his word. However, she only sighed and closed her eyes. "She's too far gone. That's no longer my sister. Do what you have to do."

"I'll fight her," I said, stepping forward. "She's mine."

"Cam, no," Zion said, fear clear in his eyes. "You can't beat a god."

"We beat Agwu," I said as rain washed down all over us. "We can beat her, too." I held my sword higher. "And I want the death blow."

Amina smiled at me from across the roof. "Then we shall fight again," she said. "And you shall die. Once and for all."

"Attack!" Makai screamed. It all became madness after that. I paid attention to none of it, my concentration focused squarely on Amina. Ramala ran with me, protecting me as much as she could. She grabbed me by the waist again, but this time throwing me straight toward Amina, over the swirling demons. We crashed into her at the same time, and Amina lifted us into the air, laughing as she did.

We struck out at her with our swords and fists. She screamed, but it was a deep and evil sound, something I hadn't ever heard from her. Amina pushed me off, and I fell to the roof while Ramala held on strong. She raised her scepter, and lightning struck Amina from above. I called for Dambe and disappeared in thin air, and found myself floating above Amina. I raised my sword above my head, screaming as I fell down toward her.

We all fell at the same time, but not before Amina swung around, smacking me straight in the face. I reeled, careening across the roof, my back hitting against the ruined plaster of the hole blasted into it. Something in my back *cracked* as I settled, pain shooting through my entire body, especially along my legs.

I gasped, realizing that I couldn't move even if I wanted to. I went in and out of consciousness, but I knew I had to do something, and since I thought I was going to die and that we would lose anyway, maybe I could do now what I thought was justice.

"Cameron?" someone whispered to me.

The pain in my legs was replaced with a deep numbness, which didn't seem like a good sign. I moaned, looking to my right in the rainy darkness lit up by dying embers. Nneka sat next to me, peering at me with large, frightened eyes.

"Cameron, don't do this."

"I have to," I croaked.

The *Book* churned in my chest as I brought all my magic to the surface; I thrust my hand in Amina's direction, a golden orb appearing in my hand.

"Cameron, listen to me," Nneka pleaded. "Do not do this. If you do, the Descendants will be lost."

My head pounded, and I felt nauseous, like my world was spinning. People were still fighting all around me, making me want to vomit again, but I continued to hold my hand aloft, trying to make my final decision.

"Wait," I whispered, as my vision dimmed again. "*The Descendants belong in the* Book*, living and dead. It's what they deserve.*" I whispered Nneka's words aloud, remembering clearly what she had said.

Nneka whipped around, standing in front of me, her hair flowing. "What did you just say?"

"What you told me," I said. "After I Summoned Bakari's

281

soul." It was all so clear now, and I felt foolish for forgetting. It would be easy now, getting Mama back. I laughed, spitting out blood. Nneka bent over, peering at me.

"Cameron, you need to be healed. You're delirious. You're going to die if you don't get help. Yell. Scream. Do something!"

"No," I moaned. "I can get Mama back. I know what to do now." I held my hand high, as the gold and shadows surrounded it, deepening my magic to the point I felt light-headed. I thrust my arm toward Amina again, still flying in the air with her sister. There was a *snap*, and something burst in the air. Amina gasped, clenching her heart as she stared at me. Ramala crashed into the cement.

Everyone froze in place as they stared at Amina, who had begun to thrash in midair. Agbala appeared in a shower of light, standing next to Nneka, but not actually seeing her.

"Descendant!" Agbala yelled, plucking from the white aura that surrounded her, blowing it in my direction. The magic whirled around my legs, giving me back feeling. With a sickening *crunch*, my spine shifted, the pain the worst I had ever experienced. But I was on a mission, and nothing could take this moment away from me. I stood and moaned as magic leeched from her, flowing through me.

"What—" she gasped.

"Cameron, what is happening?" Agbala asked, staring at my outstretched hand, shrouded in gold and shadows.

"I'm getting my mother back," I whispered, standing firmly against the concrete.

"Cameron, you cannot—"

"No!" I yelled, waving my left hand in her direction. That one, too, swirled with shadows and gold. Agbala gasped once, and then vanished, leaving me standing with Nneka.

In another second, my attention was back on the thrashing Amina, still suspended in midair.

"I know what I'm doing, Nneka," I said, determination like steel rising in me. "You said it yourself. The Descendants belong in the *Book*, but not all of them are. The *Book* is unbalanced."

"Because . . . when your mother died, her essence wasn't transferred to it," Nneka whispered, catching on.

"Yes," I said. "I've been searching for a way to save her, and this is it. When Mama died, Amina broke Agbala's rule, the loophole she created. Which means I can get her back, because she doesn't belong with Amina."

Nneka nodded once, and then disappeared as well.

I thrust forward with my magic, walking closer to Amina. Everyone watched me, demon and human alike. Amina screamed, her mouth opening, her entire neck and chest shining with diamond light. *Mama's soul.*

"Give. Me. My. Mother. Back!" I screamed, with everything inside me.

"Mmo! Protect me!" Amina yelled into the night, her voice carrying above the rain's noise.

Every last one of them still living converged around her, shadowing her from my view. But it wouldn't protect her or

Ekwensu. I was getting my mother back, one way or another. I kept my magic aimed at Amina and heard her scream one last time, Mama's soul bursting into the night, climbing higher and higher above the conflagration of shadows.

"One last thing," I said, doing my best not to look at Mama's soul. If I did, I would lose my nerve. And I couldn't lose it just yet. I thought about Anyanwu's bow and arrow, as Amina continued to scream in pure agony.

It appeared in my hands, Summoned to me, in swirls of gold and shadow.

I nocked an arrow into the bow, pulling backward.

"Your reign of terror is over," I said as the arrow pulsed with the power of the sun. I aimed it directly at the churning mmo bodies and Amina hidden in the middle. With the rest of my strength, I released it. It connected to the swarm, blasting on impact.

My entire body seemed to break, pain radiating through me. It felt like my soul were tearing into two, as if the *Book* in my chest were falling apart at the seams, its worn pages flowing in the wind.

Everything exploded around me.

CHAPTER TWENTY-NINE

"Cameron, wake up," a familiar voice whispered.

Is this what death felt like? Had I done it? Completed the mission only to die at the end? It was a peaceful experience, though, as a white light shone from behind my eyelids

The voice laughed a bit. "Cameron, you're being stubborn. Per usual."

Wait. That was weird. This no longer felt like death.

The voice spoke again. "Take him to my chambers. He will wake soon, and I will speak to him then. Someone, carry Amina's body to the lake. Ala will want to see her."

"Yes, Descendant."

My chambers? Descendant?

I forced my eyes open once, but the only thing I could see was white. I felt someone gently carrying me, their chest moving up and down. It took a while before I realized that the person holding me was crying, as their tears leaked all over my face.

When they settled me on a soft bed, I was lost for a while, going in and out of consciousness, dreaming of nothingness. For the first time, the anxiety and fear had dissipated, no other mission in front of me. When I finally opened my eyes again, I had no idea how much time had passed.

The moon's light filtered through the window, creating cascading irregular shapes along the curtains. I was in my room in the Palacia. It was ruined, but someone had placed the large, goose mattress back on its frame. But that person who had talked to me had said to take me to their chambers. What did that mean?

"My beautiful boy."

The tears started immediately as I sat up, staring around the dark room. "Mama?" I knew that voice, would always know that voice.

She stepped out of the shadows, the most beautiful thing I had ever seen in my life. She was dressed in a white robe that swept the floor as she walked, as graceful as an angel. Her braided hair fell down her shoulders and to the center of her back. A single necklace wrapped around her neck. A pinkish aura surrounded her. I thrust the cover back and ran to her as soon as her hands outstretched to me.

"My beautiful boy," she said again, as I crushed myself to her, smelling her, remembering everything that she had been to me.

"Mama," I said, not able to say anything else. "Mama." The tears fell down my cheeks, and I just let them. I didn't want to let her go. She wrapped her arms around me in a warm embrace, pulling me so close that I thought we could be one person.

"Oh, my sweet, sweet boy," she whispered, picking me up in strong arms and carrying me outside to one of the large chairs that sat near the window. I settled into her lap as she rocked me back and forth. She wiped my tears away with the sleeve of her white robe, and I got to look at her in the light. Her skin was as clear as it could be, the shade of a dark, rich brown. Her mouth was full and red, her smile reaching the ends of her eyebrows, which always seemed to arch to the sky when she talked. She was familiar in a lot of ways to me, but still different. Almost as if she were here, but still not *here* all the way.

"Thank you for saving me, my strong, sweet boy," she said.

"I had to," I said, tears welling up again. "I couldn't let you keep suffering under Amina's control."

"Oh, it was bad, at first," she said, continuing to rock me. "I won't lie to you. But after a while, I learned to shroud myself in darkness. I didn't feel any pain for a long time, Cameron. It was like I went into a deep, dark sleep. I never thought I would awaken again. But you saved me. You did what I couldn't."

"I found Daddy, too," I breathed.

"I know. Ramala and the others told me everything you've

been up to since I've been gone." She tapped my forehead with her index finger. "You're very willful, Cameron. I've told you about that. But I'm glad you are. You've saved us all."

I buried my head in the material of her robe, while she massaged her hands through my rough curls, something I always loved her doing. Her touch felt different, too, but not in any bad way.

"We can go home now," I said, closing my eyes. "It's all over."

She tensed a bit before sighing. "Cameron, I can go home with you, but I can't stay. I . . . I died, my son."

It was why she had felt different to me, but yet so much the same. I almost knew this would happen, but I had tried to shut it away. For so long, even Agbala and Ramala had told me. Surprisingly, there was no sadness, but an understanding.

"As long as you can stay with me for a while, that's all that matters."

"Of course, I can," she said, kissing my forehead. "My soul exists in Chidani, in the *Book*. You figured that out when you defeated Amina, for the last time. You did what I or your daddy couldn't do. In fact, you can *always* see me, whenever you want me. You have the *Book* inside of you, and it'll be with you forever, now that you have saved Chidani from Amina and Ekwensu. That's where my soul resides. You can pull from me anytime, my son."

That was why I felt no sadness at her leaving me again, because she wouldn't *really* be leaving me again. Nneka and the other Descendants were evidence of that, as they existed inside me. And would do so forever.

We sat there for a long while, talking, laughing, just enjoying each other's presence. After a while, she sighed.

"I am tired, Cameron," she said. "I need to rest. It's been so long since I have rested."

She picked me up, and set me down on the carpet. When she did, both of my hands swirled with gold and shadows again, beckoning me to Summon her inside the *Book*. I didn't want to let her go, wanted to have more time with her. But she was right; I would and could always see her whenever I wanted to. She took a deep breath as the magic built inside me, and then she disappeared in a shower of light, a white orb the only thing to replace her. It floated in front of me for a while before it disappeared inside my chest. Mama's magic fueled me, giving me renewed strength. The tears that fell from my face now weren't ones of sadness, but happiness. Happiness that I had saved her. Happiness that she was with me again, and would always be.

I closed my eyes for a second, sighed, and went back into my bedroom, getting underneath the covers and going back to sleep.

CHAPTER THIRTY

The mood was somber as we stood near the Palacia's lake a few days later. It was time to send Amina's soul along its way. Makai, Bakari, and Halifa carried a marble coffin between them, stopping at the lake's edge.

A splash sounded, and Daddy appeared out of the water, his tail transforming into legs. I Summoned Mama's spirit, and she appeared. My face grew hot as she ran across the sand, trying to get to him.

"A dead soul in love with a mermaid?" Zion said. "You never see that too often."

"You *would* make a joke about it all," I said, laughing a bit.

"He's the *king* of the mermaids," Aliyah pointed out. "Let's get that one straight."

"Did we really have to be here?" Zion asked, shifting his

sparkling dashiki back in place. "It's not like we actually liked her."

"Ramala insisted," I said, as we trudged along the sand. "Not many people wanted to see her bury her sister, so she needed support."

"I mean, Amina could've at least supported her sister and let her keep the gifts," Aliyah said, huffing. "She's a murderer. I don't really care for her."

By this time, we had reached the lake's edge, joining Makai, Bakari, Halifa, and Agbala, who was speaking a few words. She stopped when we finally came close.

"I think your grandmother would probably like to be here for this moment, yes?"

At first, I thought she was referring to Amina's funeral, but then I looked at Mama, who had waded into the water now, wrapping her arms around Daddy.

"Yes, I think she would."

Agbala smiled. "Good." She snapped her fingers again, and this time, a blue portal opened on the sand where Mama and Daddy were. Grandma stepped through a little while later, wearing her bathrobe and flip-flops. Zion snickered until I gave him a death glare.

"We did leave early in the morning when coming back here," I said.

"We left early all right. Early *afternoon*," Zion mumbled as Aliyah snorted.

"Cameron!" Grandma screamed, running over to me. I trudged over the sand as tears leaked from her eyes. She held me in a bear hug, picking me up—stronger than I anticipated— and then dropped me to the ground. With a flourish, she took off one of her house shoes and chased me around the sand, screaming as she did, trying to hit me. Zion's and Aliyah's yells of laughter reached me as I ran.

"Grandma, will you stop?" I said, ducking as her house shoe flew past my head.

"Don't you DARE tell me to stop!" she said, beginning to take off her second house shoe. "You left for Chidani without telling me?!"

"Mama?"

Grandma froze in place when she heard Mama's voice. I picked up her house shoe from the sand, and brought it back over to her. "Cameron, what did you do?" she whispered as she put it back on.

I laughed a bit. "I did exactly what I told you I would. Look."

Mama strolled forward, Daddy holding her hand, both dripping with the lake's water, tinged with diamond light.

"Nina?" Grandma said, staring at her. "I . . . What? *How?*" She looked to Daddy. "Lonnie . . . you too? Both of you are . . . ?"

"Cameron saved me," Mama said, holding her arms outstretched. "Are you gonna hug me, Mama?"

Grandma flew across the sand so fast that I thought she

was using Dambe. She gripped them both in the same bear hug she gave me, and they all stood there, just looking at one another, sobbing in the process.

I went back over to Zion, Aliyah, and the rest, smiling as I did.

But Ramala's carriage coming from the Royal Court washed it from my face. A servant stepped out and helped her to the ground. She was shrouded in black, a heavy kaftan covering her sadness. When she walked to the lake's edge, Agbala spoke again.

"Ekwensu has disappeared, but the gods will find him and punish him for breaking our most sacred law." She shuddered at the thought. "He was already punished before and chained in Shukti; the only thing we can do now is to take his magic, install another god in his place, and . . . destroy him into nothingness." I got a bit of satisfaction at that. Nothingness was punishment enough.

"We are sending Princess Amina on the long journey, the journey to my mother, Ala," Agbala continued. "Although major crises happened under her watch, we celebrate all of the good she did in the early days of Chidani's founding. Queen Ramala, would you like to say a few words?"

Zion clenched my hand as I turned my gaze to the sand. I did my best to drown out Ramala's words, but they were too loud, too oppressive, just like Amina.

"She wasn't the best person. We all know that. She killed the Descendant who came to help me, and harmed her spouse.

For so long, I've hated her for what she did to me, for what she did to our country. But then, I think of my own actions, and how I justified them over and over in my head as 'sacrifices' for the greater good. Now, I think that Amina may have had good reason to hate me, to hate what I had become. I think I was so consumed by my power that I forgot why and how she suffered under my rule. How she must've felt seeing our people in chains, seeing our people being whipped and pushed into the ocean to never be seen again."

Ramala cleared her throat before she spoke again. I clenched my left fist as she continued.

"It's okay, Cam," Zion said, taking my fist and flattening it. "It won't be long now."

Ramala's voice became heavy with sobs as she spoke. "I know I was wrong. I know that now. Cameron told me as much when I showed him one of Chidani's maps, even though he didn't know it at the time. I was cruel to her, just as she was cruel to our people. There was never going to be a good ending to all of this, though I tried to protect her as much as I could. She had become too corrupted to save; Ekwensu would have never let her go. But, I am glad she will transition now to Ala's home. At least, there, she will become the person she was always meant to be."

She turned to me now, her eyes softening when they met mine. "And I want to say that I thank you, Cameron. You did what needed to be done. And I ask you to forgive me."

"I forgive you," I responded.

I didn't want to see the rest of Amina's funeral; I still felt too close to what had happened and the evil she had done. I went away, walking back to the Palacia alone.

Aliyah and Zion joined me not too long after, putting arms around my waist and helping me into the palace, and upstairs to Mama's bedding chambers, where we prepared our things to leave Chidani.

I took the sprite out of my pack, leaving it to fly around my chambers and then out the window. It flew away, sending sparkles falling from the air.

CHAPTER THIRTY-ONE

"Cam, can you set the picnic table?" Grandma yelled from the kitchen a few weeks after we had returned home.

I rolled my eyes and pressed the volume up on my game in my bedroom.

"Cameron Battle! I know you pushed that volume up! Don't make me come up there and get you! Aliyah and Zion will be here any second!"

With a heavy sigh, I threw the game controller on the floor, turned the television off, and trudged down the steps to the kitchen. "Yes, ma'am. What did you need me to take out?"

Grandma stood at the kitchen sink, apron around her waist, with a dish towel hanging out of her blue jeans. She looked twenty years younger, bounding around the space like a teenager. She gestured to the table. "All of that stuff. And make sure you put down a tablecloth. You know I don't like no food droppings on my good wood." *Trill, trill, trill.* The house phone on the countertop by the stove rang. "But answer the phone before you do that."

"Hello," I said after picking up the phone.

"Um . . . hello?" a familiar timid voice spoke.

"Yeah, hello," I responded, allowing annoyance to seep into my tone. "Who is this?"

"This is . . . Vince. I'm calling to speak to Cameron."

I tossed a quick glance at Grandma before I took the phone into the living room so she couldn't hear me. "Yeah, this is Cameron. How did you get this number?" My heart beat so fast and loud that I could hear it in my ears. *What does he want?*

"Your friend Zion gave it to me. I asked him how to get in touch with you." *What does he remember?* Agbala had said she had erased his memory before sending him home, but what if she had made a mistake? What if her magic wasn't strong enough?

"What do you want, Vince?"

"I've been having these . . . dreams . . . I guess. I can't explain it," he said. "Bad dreams. You and your friends were in them."

I almost dropped the phone. I didn't know what to say, couldn't say anything.

"Anyway, I guess it's just my mind helping me to remember how I acted when we first met. I wasn't the nicest person to you. I don't know how or why I acted like that; I wanted you to know that I'm not a bully. I don't know what came over me."

I still couldn't say anything, didn't know how to respond to him. Relief flooded me that he didn't remember Chidani as a real place, but his call still unnerved me.

"Cameron?" he said.

"Yes," I whispered.

"I just wanted to know if you could forgive me? If maybe we could be friends? Or at least we could talk more at school. I see how you and Zion and Aliyah hang out with each other, and I think it's cool. Mama has always told me to never ask for forgiveness if I can't also make it right, to pay restitution for what I did. I'd like you to give me that chance."

"Yeah . . . I mean, sure," I said. "I'll see you around at school."

"Cool, 'bye," he said, hanging up the phone on his end.

"Cameron!" Grandma called again.

"I'm coming, I'm coming," I said, stepping back into the kitchen and putting the phone back in its cradle.

"Who was that?" she asked.

I shrugged. "Just a friend from school."

I looked at the table; barbeque and hot wings, baked beans, collard greens, candied yams, potato salad, deviled eggs, buttered rolls, and green beans filled it. Grandma went to open the stove, while I opened one of the drawers to remove the red tablecloth she liked to use on special occasions. As soon as I turned around with it, she thrust a huge pan of bubbling baked macaroni and cheese into my hands as well.

"Take this out first, and then come and get the rest of the stuff."

"Yes, ma'am," I said, stepping outside into the backyard. It had been a few weeks since we had returned to our world, and this would be the first time that we all gathered. Daddy wanted to come immediately, but Mama still needed rest from everything she had been through. I felt her inside me sometimes when I thought hard enough; her soul felt like a beating heart next to mine, healing the part that broke when I lost her.

After stepping outside, I closed my eyes as the sun's rays energized me with warmth, a sure sign that everything we had been through was over, that the barrier was closed, that we had saved Chidani.

After opening them, I walked into the woods and neared the pond that had suspiciously grown deeper since we had returned. I grinned at the flowing water, knowing exactly what that would mean in just an hour or so. The picnic table Grandma had installed rose from the ground, large and imposing, made from blocks of iroko wood she had taken with her from Chidani for this special occasion.

"I remember how beautiful this was," she had said, thinking about her time as the Descendant. I don't know how she built the picnic bench, but I suspected Dambe was the answer. I put the pan of macaroni down on the seat before setting the tablecloth on the table, spreading it smooth with my hands.

After, I spent a few moments in the woods, remembering how they had scared me so long ago, the first time I had seen a mmo. All of that seemed so far away now, after everything we had been through.

Beep, beep, beep. That would be Zion and Aliyah arriving for dinner. Afterward, we would have our traditional sleepover.

I ran back to the house to see them, but as soon as I made the turn to the driveway, Grandma opened the back door.

"Cameron!" she screamed. "There's still food that needs to be taken out. I'll get the front door."

"But, Gran—"

"Cameron!" she warned.

"Okay, okay, okay," I mumbled, going back into the house to get the rest of the dishes.

Whoosh. In a rush of air, Zion appeared right next to me. I screamed, and jumped, dropping the bowl of baked beans. In a split second, he grabbed the bowl and set it neatly back on the kitchen table.

"Whew, that was close," he said, his eyes widening.

"Ziiioon," I said, pushing his shoulder a bit. "You know you're not supposed to be using Dambe with people around."

"Hey," he said, crossing his arms. "I heard your grandma yelling at you. I thought I would at least help you with the food. You should thank me."

I raised an eyebrow. "You gave Vince my number?"

He shrugged. "He doesn't remember anything that happened. You've been ignoring him at school like the plague. He stopped me in the hallway and said he wanted to apologize to you, well apologize to us both, but you weren't giving him the chance. Plus, I pretty much live here, anyway. It's practically *my* number, too."

I mean, you do have a point there.

"Well, he did do something wrong."

"But it wasn't really him," Zion said, shuddering a bit. "He's actually nice once you get to know him. Did he call today?"

"Yeah, he did. He apologized for bullying us. I forgave him, of course, but I still can't stop thinking about everything that's happened."

"Remember, your mom was a mmo. There's no telling what Amina put her through. At least Vince is sorry for his behavior. Amina wasn't."

"You're right," I sighed. "I'll give him a chance."

Zion leaned against the side of the refrigerator. "Now, do you want my help or not?"

I laughed and opened my arms. "Of course, you can help me. Thank you." He snuggled in my arms, pulling close.

"I've missed this," he breathed. "Being next to you all of the time."

"I know," I said, kissing his forehead and twirling my fingers through his curly hair. "But we're back now. And the sleepovers shall continue!"

"Yeah," he said.

"Zion," I said, pulling away a bit. "I need to tell you something."

"What?"

"I—I just want to thank you for everything. For being there for me. Through it all. I never got to tell you that . . . even though I'm the Descendant, you're stronger than me. Always have been."

"Thanks, Cameron." He sighed a bit. "Now, before I lose my nerve." With a flourish, he grabbed my shoulders and planted a dry kiss on my lips. It was quick, but it made all the difference. And I returned it. "There, I did it."

I smiled. "Good. Now, come on, help me with this stuff."

When we stepped outside with the rest of the dishes, Aliyah joined us, talking furiously about everything that had happened since she had been home. I wasn't really paying attention to her words; it was just good to see her talking animatedly, as if all we had been through hadn't scarred her. Grandma said that our experiences probably would, but that the wounds might not show up for a while.

For me, Daddy's and Mama's presence kept me centered, although I couldn't see them as much as I wanted. But seeing them made all the difference.

As soon as we finished setting the table, I heard a splash from the deep pond. I ran back in the house and rummaged around Grandma's room for one of Daddy's shirts. I went back to the pond alone and watched as a whirlpool appeared first, and then a silhouette of a large tail, infused with diamonds and rubies. The rest of Daddy came last, appearing in a shower of water, his chest bare.

He was completely dry as he stepped forward, and I handed him his shirt with a smile on my face. After he put it on, he picked me up in a hug first and then threw me high into the air, where I yelled in delight before he set me back down on the ground.

"Lonnie, you know you don't know your own strength," Grandma said, coming into the picnic area.

"Oh, it'll be fine. Cameron's strong, ain't you?" he asked me.

"Yes, Daddy," I said, doing my best to smooth down my hair, which had gone every which way.

I looked at them as Daddy strolled over to the picnic table and sat down with the rest of them. There they were, my new family. Zion sat, trying to grab on to a hot wing, but not before Grandma gently slapped his hands with her own. Then there was Aliyah, shuffling her Pokémon cards, passing them out between her and Daddy to play.

But everyone wasn't here, yet. While they talked among themselves, I went behind a large oak tree, centering myself, before Summoning Mama to me. The wind whistled in the trees, kicking up where I was standing, sending dead leaves flying around me. She stood in front of me, wearing a flowy white gown, her hair flying in the wind. A white ethereal light surrounded her, a heavenly aroma drifting from her. She was the most magnificent thing I had ever seen, and probably would ever see.

"My beautiful boy," she said, her hands outstretched to me. I hugged her, and she enfolded strong arms around me. She smelled my hair as she leaned closer.

"How are you?"

"I'm fine, Mama. More than fine, actually."

"I'm always glad to hear that."

"Are you ready to eat?" I asked.

She chuckled. "I don't have a need to eat anymore, but I'm so glad that I can still taste. And be with family whenever you need me." She played with my hair, curling her hands around the kinks, massaging them as she always did. "Living inside of you teaches me a lot about you, Cameron."

"What did you learn?"

She gently pushed me away, keeping both her hands on my shoulders. "I know that you love Zion. And I know that he loves you, too. Especially by the way he looks at you. And that kiss in the kitchen . . ."

My face grew hot. "Mama, I don't wanna talk about that."

She laughed again. "Well, you should take the *Book* out and leave it in the attic, where your grandmother kept it. If you don't, I'll be able to see your every emotion when I'm that close to you in your soul." She turned solemn eyes to me now, as if she recognized something for the first time. "Cameron, I'm fine. I live in the *Book* now. And I'm happier than I've ever been. I can see you whenever I want.

I can see your daddy whenever you allow me to. I get to fellowship and love with the previous Descendants. And . . . I actually get to rest. I no longer have to fight any longer. I'm more at peace than I've ever been. Please, you have to believe me."

She always knew me more than anybody else ever had. And she was right; I had kept the *Book* close to me, because her presence was comforting. And I somehow believed that if I ever put it back in the attic, I would never see her again. That I would somehow forget her. And I couldn't live with the guilt if that ever happened.

"Promise me," she said, taking my hands and leaning down. "Promise me that you will live your life for yourself. Not for me. I know you love me, and I know you'll always be here. But, son, you have to live your life. Love Zion. Love him so fiercely and hold him closely to you."

"But I don't wanna ever forget you."

"Nonsense," she said, shaking her head. "You could never forget me. And even if you did, it wouldn't matter. Because one day, when you pass away, you'll join me. And you'll see how beautiful it is in the *Book*."

"Okay, Mama," I said. "I promise that I will live my life. But I will never forget you. I'll put the *Book* in the attic and make Grandma read to me every week. And every few weeks, I'll take you to see Daddy, too."

She squeezed my arms while standing. "Good. I'll take that bet."

She pulled me close one more time, sing-whispering the last sweet refrain of the song she had always taught me:

"Those who open the histories will hear a sound
What was lost has finally been found."

And with that, we walked in front of the oak tree, hand in hand, continuing to the picnic table with the others.

"'Bout time!" Zion yelled from his seat.

We joined them at the table. Mama sat beside Daddy, who put strong arms around her. I grabbed Zion's hand under the table, feeling the warmth there. He gave me a mischievous smile, swiping his thumb across my palm.

And then we ate and laughed and ate and laughed and ate and laughed until the sun set in the sky.

ACKNOWLEDGMENTS

Whew, what a roller coaster ride! Writing this sequel took a lot out of me and pushed me to my limits, especially after how cathartic writing the first book was for me. As authors, writing can be such a solitary thing, but I do want to thank a few people who have helped me along this journey to getting this series completed.

To Mary Kate Castellani and Kei Nakatsuka, thank you for helping me get this book into shape. Your words, insight, and wisdom have assisted in creating something beautiful for Black boys, a series they can see themselves in. Thank you for your tireless support of Cameron Battle from the beginning all the way to now. This series has gotten into so many children's hands because of you, and the amazing work you are doing at Bloomsbury in shepherding children's literature into the world is awe-inspiring.

To my agent, Caitie Flum, thank you for being my rock throughout this process. Thank you for putting up with my many questions, my nervousness, and my anxiousness with such grace. You truly are a friend to me in this industry, and I cannot wait to keep putting more and more books out there with you.

To Marquis Vince Dixon—whew, you are everything to me. Thank you for coming into my life when I needed you. You are truly my best friend in this world, and I love you to the moon and back.

To Mighty Fine—the love in my soul for you knows no bounds. Thank you for your jokes, the many laughs we have, and the hours-long phone calls. The way you constantly put your ego aside for other people (and me) is nothing short of amazing.

To Jamond D. Perry—my twin brother, my lifeblood, my best friend. You are everything and more to me. What more can I say? My love for you is as deep as the deepest ocean, and as wide as the infinite universe. Onward and upward.

I wrote this book for Black boys, but I would be remiss if I wasn't honest in saying that I also wrote this for me. I was a lonely child, someone who was always searching for love, to feel accepted and wanted. Writing this series is getting me one step closer to my happy, to finding inner peace and love. It has helped me on my journey to self-love. I am so happy that Cameron Battle has gotten into the hearts and minds of so many readers; this process has helped me on my own journey to find myself. Ultimately, Cameron Battle finds his true magic in himself and his friends. I can't wait to find that for myself as well.

I'm well on my way!